THE LIMITLESS VISION

It would be surprising if scientists did not write science fiction. The same talents are required: creativeness, an open mind, imagination . . .

And many do. This collection represents the very best of them.

"Excellent science fiction . . . intensely human, keenly understanding."

Wilmington News Journal

THE EXPERT DREAMERS

EDITED BY
FREDERIK POHL

AN AVON BOOK

AVON BOOKS
A division of
The Hearst Corporation
959 Eighth Avenue
New York, New York 10019

First Avon Printing, September, 1968

Cover illustration by Don Crowley

Printed in the U.S.A.

ACKNOWLEDGMENTS

"At the End of the Orbit" by Arthur C. Clarke. Copyright, 1961, by Digest Productions Corporation. From *If Science Fiction*. Reprinted by permission of the author and the author's agent, Scott Meredith Literary Agency, Inc.

"On the Feasibility of Coal-Driven Power Stations" by O. R. Frisch. Copyright, 1956, by Scientific American, Inc. From *Scientific American*. Reprinted by permission of Scientific American, Inc.

"A Feast of Demons" by William Morrison. Copyright, 1958, by Galaxy Publishing Corporation. From *Galaxy Magazine*. Reprinted by permission of the author.

"The Heart on the Other Side" by George Gamow. Reprinted by permission of the author.

"Lenny" by Isaac Asimov. Copyright, 1957, by Royal Publications, Inc. From *Infinity Science Fiction*. By permission of the author.

"The Singers" by W. Grey Walter. Reprinted from *The Curve of the Snowflake*, by W. Grey Walter, by permission of W. W. Norton, Inc. Copyright, 1956, by W. W. Norton & Company, Inc.

"The Invasion" by Robert Willey. Copyright, 1940, by Fictioneers, Inc. From *Super Science Stories*. Reprinted by permission of the author.

"To Explain Mrs. Thompson" by Philip Latham. Copyright, 1951, by Street & Smith Publications, Inc. From *Astounding Science Fiction*. Reprinted by permission of the author and the author's agent, Scott Meredith Literary Agency, Inc.

"Adrift on the Policy Level" by Chandler Davis. Copyright, 1959, by Ballantine Books, Inc. From *Star Science Fiction*. Reprinted by permission of the author.

"The Black Cloud" by Fred Hoyle. From *The Black Cloud* by Fred Hoyle. Copyright © 1957 by Fred Hoyle. Reprinted by permission of Harper & Brothers.

"Chain Reaction" by Boyd Ellanby. Copyright, 1956, by Galaxy Publishing Corporation. From *Galaxy Magazine*. By permission of the authors.

"The Miracle of the Broom Closet" by W. Norbert. Copyright, 1952, by Tech Engineering News (MIT). Reprinted by permission of the author.

"Heavyplanet" by Lee Gregor. Copyright, 1958, by Street & Smith Publications, Inc. From *Astounding Science Fiction*. Reprinted by permission of the author.

"The Test Stand" by Lee Correy. Copyright, 1955, by Street & Smith Publications, Inc. From *Astounding Science Fiction*. Reprinted by permission of the author's agent, Lurton Blassingame.

"Amateur in Chancery" by George O. Smith. Copyright, 1961, by Galaxy Publishing Corporation. From *Galaxy Magazine*. Reprinted by permission of the author's agent, Lurton Blassingame.

"The Mark Gable Foundation" by Leo Szilard. From *The Voice of the Dolphins*. Five Stories of Political & Social Satire. Copyright © 1961 by Leo Szilard. Reprinted by permission of Simon and Schuster, Inc. Paperback edition available at $1.00.

CONTENTS

INTRODUCTION

By way of introducing the stories in this collection I would like to set down a personal note. The men (and woman) who wrote them are what are called "scientists." I am not. Barring some chemistry which I have long forgotten and some glimmerings of mathematics and star-watching which I have pursued for entertainment, I am at the most a spectator of science. Unlike most of these contributors, I am not now nor ever will be one who unlocks a new domain of knowledge for the human race. My training is slight and my aptitudes minimal.

These are not the qualifications that make a great artist in the realm of science. But perhaps they will do for the paid guide who conducts the travelers through the chambers lined with works by the masters.

Science in this latter half of the twentieth century has grown large and bewildering. At its farthest reach it looks out on such wonderful and strange things that language no longer suffices to carry the burden of thought. A squiggle on a blackboard represents a question about the growth of suns; a cascade of pulses from the transistorized cells of a computer represents its answer.

We laymen not only do not have the words to express what the farthest investigators have found, we can hardly frame the questions to ask what they are doing. All the "common-sense" evidence of our eyes is a liar—the Earth is not flat, matter is not solid, space is curved, time is relative—and we are the prisoners of our sense and our habits, lacking the mathematical keys that will allow us to escape.

Most of us have learned to accept the reality of atomic energy—well, we've seen the thing work—the motion pictures of hydrogen-bomb tests showed something very big and very wonderful. Whether we understand what we are accepting is another question. It is more a condition of anesthesia than of

comprehension. We don't so much grasp the concepts involved as we encyst them.

Such other questions as the origin of the universe (did it
begin in a single enormous explosion of a giant atom?—and
if so where did the atom come from? does it go on renewing
itself by constant growth as Hoyle's steady-state theory sug-
gests? or by contracting back to the atom and exploding
again, as Öpik imagines?); or Gödel's logical proof that some
things are forever unprovable; or the cyberneticians' remarkable machines that grow and reproduce themselves—these
things we may not even encyst. We can hardly take them in
in any form. We reject them as "not of practical concern" if
we are lazy-minded (though no commodity is of more practical value than knowledge!); or we try to follow them . . .
and lose ourselves in mathematics.

What most of us do not do, because we can't, is to understand them and their implications.

But this is by no means the same thing as saying that these
things have no implications. "Science" is a way of finding,
storing and making available new knowledge. What these
people are doing is learning. What they find will change our
lives very drastically—may kill us tomorrow with nuclear fallout or blast, or may on the day after tomorrow give every
man and woman of us perfect health and all but eternal life.

That is what we mean when we talk about "science."
Should we now consider what we mean by "science fiction"?

The definitions of science fiction will always be endless,
since its practitioners and aficionados, a thorny breed, find no
greater joy than to quarrel with authority and thus are most
unlikely ever themselves to agree on an authoritative definition. It may be that this state is what defines science fiction.
We can follow that thought in a moment; but let us first see
what science fiction is not.

It is not, for example, "gadget" fiction. To those who think
that "science" is automatic toasters and jet planes, be it
known that science fiction is only cosmetically concerned
with such trivia. The gadgets may dress up the story; but the
story is more than the gadgets.

Neither is it social commentary—although books have
been written to say that it is. Neither dramatized predictions
of the future; neither bloody, fast-paced literature of escape.
Oh, it may be any of these things. It may be all of them. But
science fiction does not limit itself . . . any more than science does.

It has been said a thousand times that "science fiction" is a misnomer. I do not agree. The term is quite apt—accidentally, if you will, since it was the "gadget" view of science fiction that prevailed decades ago when the term was coined —but it is apt all the same. For what is science? It is a *way* of doing things. Its heart is the "scientific method"—accumulate facts, make deductions, frame an explanation, test the explanation by making predictions, test the predictions by experiment.

Come back to the thought we postponed a moment ago. What almost all science fiction writers have in common is a capacity for looking at things from outside. Call it objectivity. Call it extrapolation. It is a talent for looking at things through fresh eyes, and setting down the results in the form of an entertaining story.

This is in essence what a scientist must do, must reject "what everybody knows" and concentrate on the evidence secured by experiment and observation. If the evidence forces him to conclude that the Earth is indeed not the center of the universe—that disease is after all not caused by the natural decay of the human effluvium, but by bacteria—that time and space are relative quantities—whatever—then he must follow his conclusions to the end. So must a science fiction writer. He cannot assume that human nature does not change. He changes it for every story he writes. He can't accept the bland view that life moves constantly onward and upward toward Utopia. If the evidence he is considering points the other way, his story cannot have a happy ending.

We are, after all, at a nexus point of some sort in the development of the human race. It is not merely a matter of H-bombs or population explosion which may annihilate us or starve us; whether or not we solve problems like these, we have many other problems in sight for which we have no solution at all. We can't have a solution. We don't yet know enough about the problems, since they are just beginning to appear. The questions that will be as real to our grandchildren as fallout shelters and technological unemployment are to us are the proper concerns of science fiction: the aliens we may some day meet in space; the effects on our lives of uncontrolled plenty. It is only a century since nearly all the world lived in a way almost indistinguishable from that of neolithic man—his hut was warmer and his crops better, but the nineteenth century peasant was tied to the soil unendingly, and when drought came he died. He had neither leisure nor medicine. Now we have given him some of both and will soon give him a great deal. What will he make of it? What will we make of him?

These are the questions—a very few of the questions—that science fiction is exploring, bit by bit.

It must be admitted that sometimes science fiction concerns itself with lesser questions. Sometimes it doesn't appear to be concerning itself with anything at all—except maybe blood and thunder thrills, or cheap comedy. We have been talking as though all science fiction conforms to the standards of excellence of its best examples, and that is demonstrably false. Probably ninety per cent of all science fiction is trash, unwelcome as that admission is to many of us who admire it.

Probably so. But one of the best science fiction writers, Theodore Sturgeon, has included that observation in what has come to be called Sturgeon's Ninety Per Cent Law: "90% of *everything* is trash." This statement is so obvious that it hardly needs to be amplified. Are you fond of the dance? Then you have seen at least nine clumsy lines of chorus ponies for every admirable ballet troupe. Music? There are many more than nine Ozark doggerel chants for every Bach fugue —for that matter, nine rock-and-roll wails for every *Stardust*. Politics? Painting? Name it; the 90% law applies.

So maybe there are in every ten science fiction stories one which is really good—and three which are horrible—but that one in ten is very precious to its admirers, and well worth the examination of even those who are not.

There is one other useful trait of science fiction. Look forward twenty years to see what it is.

What hope for a happy future our race has lies in the hands of those who will then probe out the answers to questions we are at the present time barely able to form. In twenty years there will be hundreds and thousands of skilled, brilliant minds at work in the world's laboratories. It will be up to them to find out for us the *How* of space travel, the *Why* of the expanding universe, the *How*—in a different vein—of controlling the violent interactions of humanity with itself.

Who will these men and women be?

Why, it is a fair chance that more than one of them will be holding this book in his hands in 1962. For science fiction is among its other attributes a well known love of the science-minded teen-ager; and it is from that group that tomorrow's scientists must come. It has been so in the past. There is, for example, a man in the laboratory of the National Bureau of Standards now who is there because when he was very young —in 1928—he read a science fiction story, *The Skylark of Space,* whose hero, Richard Seaton, had just that job in just that place. Turn back the clock and you will find others like him. Twenty years ago, a good many present-day scientists were young science fiction fans, showing no other visible trace of the technical skills they were yet to develop.

Several such, in fact, are represented in this book.

So it is not strange, after all, that scientists should write science fiction stories. Here is the evidence to prove it. The stories in this volume are by men who work with science, in one discipline or other, in their daily lives . . . men, some of them, who have themselves advanced to occupy some of the farthest outposts of our present scientific knowledge.

It must not be thought that every scientist who ever wrote a science fiction story is represented here. There isn't that much room. The list may not be endless, but it is huge. Probably no other branch of writing—fiction, anyway—has as high a percentage of writers who are entitled to be called "doctor" in some discipline. But these are the ones whose stories have struck me as most interesting; and I hope that this interest will be shared.

FREDERIK POHL

Red Bank, 1962

AT THE END
OF THE ORBIT

ARTHUR C. CLARKE

Hoyle, Frisch, Gamow, and most of the others of the contributors to this volume are scientists first, who happen once in a while to feel the need to write a science fiction story. Arthur C. Clarke turns the equation around. He is a writer who finds himself, more or less as a hobby, from time to time a scientist. He took his degree—with First Class Honors—in physics and mathematics; but his accomplishments have been remote from those fields. His best-selling book on space medicine shows one facet of his career; his role as one of the early builders of the British Interplanetary Society shows another. A Fellow of the Royal Astronomical Society, his principal present investigations are—of course!—in the line of marine biology, skin-diving off the shores of Ceylon and along Australia's Great Barrier Reef.

But more than anything else, Clarke is a science fiction writer . . . and one of the very best.

I

Tibor didn't see the thing. He was asleep, and dreaming his inevitable painful dream.

Only Joey was awake on deck, in the cool stillness before dawn, when the meteor came flaming out of the sky above New Guinea. He watched it climb up the heavens until it passed directly overhead, routing the stars and throwing swift-moving shadows across the crowded deck. The harsh light outlined the bare rigging, the coiled ropes and air-hoses, the copper diving-helmets neatly snugged down for the night —even the low, pandanus-clad island half a mile away. As it passed into the southwest, out over the emptiness of the Pacific, it began to disintegrate.

15

Incandescent globules broke off, burning and guttering in a trail of fire that stretched a quarter of the way across the sky. It was already dying when it raced out of sight. But Joey did not see its end. Still blazing furiously, it sank below the horizon, as if seeking to hurl itself into the face of the hidden sun.

If the sight was spectacular, the utter silence was unnerving. Joey waited and waited and waited, but no sound came from the riven heavens. When, minutes later, there was a sudden splash from the sea, close at hand, he gave an involuntary start of surprise—then cursed himself for being frightened by a manta. (A mighty big one, though, to have made so much noise when it jumped.) There was no other sound, and presently he went back to sleep.

In his narrow bunk just aft of the air compressor, Tibor heard nothing. He slept so soundly after his day's work that he had little energy even for dreams. And when they came, they were not the dreams he wanted. In the hours of darkness, as his mind roamed back and forth across the past, it never came to rest amid memories of desire. He had women in Sydney and Brisbane and Darwin and Thursday Island—but none in his dreams. All that he ever remembered when he woke, in the fetid stillness of the cabin, was the dust and fire and blood as the Russian tanks rolled into Budapest. His dreams were not of love, but only of hate.

When Nick shook him back to consciousness, he was dodging the guards on the Austrian border. It took him a few seconds to make the ten-thousand-mile journey to the Great Barrier Reef. Then he yawned, kicked away the cockroaches that had been nibbling at his toes and heaved himself out of his bunk.

Breakfast, of course, was the same as always—rice, turtle eggs and bully-beef, washed down with strong, sweet tea. The best that could be said of Joey's cooking was that there was plenty of it. Tibor was used to the monotonous diet. He made up for it, and for other deprivations, when he was back on the mainland.

The sun had barely cleared the horizon when the dishes were stacked in the tiny galley and the lugger got under way. Nick sounded cheerful as he took the wheel and headed out from the island. The old pearling-master had every right to be, for the patch of shell they were working was the richest that Tibor had ever seen. With any luck, they would fill their hold in another day or two, and sail back to T.I. with half a ton of shell on board. And then, with a little more luck, he could give up this stinking, dangerous job and get back to civilization.

Not that he regretted anything. The Greek had treated him well, and he'd found some good stones when the shells were opened. But he understood now, after nine months on the Reef, why the number of white divers could be counted on the fingers of one hand. Japs and Kanakas and Islanders could take it—but damn few Europeans.

The diesel coughed into silence and the *Arafura* coasted to rest.

They were some two miles from the island, which lay low and green on the water, yet sharply divided from it by its narrow band of dazzling beach. It was no more than a nameless sand bar that a tiny forest had managed to capture. Its only inhabitants were the myriads of stupid muttonbirds that riddled the soft ground with their burrows and made the night hideous with their banshee cries.

There was little talk as the three divers dressed. Each man knew what to do, and wasted no time in doing it. As Tibor buttoned on his thick twill jacket, Blanco, his tender, rinsed out the faceplate with vinegar so that it would not become fogged. Then Tibor clambered down the rope ladder, while the heavy helmet and lead corselet were placed over his head.

Apart from the jacket, whose padding spread the weight evenly over his shoulders, he was wearing his ordinary clothes. In these warm waters there was no need for rubber suits. The helmet simply acted as a tiny diving-bell held in position by its weight alone. In an emergency the wearer could—if he was lucky—duck out of it and swim back to the surface unhampered. Tibor had seen this done. But he had no wish to try the experiment for himself.

Each time he stood on the last rung of the ladder, gripping his shell-bag with one hand and his safety line with the other, the same thought flashed through Tibor's mind. He was leaving the world he knew; but was it for an hour—or was it forever?

Down there on the sea bed was wealth and death, and one could be sure of neither. The chances were that this would be another day of uneventful drudgery, as were most of the days in the pearl-diver's unglamorous life. But Tibor had seen one of his mates die, when his air-hose tangled in the *Arafura*'s prop. And he had watched the agony of another, as his body twisted with the bends. In the sea, nothing was ever safe or certain. You took your chances with open eyes.

And if you lost there was no point in whining.

He stepped back from the ladder, and the world of sun

and sky ceased to exist. Top-heavy with the weight of his helmet, he had to back-pedal furiously to keep his body upright.
He could see nothing but a featureless blue mist as he sank
towards the bottom. He hoped that Blanco would not play
out the safety line too quickly. Swallowing and snorting, he
tried to clear his ears as the pressure mounted. The right one
"popped" quickly enough, but a piercing, intolerable pain
grew rapidly in the left, which had bothered him for several
days. He forced his hand up under the helmet, gripped his
nose and blew with all his might. There was an abrupt,
soundless explosion somewhere inside his head, and the pain
vanished instantly. He'd have no more trouble on this dive.

   Tibor felt the bottom before he saw it.
   Unable to bend over lest he risk flooding the open helmet,
his vision in the downwards direction was very limited. He
could see around, but not immediately below. What he did
see was reassuring in its drab monotony—a gently undulat-
ing, muddy plain that faded out of sight about ten feet ahead.
A yard to his left a tiny fish was nibbling at a piece of coral
the size and shape of a lady's fan. That was all. There was no
beauty, no underwater fairyland here. But there was money.
That was what mattered.
   The safety line gave a gentle pull as the lugger started to
drift downwind, moving broadside-on across the patch, and
Tibor began to walk forward with the springy, slow-motion
step forced on him by weightlessness and water resistance. As
Number Two diver, he was working from the bow. Amidships was Stephen, still comparatively inexperienced, while at
the stern was the head diver, Billy. The three men seldom
saw each other while they were working; each had his own
lane to search as the *Arafura* drifted silently before the wind.
Only at the extremes of their zigzags might they sometimes
glimpse one another as dim shapes looming through the mist.
   It needed a trained eye to spot the shells beneath their
camouflage of algae and weeds, but often the molluscs be-
trayed themselves. When they felt the vibrations of the approaching diver, they would snap shut—and there would be a
momentary, nacreous flicker in the gloom. Yet even then
they sometimes escaped, for the moving ship might drag the
diver past before he could collect the prize just out of reach.
In the early days of his apprenticeship, Tibor had missed
quite a few of the big silver-lips, any one of which might
have contained some fabulous pearl. Or so he had imagined,
before the glamor of the profession had worn off, and he

realized that pearls were so rare that you might as well forget
them.

The most valuable stone he'd ever brought up had been
sold for twenty pounds, and the shell he gathered on a good
morning was worth more than that. If the industry had de-
pended on gems instead of mother-of-pearl, it would have
gone broke years ago.

There was no sense of time in this world of mist. You
walked beneath the invisible, drifting ship, with the throb of
the air compressor pounding in your ears, the green haze
moving past your eyes. At long intervals you would spot a
shell, wrench it from the sea bed and drop it in your bag. If
you were lucky, you might gather a couple of dozen on a single drift across the patch. On the other hand, you might not
find a single one.

You were alert for danger, but not worried by it. The real
risks were simple, unspectacular things like tangled air-hoses
or safety lines—not sharks, groupers or octopi. Sharks ran
when they saw your air bubbles, and in all his hours of div-
ing Tibor had seen just one octopus, every bit of two feet
across. As for groupers—well, *they* were to be taken seriously, for they could swallow a diver at one gulp if they felt
hungry enough. But there was little chance of meeting them
on this flat and desolate plain. There were none of the coral
caves in which they could make their homes.

The shock would not have been so great, therefore, if this
uniform, level grayness had not lulled him into a sense of security.

At one moment he was walking steadily towards an un-
reachable wall of mist, that retreated as fast as he approached. And then, without warning, his private nightmare
was looming above him.

II

Tibor hated spiders, and there was a certain creature in the
sea that seemed deliberately contrived to take advantage of
that phobia. He had never met one, and his mind had always
shied away from the thought of such an encounter, but Tibor
knew that the Japanese spider crab can span twelve feet
across its spindly legs. That it was harmless mattered not in
the least. A spider as big as a man simply had no right to
exist.

As soon as he saw that cage of slender, jointed limbs
emerge from the all-encompassing grayness, Tibor began to

scream with uncontrollable terror. He never remembered
jerking his safety line, but Blanco reacted with the instanta-
neous perception of the ideal tender. His helmet still echoing
to his screams, Tibor felt himself snatched from the sea bed,
lifted towards light and air—and sanity. As he swept upwards, he saw both the strangeness and the absurdity of his
mistake, and regained a measure of control. But he was still
trembling so violently when Blanco lifted off his helmet that
it was some time before he could speak.

"What the hell's going on here?" demanded Nick. "Everyone knocking off work early?"

It was then that Tibor realized that he was not the first to
come up. Stephen was sitting amidships, smoking a cigarette
and looking completely unconcerned. The stern diver, doubt-
less wondering what had happened, was being hauled up wil-
ly-nilly by his tender, since the *Arafura* had come to rest and
all operations had been suspended until the trouble was resolved.

"There's some kind of wreck down there," said Tibor. "I
ran right into it. All I could see were a lot of wires and
rods."

To his annoyance and self-contempt, the memory set him
trembling again.

"Don't see why *that* should give you the shakes," grumbled
Nick. Nor could Tibor—here on this sun-drenched deck. It
was impossible to explain how a harmless shape glimpsed
through the mist could set one's whole mind jangling with
terror.

"I nearly got hung up on it," he lied. "Blanco pulled me
clear just in time."

"Hmm," said Nick, obviously not convinced. "Anyway, it
ain't a ship." He gestured towards the midships diver. "Steve
ran into a mess of ropes and cloth—like thick nylon, he says.
Sounds like some kind of parachute." The old Greek stared
in disgust at the soggy stump of his cigar, then flicked it overboard. "Soon as Billy's up, we'll go back and take a look.
Might be worth something—remember what happened to Jo
Chambers."

Tibor remembered; the story was famous the length of the
Great Barrier Reef. Jo had been a lone-wolf fisherman who,
in the last months of the War, had spotted a DC-3 lying in
shallow water a few miles off the Queensland coast. After
prodigies of single-handed salvage, he had broken into the
fuselage and started unloading boxes of taps and dies, perfectly protected by their greased wrappings. For a while he

had run a flourishing import business, but when the police caught up with him he reluctantly revealed his source of supply. Australian cops can be very persuasive.

And it was then, after weeks and weeks of backbreaking underwater work, that Jo discovered what his DC-3 had been carrying besides the miserable few thousand dollars' worth of tools he had been flogging to garages and workshops on the mainland.

The big wooden crates he'd never got round to opening held a week's payroll for the U.S. Pacific Forces.

No such luck here, thought Tibor as he sank over the side again. But the aircraft—or whatever it was—might contain valuable instruments, and there could be a reward for its discovery. Besides, he owed it to himself. He wanted to see exactly what it was that had given him such a fright.

Ten minutes later, he knew it was no aircraft. It was the wrong shape, and it was much too small—only about twenty feet long and half that in width. Here and there on the gently-tapering body were access hatches and tiny ports through which unknown instruments peered at the world. It seemed unharmed, though one end had been fused as if by terrific heat. From the other sprouted a tangle of antennae, all of them broken or bent by the impact with the water. Even now, they bore an incredible resemblance to the legs of a giant insect.

Tibor was no fool. He guessed at once what the thing was.

Only one problem remained, and he solved that with little difficulty. Though they had been partly charred away by heat, stenciled words could still be read on some of the hatch-covers. The letters were Cyrillic, and Tibor knew enough Russian to pick out references to electrical supplies and pressurizing systems.

"So they've lost a sputnik," he told himself with satisfaction.

He could imagine what had happened. The thing had come down too fast, and in the wrong place. Around one end were the tattered remnants of flotation bags; they had burst under the impact, and the vehicle had sunk like a stone.

The *Arafura*'s crew would have to apologize to Joey. He hadn't been drinking grog. What he'd seen burning across the stars must have been the rocket carrier, separated from its payload and falling back unchecked into the Earth's atmosphere.

For a long time Tibor hovered on the sea bed, knees bent in the diver's crouch, as he regarded this space creature now trapped in an alien element. His mind was full of half-formed plans, but none had yet come clearly into focus.

He no longer cared about salvage money. Much more important were the prospects of revenge.

Here was one of the proudest creations of Soviet technology—and Szabo Tibor, late of Budapest, was the only man on earth who knew.

There must be some way of exploiting the situation—of doing harm to the country and the cause he now hated with such smoldering intensity. In his waking hours, he was seldom conscious of that hate. Still less did he ever stop to analyze its real cause. Here in this lonely world of sea and sky, of streaming mangrove swamps and dazzling coral strands, there was nothing to recall the past. Yet he could never escape it. And sometimes the demons in his mind would awake, lashing him into a fury of rage or vicious, wanton destructiveness. So far he had been lucky; he had not killed anyone. But some day . . .

An anxious jerk from Blanco interrupted his reveries of vengeance.

He gave a reassuring signal to his tender, and started a closer examination of the capsule. What did it weigh? Could it be hoisted easily? There were many things he had to discover, before he could settle on any definite plans.

He braced himself against the corrugated metal wall and pushed cautiously. There was a definite movement as the capsule rocked on the sea bed. Maybe it could be lifted, even with the few pieces of tackle that the *Arafura* could muster. It was probably lighter than it looked.

Tibor pressed his helmet against a flat section of the hull, and listened intently.

He had half expected to hear some mechanical noise, such as the whirring of electric motors. Instead, there was utter silence. With the hilt of his knife, he rapped sharply on the metal, trying to gauge its thickness and to locate any weak spots. On the third try, he got results: but they were not what he had anticipated.

In a furious, desperate tattoo, the capsule rapped back at him.

Until this moment, Tibor had never dreamed that there might be someone inside. The capsule had seemed far too small.

Then he realized that he had been thinking in terms of conventional aircraft. There was plenty of room here for a little pressure cabin in which a dedicated astronaut could spend a few cramped hours.

As a kaleidoscope can change its pattern completely in a single moment, so the half-formed plans in Tibor's mind dissolved and then crystallized into a new shape. Behind the thick glass of his helmet, he ran his tongue lightly across his lips. If Nick could have seen him now, he would have wondered—as he had sometimes done before—whether his Number Two diver was wholly sane. Gone were all thoughts of a remote and impersonal vengeance against something as abstract as a nation or a machine.

Now it would be man to man.

III

"Took your time, didn't you?" said Nick. "What did you find?"

"It's Russian," said Tibor. "Some kind of sputnik. If we get a rope around it, I think we can lift it off the bottom. But it's too heavy to get aboard."

Nick chewed thoughtfully on his eternal cigar.

The pearling master was worried about a point that had not occurred to Tibor. If there were any salvage operations round here, everyone would know where the *Arafura* had been drifting. When the news got back to Thursday Island, his private patch of shell would be cleaned out in no time.

They'd have to keep quiet about the whole affair, or else haul the damn thing up themselves and not say where they'd found it. Whatever happened, it looked like being more of a nuisance than it was worth. Nick, who shared most Australians' profound suspicion of authority, had already decided that all he'd get for his trouble would be a nice letter of thanks.

"The boys won't go down," he said. "They think it's a bomb. Want to leave it alone."

"Tell 'em not to worry," replied Tibor. "I'll handle it."

He tried to keep his voice normal and unemotional, but this was too good to be true. If the other divers heard the tapping from the capsule, his plans would have been frustrated.

He gestured to the island, green and lovely on the skyline.

"Only one thing we can do. If we can heave it a couple of feet off the bottom, we can run for the shore. Once we're in shallow water, it won't be too hard to haul it up on the beach. We can use the boats, and maybe get a block and tackle on one of those trees."

Nick considered the idea without much enthusiasm. He

doubted if they could get the sputnik through the reef, even on the leeward side of the island. But he was all in favor of lugging it away from this patch of shell. They could always dump it somewhere else, buoy the place and still get whatever credit was going.

"Okay," he said. "Down you go. That two-inch rope's the strongest we've got—better take that. Don't be all bloody day; we've lost enough time already."

Tibor had no intention of being all day. Six hours would be quite long enough. That was one of the first things he had learned, from the signals through the wall.

It was a pity that he could not hear the Russian's voice; but the Russian could hear him, and that was what really mattered. When he pressed his helmet against the metal and shouted, most of his words got through. So far, it had been a friendly conversation; Tibor had no intention of showing his hand until the right psychological moment.

The first move had been to establish a code—one knock for "Yes," two for "No." After that, it was merely a matter of framing suitable questions. Given time, there was no fact or idea that could not be communicated by means of these two signals.

It would have been a much tougher job if Tibor had been forced to use his indifferent Russian. He had been pleased, but not surprised, to find that the trapped pilot understood English perfectly.

There was air in the capsule for another five hours; the occupant was uninjured; yes, the Russians knew where it had come down.

That last reply gave Tibor pause. Perhaps the pilot was lying, but it might very well be true. Although something had obviously gone wrong with the planned return to Earth, the tracking ships out in the Pacific must have located the impact point—with what accuracy, he could not guess. Still, did that matter? It might take them days to get here, even if they came racing straight into Australian territorial waters without bothering to get permission from Canberra. He was master of the situation. The entire might of the U.S.S.R. could do nothing to interfere with his plans—until it was much too late.

The heavy rope fell in coils on the sea-bed, stirring up a cloud of silt that drifted like smoke down the slow current. Now that the sun was higher in the sky, the underwater world was no longer wrapped in a gray, twilight gloom. The sea-bed was colorless but bright, and the boundary of vision was now almost fifteen feet away.

For the first time, Tibor could see the space-capsule in its entirety. It was such a peculiar-looking object, being designed for conditions beyond all normal experience, that there was an eye-teasing wrongness about it. One searched in vain for a front or a rear. There was no way of telling in what direction it pointed as it sped along its orbit.

Tibor pressed his helmet against the metal and shouted.

"I'm back," he called. "Can you hear me?"

Tap.

"I've got a rope, and I'm going to tie it on to the parachute cables. We're about three kilometres from an island. As soon as we've made you fast we'll head towards it. We can't lift you out of the water with the gear on the lugger, so we'll try to get you up on the beach. You understand?"

Tap.

It took only a few moments to secure the rope; now he had better get clear before the *Arafura* started to lift.

But there was something he had to do first.

"Hello!" he shouted. "I've fixed the rope. We'll lift in a minute. D'you hear me?"

Tap.

"Then you can hear this too. You'll never get there alive. I've fixed *that* as well."

Tap, tap.

"You've got five hours to die. My brother took longer than that, when he ran into your mine field. You understand? I'm from Budapest! I hate you and your country and everything it stands for. You've taken my home, my family, made my people slaves. I wish I could see your face now! I wish I could watch you die, as I had to watch Theo. When you're halfway to the island, this rope is going to break where I cut it. I'll go down and fix another—and that'll break, too. You can sit in there and wait for the bumps."

Tibor stopped abruptly, shaken and exhausted by the violence of his emotion.

There was no room for logic or reason in this orgasm of hate. He did not pause to think, for he dared not. Yet somewhere far down inside his mind the real truth was burning its way up towards the light of consciousness.

It was not the Russians he hated, for all that they had done. It was himself, for he had done more.

The blood of Theo, and of ten thousand countrymen, was upon his own hands. No one could have been a better communist than he was, or have more supinely believed the propaganda from Moscow. At school and college, he had been the first to hunt out and denounce "traitors" (how many had he sent to the labor camps or the AVO torture chambers?). When he had seen the truth, it was far, far too late. And even then he had not fought. He had run.

He had run across the world, trying to escape his guilt; and the two drugs of danger and dissipation had helped him to forget the past. The only pleasure life gave him now were the loveless embraces he sought so feverishly when he was on the mainland, and his present mode of existence was proof that these were not enough.

If he now had the power to deal out death, it was only because he had come here in search of it himself.

There was no sound from the capsule. Its silence seemed contemptuous, mocking. Angrily, Tibor banged against it with the hilt of his knife.

"Did you hear me?" he shouted. "Did you hear me?"

No answer.

"Damn you! I know you're listening! If you don't answer, I'll hole you and let the water in!"

He was sure that he could, with the sharp point of his knife. But that was the last thing he wanted to do; that would be too quick, too easy an ending.

There was still no sound; maybe the Russian had fainted. Tibor hoped not, but there was no point in waiting any longer. He gave a vicious parting bang on the capsule, and signaled to his tender.

Nick had news for him when he broke the surface.

"T.I. radio's been squawking," he said. "The Ruskis are asking everyone to look out for one of their rockets. They say it should be floating somewhere off the Queensland coast. Sounds as if they want it badly."

"Did they say anything else about it?" Tibor asked anxiously.

"Oh, yes. It's been round the Moon a couple of times."

"That all?"

"Nothing else that I remember. There was a lot of science stuff I didn't get."

That figured; it was just like the Russians to keep as quiet as they could about an experiment that had gone wrong.

"You tell T.I. that we'd found it?"

"Are you crazy? Anyway, the radio's crook; couldn't if we wanted to. Fixed that rope properly?"

"Yes—see if you can haul her off the bottom."

The end of the rope had been wound round the mainmast, and in a few seconds it had been drawn taut. Although the sea was calm, there was a slight swell and the lugger was rolling ten or fifteen degrees. With each roll, the gunwales would rise a couple of feet, then drop again. There was a lift here of several tons, but one had to be careful in using it.

The rope twanged, the woodwork groaned and creaked, and for a moment Tibor was afraid that the weakened line would part too soon. But it held, and the load lifted.

They got a further hoist on the second roll—and on the third. Then the capsule was clear of the sea-bed, and the *Arafura* was listing slightly to port.

"Let's go," said Nick, taking the wheel. "Should be able to get her half a mile before she bumps again."

The lugger began to move slowly towards the island, carrying its hidden burden beneath it.

As he leaned on the rails, letting the sun steam the moisture from his sodden clothing, Tibor felt at peace for the first time in—how many months? Even his hate had ceased to burn like fire in his brain. Perhaps, like love, it was a passion that could never be satisfied. But for the moment, at least, it was satiated.

There was no weakening of his resolve. He was implacably set upon the vengeance that had been so strangely—so miraculously—placed within his power. Blood called for blood, and now the ghosts that haunted him might rest at last.

IV

He began to worry when they were two-thirds of the way to the island, and the rope had not parted.

There were still four hours to go. That was much too long. For the first time it occurred to him that his entire plan might miscarry, and might even recoil on his head. Suppose that, despite everything, Nick managed to get the capsule up on the beach before the deadline?

With a deep *twang* that set the whole ship vibrating, the rope came snaking out of the water, scattering spray in all directions.

"Might have guessed," muttered Nick. "She was just starting to bump. You like to go down again, or shall I send one of the boys?"

"I'll take it," Tibor hastily answered. "I can do it quicker than they can."

That was perfectly true, but it took him twenty minutes to locate the capsule. The *Arafura* had drifted well away from it before Nick could stop the engine, and there was a time when Tibor wondered if he would ever find it again.

He quartered the sea-bed in great arcs, and it was not until he had accidentally tangled in the trailing parachute that his search was ended. The shrouds lay pulsating slowly in the current like some weird and hideous marine monster—but there was nothing that Tibor feared now except frustration and his pulse barely quickened as he saw the whitely looming mass ahead.

The capsule was scratched and stained with mud, but appeared undamaged. It was lying on its side now, looking rather like a giant milk-churn that had been tipped over. The passenger must have been bumped around. But if he'd fallen all the way back from the Moon he must have been well padded and was probably still in good shape. Tibor hoped so. It would be a pity if the remaining three hours were wasted.

Once again he rested the verdigrised copper of his helmet against the no-longer-quite-so-brightly-gleaming metal of the capsule.

"Hello!" he shouted. "Can you hear me?"

Perhaps the Russian would try to balk him by remaining silent—but that, surely, was asking too much of any man's self-control. Tibor was right. Almost at once there was the sharp knock of the reply.

"So glad you're there," he called back. "Things are working out just the way I said, though I guess I'll have to cut the rope a little deeper."

The capsule did not answer it. It never answered again, though Tibor banged and banged on the next dive—and on the next.

But he hardly expected it to then, for they'd had to stop for a couple of hours to ride out a squall, and the time-limit had expired long before he made his final descent.

He was a little annoyed about that, for he had planned a farewell message. He shouted it just the same, though he knew he was wasting his breath.

By early afternoon, the *Arafura* had come in as close as she dared. There were only a few feet of water beneath her, and the tide was falling. The capsule broke surface at the bottom of each wave trough, and was now firmly stranded on a sandbank. There was no hope of moving it any further. It was stuck until a high sea dislodged it.

Nick regarded the situation with an expert eye.

"There's a six-foot-tide tonight," he said. "The way she's lying now, she'll be in only a couple of feet of water at low. We'll be able to get at her with the boats."

They waited off the sandbank while the sun and the tide

went down and the radio broadcast intermittent reports of a search that was coming closer but was still far away. Late in the afternoon the capsule was almost clear of the water. The crew rowed the small boat towards it with a reluctance which Tibor found himself sharing, to his annoyance.

"It's got a door in the side," said Nick suddenly. "Jeeze— think there's anyone in it?"

"Could be," answered Tibor, his voice not as steady as he thought.

Nick glanced at him curiously. His diver had been acting strangely all day, but he knew better than to ask him what was wrong. In this part of the world, you soon learned to mind your own business.

The boat, rocking slightly in the choppy sea, had now come alongside the capsule. Nick reached out and grabbed one of the twisted antenna stubs. Then, with catlike agility, he clambered up the curved metal surface. Tibor made no attempt to follow him, but watched silently from the boat as he examined the entrance hatch.

"Unless it's jammed," Nick muttered, "there must be some way of opening it from outside. Just our luck if it needs special tools."

His fears were groundless. The word "Open" had been stencilled in ten languages round the recessed doorcatch, and it took only seconds to deduce its mode of operation. As the air hissed out Nick said "Phew!" and turned suddenly pale. He looked at Tibor as if seeking support, but Tibor avoided his eye.

Then, reluctantly, Nick lowered himself into the capsule.

He was gone for a long time. At first, they could hear muffled bangings and bumpings from the inside, followed by a string of bi-lingual profanity.

And then there was a silence that went on and on and on.

When at last Nick's head appeared above the hatchway, his leathery, wind-tanned face was gray and streaked with tears. As Tibor saw this incredible sight, he felt a sudden ghastly premonition. Something had gone horribly wrong, but his mind was too numb to anticipate the truth. It came soon enough, when Nick handed down his burden, no larger than an oversized doll.

Blanco took it, as Tibor shrank to the stern of the boat.

As he looked at the calm, waxen face, fingers of ice seemed to close not only upon his heart, but round his loins. In the same moment, both hate and desire died forever within him, as he knew the price of his revenge.

The dead astronaut was perhaps more beautiful in death than she had been in life. Tiny though she was, she must have been tough as well as highly-trained to qualify for this mission. As she lay at Tibor's feet she was neither a Russian, nor the first female human being to have seen the far side of the Moon. She was merely the girl that he had killed.

Nick was talking from a long way off.

"She was carrying this," he said, in an unsteady voice. "Had it tight in her hand. Took me a long time to get it out."

Tibor scarcely heard him, and never even glanced at the tiny spool of tape lying in Nick's palm. He could not guess, in this moment beyond all feeling, that the Furies had yet to close in upon his soul—and that soon the whole world would be listening to an accusing voice from beyond the grave, branding him more irrevocably than any man since Cain.

ON THE FEASIBILITY OF COAL-DRIVEN POWER STATIONS

O. R. FRISCH

Atomic energy has many fathers—or men who have been so labeled—from Democritus to General Grove; but few have so clear a title to the name as O. R. Frisch. With Lise Meitner, Dr. Frisch was the first to identify the uranium-fission effect which led by a straight line of studies to Los Alamos and Hiroshima. Here Dr. Frisch moves three thousand years into the future to imagine another scientist making that same stunning discovery—the threshold of a new source of power.

(EDITOR'S NOTE: The followng article is reprinted from the Yearbook of the Royal Institute for the Utilization of Energy Sources for the Year 4995. In view of the acute crisis caused by the threat of exhaustion of uranium and thorium from the Earth and Moon Mining System, the Editors thought it advisable to give the new information contained in the article the widest possible distribution.)

Introduction. The recent discovery of coal (black, fossilized plant remains) in a number of places offers an interesting alternative to the production of power from fission. Some of the places where coal has been found indeed show signs of previous exploitation by prehistoric men who, however, prob-

31

ably used it for jewels and to blacken their faces at tribal ceremonies.

The power potentialities depend on the fact that coal can be readily oxidized, with the production of a high temperature and an energy of about 0.0000001 megawattday per gram. That is, of course, very little, but large amounts of coal (perhaps millions of tons) appear to be available.

The chief advantage is that the critical amount is very much smaller for coal than for any fissile material. Fission plants become, as is well known, uneconomical below 50 megawatts, and a coal-driven plant may be competitive for communities with small power requirements.

Design for a Coal Reactor. The main problem is to achieve free, yet controlled, access of oxygen to the fuel elements. The kinetics of the coal-oxygen reaction are much more complicated than fission kinetics, and not yet completely understood. A differential equation which approximates the behavior of the reaction has been set up, but its solution is possible only in the simplest cases.

It is therefore proposed to make the reaction vessel in the form of a cylinder, with perforated walls to allow the combustion gases to escape. A concentric inner cylinder, also perforated, serves to introduce the oxygen, while the fuel elements are placed between the two cylinders. The necessary presence of end plates poses a difficult but not insoluble mathematical problem.

Fuel Elements. It is likely that these will be easier to manufacture than in the case of fission reactors. Canning is unnecessary and indeed undesirable since it would make it impossible for the oxygen to gain access to the fuel. Various lattices have been calculated, and it appears that the simplest of all—a close packing of equal spheres—is likely to be satisfactory. Computations are in progress to determine the optimum size of the spheres and the required tolerances. Coal is soft and easy to machine; so the manufacture of the spheres should present no major problem.

Oxidant. Pure oxygen is of course ideal but costly; it is therefore proposed to use air in the first place. However, it must be remembered that air contains 78 per cent of nitrogen. If even a fraction of that combined with the carbon of the coal to form the highly toxic gas cyanogen this would constitute a grave health hazard (see below).

Operation and Control. To start the reaction one requires a fairly high temperature of about 988 degrees F.; this is most conveniently achieved by passing an electric current between the inner and outer cylinder (the end plates being made of insulating ceramic). A current of several thousand amps is needed, at some 30 volts, and the required large storage battery will add substantially to the cost of the installation.

Once the reaction is started its rate can be controlled by adjusting the rate at which oxygen is admitted; this is almost as simple as the use of control rods in a conventional fission reactor.

Corrosion. The walls of the reactor must withstand a temperature of well over 1,000 degrees F. in the presence of oxygen, nitrogen, carbon monoxide and dioxide, as well as small amounts of sulphur dioxide and other impurities, some still unknown. Few metals or ceramics can resist such grueling conditions. Niobium with a thin lining of nickel might be an attractive possibility, but probably solid nickel will have to be used. For the ceramic, fused thoria appears to be the best bet.

Health Hazards. The main health hazard is attached to the gaseous waste products. They contain not only carbon monoxide and sulphur dioxide (both highly toxic) but also a number of carcinogenic compounds such as phenanthrene and others. To discharge those into the air is impossible; it would cause the tolerance level to be exceeded for several miles around the reactor.

It is therefore necessary to collect the gaseous waste in suitable containers, pending chemical detoxification. Alternatively the waste might be mixed with hydrogen and filled into large balloons which are subsequently released.

The solid waste products will have to be removed at frequent intervals (perhaps as often as daily!), but the health hazards involved in that operation can easily be minimized by the use of conventional remote-handling equipment. The waste could then be taken out to sea and dumped.

There is a possibility—though it may seem remote—that the oxygen supply may get out of control; this would lead to melting of the entire reactor and the liberation of vast amounts of toxic gas. Here is a grave argument against the use of coal and in favor of fission reactors which have proved their complete safety over a period of several thousand years. It will probably take decades before a control system of sufficient reliability can be evolved.

A FEAST
OF DEMONS

WILLIAM MORRISON
(Joseph Samachson)

As a chemist, Joseph Samachson's published papers have covered a score of research projects, of which the most intelligible to the layman has to do with the body retention of that familiar nemesis of nuclear testing, strontium-90. As a science fiction writer, he has been a steady contributor to most of the leading science fiction magazines for some two decades. Readers of Star of Stars *will remember his remarkable* Country Doctor, *in which Dr. (of biochemistry) Samachson painted a moving and convincing portrait of a doctor (of medicine) confronted with the problem of healing a sick alien creature somewhat larger than a whale. Samachson's science fiction has appeared under pseudonyms, the best known of them being "William Morrison," under which the present story was first published.*

I

That year we were all Romans, and I have to tell you that I look awful in a toga and short sword, but not nearly as awful as the Greek.

You go to one of the big schools and naturally you turn out for the Class Reunion. Why not? There's money there, and good fellowship, and money, and the chance of a business contact that will do you some good. And money.

Well, I wasn't that fortunate—and you can say that again because it's the story of my life: I wasn't that fortunate.

I didn't go to Harvard, Princeton or Yale. I didn't even go

34

to Columbia, U.C.L.A. or the University of Chicago. What I
went to was Old Ugly. Don't lie to me—you never heard of
Old Ugly, not even if I tell you it's Oglethorpe A. & M.
There were fifty-eight of us in my graduating class—that's
1940—and exactly thirty turned up for the tenth reunion.

Wouldn't that turn your stomach? Only thirty Old Grads
with enough loyalty and school feeling to show up for that
tenth reunion and parade around in Roman togas and drink
themselves silly and renew old school ties. And, out of that
thirty, the ones that we all really wanted to see for sentimental reasons—I refer to Feinbarger of Feinbarger Shipping,
Schroop of the S.S.K. Studios in Hollywood, Dixon of the
National City Bank and so on—they didn't show up at all. It
was terribly disappointing to all of us, especially to me.

In fact, at the feast that evening, I found myself sitting
next to El Greco. There simply wasn't anyone else there. You
understand that I don't refer to that Spanish painter—I believe he's dead, as a matter of fact. I mean Theobald Greco,
the one we called the Greek.

I introduced myself and he looked at me blearily through
thick glasses. "Hampstead? Hampstead?"

"*Virgil* Hampstead," I reminded him. "You remember me.
Old Virgie."

He said, "Sure. Any more of that stuff left in the bottle,
Old Virgie?"

I poured for him. It was my impression, later borne out by
evidence, that he was not accustomed to drinking.

I said, "It's sure great to see all the fellows again, isn't it?
Say, look at Pudge Detweiler there! Ever see anything so
comical as the lampshade he's wearing for a hat?"

"Just pass me the bottle, will you?" Greco requested. "Old
Virgie, I mean."

"Still in research and that sort of thing?" I asked. "You
always were a brain, Greek. I can't tell you how much I've
envied you creative fellows. I'm in sales myself. Got a little territory right here that's a mint, Greek. A mint. If I only knew
where I could lay my hands on a little capital to expand it
the way—But I won't bore you with shop talk. What's your
line these days?"

"I'm in transmutation," he said clearly, and passed out face
down on the table.

Now nobody ever called me a dope—other things, yes, but
not a dope.

I knew what transmutation meant. Lead into gold, tin into

platinum, all that line of goodies. And accordingly the next
morning, after a certain amount of Bromo and black coffee, I
asked around the campus and found out that Greco had a
place of his own not far from the campus. That explained
why he'd turned up for the reunion. I'd been wondering.

I borrowed cab fare from Old Pudge Detweiler and headed
for the address I'd been given.

It wasn't a home. It was a beat-up factory and it had a sign
over the door:

T. GRECO
Plant Foods & Organic Supplies

Since it was Sunday, nobody seemed to be there, but I
pushed open the door. It wasn't locked. I heard something
from the basement, so I walked down a flight of steps and
looked out into a rather smelly laboratory.

There was the Greek. Tall, thin, wide-eyed and staggering,
he appeared to be chasing butterflies.

I cleared my throat, but he didn't hear me. He was racing
around the laboratory, gasping and muttering to himself,
sweeping at empty air with what looked to me like an electric
toaster on a stick. I looked again and, no, it wasn't an electric
toaster, but exactly what it was defied me. It appeared to
have a recording scale on the side of it, with a needle that
flickered wildly.

I couldn't see what he was chasing.

The fact was that, as far as I could see, he wasn't chasing
anything at all.

You have to get the picture: Here was Greco, racing
around with one eye on the scale and one eye on thin air; he
kept bumping into things, and every now and then he'd stop,
and stare around at the gadgets on the lab benches, and
maybe he'd throw a switch or turn a dial, and then he'd be
off again.

He kept it up for ten minutes and, to tell you the truth, I
began to wish that I'd made some better use of Pudge Detweiler's cab fare. The Greek looked as though he'd flipped,
nothing less.

But there I was. So I waited.

And by and by he seemed to get whatever it was he was
looking for and he stopped, breathing heavily.

I said, "Hi there, Greek."

He looked up sharply. "Oh," he said, "Old Virgie."

He slumped back against a table, trying to catch his breath.

"The little devils," he panted. "They must have thought they'd got away that time. But I fixed them!"

"Sure you did," I said. "You bet you did. Mind if I come in?"

He shrugged. Ignoring me, he put down the toaster on a stick, flipped some switches and stood up. A whining sound dwindled and disappeared; some flickering lights went out. Others remained on, but he seemed to feel that, whatever it was he was doing, it didn't require his attention now.

In his own good time, he came over and we shook hands. I said appreciatively, "Nice-looking laboratory you have here, Greek. I don't know what the stuff is for, but it looks ex-pen—it looks very efficient."

He grunted. "It is. Both. Expensive and efficient."

I laughed. "Say," I said, "you were pretty loaded last night. Know what you told me you were doing here?"

He looked up quickly. "What?"

"You said you were in transmutation." I laughed harder than ever.

He stared at me thoughtfully, and for a second I thought —well, I don't know what I thought, but I was worried. He had a lot of funny-looking things there, and his hand was stretching out toward one of them.

But then he said, "Old Virgie."

"That's me," I said eagerly.

"I owe you an apology," he went on.

"You do?"

He nodded. "I'd forgotten," he confessed, ashamed. "I didn't remember until just this minute that you were the one I talked to in my senior year. My only confidant. And you've kept my secret all this time."

I coughed. "It was nothing," I said largely. "Don't give it a thought."

He nodded in appreciation. "That's just like you," he reminisced. "Ten years, eh? And you haven't breathed a word, have you?"

"Not a word," I assured him. And it was no more than the truth. I hadn't said a word to anybody. I hadn't even said a word to myself. The fact of the matter was, I had completely forgotten what he was talking about. Kept his secret? I didn't even *remember* his secret. And it was driving me nuts!

"I was sure of you," he said, suddenly thawing. "I knew I

could trust you. I must have—otherwise I certainly wouldn't
have told you, would I?"

I smiled modestly. But inside I was fiercely cudgeling my
brain.

He said suddenly, "All right, Virgie. You're entitled to
something for having kept faith. I tell you what I'll do—I'll
let you in on what I'm doing here."

All at once, the little muscles at the back of my neck
began to tense up.

He would do *what?* "Let me in" on something? It was an
unpleasantly familiar phrase. I had used it myself all too
often.

"To begin with," said the Greek, focusing attentively on
me, "you wonder, perhaps, what I was doing when you came
in."

"I do," I said.

He hesitated. "Certain—particles, which are of importance
to my research, have a tendency to go free. I can keep them
under a measure of control only by means of electrostatic
forces, generated in this." He waved the thing that looked
like a toaster on a stick. "And as for what they do—well,
watch."

El Greco began to putter with gleamy, glassy gadgets on
one of the tables and I watched him with, I admit, a certain
amount of suspicion.

"What are you doing, Greek?" I asked pretty bluntly.

He looked up. Surprisingly, I saw that the suspicion was
mutual; he frowned and hesitated. Then he shook his head.

"No," he said. "For a minute I—but I can trust you, can't
I? The man who kept my secret for ten long years."

"Of course," I said.

"All right." He poured water out of a beaker into a U-
shaped tube, open at both ends. "Watch," he said. "Remember any of your college physics?"

"The way things go, I haven't had much time to keep up
with—"

"All the better, all the better," he said. "Then you won't be
able to steal anything."

I caught my breath. "Now *listen*—"

"No offense, Virgie," he said earnestly. "But this is a billion dollars and— No matter. When it comes right down to
cases, you could know as much as all those fool professors of
ours put together and it still wouldn't help you steal a thing."

He bobbed his head, smiled absently and went back to his
gleamy gadgets. I tell you, I *steamed*. That settled it, as far as

I was concerned. There was simply no excuse for such unjustified insults to my character. I certainly had no intention of attemping to take any unfair advantage, but if he was going to act that way . . .

He was asking for it. Actually and literally asking for it.

He rapped sharply on the U-tube with a glass stirring rod, seeking my attention.

"I'm watching," I told him, very amiable now that he'd made up my mind for me.

"Good. Now," he said, "you know what I do here in the plant?"

"Why—you make fertilizer. It says so on the sign."

"Ha! No," he said. "That is a blind. What I do is, I separate optical isomers."

"That's very nice," I said warmly. "I'm glad to hear it, Greek."

"Shut up," he retorted unexpectedly. "You don't have the foggiest notion of what an optical isomer is and you know it. But try and think. This isn't physics; it's organic chemistry. There are compounds that exist in two forms—apparently identical in all respects, except that one is the mirror image of the other. Like right-hand and left-hand gloves; one is the other, turned backards. You understand so far?"

"Of course," I said.

He looked at me thoughtfully, then shrugged. "No matter. They're called d- and l-isomers—d for dextro, l for levo; right and left, you see. And although they're identical except for being mirror-reversed, it so happens that sometimes one isomer is worth much more than the other."

"I see that," I said.

"I thought you would. Well, they can be separated—but it's expensive. Not my way, though. My way is quick and simple. I use demons."

"Oh, now, Greek. *Really.*"

He said in a weary tone. "Don't talk, Virgie. Just listen. It won't tire you so much. But bear in mind that this is simply the most trifling application of my discovery. I could use it for separating U-235 from U-238 just as easily. In fact, I already—" He stopped in mid-sentence, cocked his head, looked at me and backtracked. "Never mind that. But you know what a Maxwell demon is?"

"No."

"Good for you, Virgie. Good for you!" he applauded. "I knew I'd get the truth out of you if I waited long enough." *Another* ambiguous remark, I thought to myself. "But you surely know the second law of thermodynamics."

"Surely."

"I thought you'd say that," he said gravely. "So then you know that if you put an ice cube in a glass of warm water, for instance, the ice melts, the water cools, and you get a glass with no ice but with all the water lowered in temperature. Right? And it's a one-way process. That is, you can't start with a glass of cool water and, hocus-pocus, get it to separate into warm water and ice cube, right?"

"Naturally," I said, "for heaven's sake. I mean that's silly."

"*Very* silly," he agreed. "You know it yourself, eh? So watch."

He didn't say hocus-pocus. But he did adjust something on one of his gadgets.

There was a faint whine and a gurgling spluttering sound, like fat sparks climbing between spreading electrodes in a Frankenstein movie.

The water began to steam faintly.

But only at one end! That end was steam; the other was—was—

It was ice. A thin skin formed rapidly, grew thicker; the other open end of the U-tube began to bubble violently. Ice at one end, steam at the other.

Silly?

But I was seeing it!

I must say, however, that at the time I didn't really know that that was all I saw.

The reason for this is that Pudge Detweiler came groaning down the steps to the laboratory just then.

"Ah, Greek," he wheezed. "Ah, Virgie. I wanted to talk to you before I left." He came into the room and, panting, eased himself into a chair, a tired hippopotamus with a hangover.

"What did you want to talk to me about?" Greco demanded.

"You?" Pudge's glance wandered around the room; it was a look of amused distaste, the look of a grown man observing the smudgy mud play of children. "Oh, not you, Greek. I wanted to talk to Virgie. That sales territory you mentioned, Virgie. I've been thinking. I don't know if you're aware of it, but when my father passed away last winter, he left me— well, with certain responsibilities. And it occurred to me that you might be willing to let me invest some of the—"

I didn't even let him finish. I had him out of there so fast, we didn't even have a chance to say good-by to Greco. And all that stuff about demons and hot-and-cold water and so on, it all went out of my head as though it had never been. Old Pudge Detweiler! How was *I* to know that his father had left him thirty thousand dollars in one attractive lump of cash!

II

Well, there were business reverses. Due to the reverses, I was forced to miss the next few reunions. But I had a lot of time to think and study, in between times at the farm and the shop where we stamped out license plates for the state.

When I got out, I began looking for El Greco.

I spent six months at it, and I didn't have any luck at all. El Greco had moved his laboratory and left no forwarding address.

But I wanted to find him. I wanted it so badly, I could taste it, because I had begun to have some idea of what he was talking about, and so I kept on looking.

I never did find him, though. He found me.

He came walking in on me in a shabby little hotel room, and I hardly recognized him, he looked so prosperous and healthy.

"You're looking just great, Greek," I said enthusiastically, seeing it was true. The years hadn't added a pound or a wrinkle—just the reverse, in fact.

"You're not looking so bad yourself," he said, and gazed at me sharply. "Especially for a man not long out of prison."

"Oh." I cleared my throat. "You know about that."

"I heard that Pudge Detweiler prosecuted."

"I see." I got up and began uncluttering a chair. "Well," I said, "it's certainly good to— How did you find me?"

"Detectives. Money buys a lot of help. I've got a lot of money."

"Oh." I cleared my throat again.

Greco looked at me, nodding thoughtfully to himself. There was one good thing; maybe he knew about my trouble with Pudge, but he also had gone out of his way to find me. So *he* wanted something out of *me*.

He said suddenly, "Virgie, you were a damned fool."

"I was," I admitted honestly. "Worse than you know. But I am no longer. Greek, old boy, all this stuff you told me about those demons got me interested. I had plenty of time for reading in prison. You won't find me as ignorant as I was the last time we talked."

He laughed sourly. "That's a hot one. Four years of college leave you as ignorant as the day you went in, but a couple years of jail make you an educated man."

"Also a reformed one."

He said mildly, "Not too reformed, I hope."

"Crime doesn't pay—except when it's within the law. That's the chief thing I learned."

"Even then it doesn't pay," he said moodily. "Except in money, of course. But what's the use of money?"

There wasn't anything to say to *that*. I said, probing delicately, "I figured you were loaded. If you can use your demons to separate U-235 from U-238, you can use them for separating gold from sea water. You can use them for damn near anything."

"Damn near," he concurred. "Virgie, you may be of some help to me. Obviously you've been reading up on Maxwell."

"Obviously."

It was the simple truth. I had got a lot of use out of the prison library—even to the point of learning all there was to learn about Clerk Maxwell, one of the greatest of physicists, and his little demons. I had rehearsed it thoroughly for El Greco.

"Suppose," I said, "that you had a little compartment inside a pipe of flowing gas or liquid. That's what Maxwell said. Suppose the compartment had a little door that allowed molecules to enter or leave. You station a demon—that's what Maxie called them himself—at the door. The demon sees a hot molecule coming, he opens the door. He sees a cold one, he closes it. By and by, just like that, all the hot molecules are on one side of the door, all the cold ones—the slow ones, that is—on the other. Steam on one side, ice on the other, that's what it comes down to."

"That was what you saw with your own eyes," Theobald Greco reminded me.

"I admit it," I said. "And I admit I didn't understand. But I do now."

I understood plenty. Separate isotopes—separate elements, for that matter. Let your demon open the door to platinum, close it to lead. He could make you rich in no time.

He had, in fact, done just that for Greco.

Greco said, "Here. First installment." He pulled something out of his pocket and handed it to me. It was metallic—about the size of a penny slot-machine bar of chocolate, if you remember back that far. It gleamed and it glittered. And it was ruddy yellow in color.

"What's that?" I asked.

"Gold," he said. "Keep it, Virgie. It came out of sea water, like you said. Call it the down payment on your salary."

I hefted it. I bit it. I said, "By the way, speaking of salary . . ."

"Whatever you like," he said wearily. "A million dollars a year? Why not?"

"Why not?" I echoed, a little dazed.

And then I just sat there listening, while he talked. What else was there to do? I won't even say that I was listening, at least not with the very fullest of attention, because that thought of a million dollars a year kept coming between me and his words. But I got the picture. The possibilities were endless. And how well I knew it!

Gold from the sea, sure. But energy—free energy—it was there for the taking. From the molecules of the air, for instance. Refrigerators could be cooled, boilers could get up steam, homes could be heated, forges could be fired—and all without fuel. Planes could fly through the air without a drop of gasoline in their tanks. Anything.

A million dollars a year . . .

And it was only the beginning.

I came to. "What?"

He was looking at me. He repeated patiently, "The police are looking for me."

I stared. "You?"

"Did you hear about Grand Rapids?"

I thought. "Oh— Wait. A fire. A big one. And that was you?"

"Not me. My demons. Maxwell demons—or Greco demons, they should be called. He talked about them; I use them. When they're not using me. This time, they burned down half the city."

"I remember now," I said. The papers had been full of it.

"They got loose," he said grimly. "But that's not the worst. You'll have to earn your million a year, Virgie."

"What do you mean, they got loose?"

He shrugged. "Controls aren't perfect. Sometimes the demons escape. I can't help it."

"How do you control them in the first place?"

He sighed. "It isn't really what you would call controls," he said. "It's just the best I can do to keep them from spreading."

"But—you said sometimes you separate metals, sometimes you get energy. How do the demons know which you want them to do, if you say you can't control them?"

"How do you make an apple tree understand whether you
want it to grow Baldwins or Macintoshes?"

I gawked at him. "Why—but you don't, Greek! I mean it's
either one or the other!"

"Just so with demons! You're not so stupid after all, are
you? It's like improving the breed of dogs. You take a common ancestral mutt, and generations later you can develop an
Airedale, a dachshund or a Spitz. How? By selection. My
demon entities grow, they split, the new entities adapt themselves to new conditions. There's a process of evolution. I
help it along, that's all."

He took the little slab of gold from me, brooding.

Abruptly he hurled it at the wall. "Gold!" he cried wildly.
"But who wants it? I need *help*, Virgie! If gold will buy it
from you, I'll pay! But I'm desperate. You'd be desperate too,
with nothing ahead but a sordid, demeaning death from
young age and a—"

I interrupted him. "What's that?"

It was a nearby raucous hooting, loud and mournful.

Greco stopped in mid-sentence, listening like a hunted
creature. "My room," he whispered. "All my equipment—on
the floor above—"

I stepped back, a little worried. He was a strange man,
skinny and tall and wild-eyed. I was glad he was so thin; if
he'd been built solidly in proportion to his height, just then
he would have worried me, with those staring, frightened
eyes and that crazy way of talking. But I didn't have time to
worry, in any case. Footsteps were thundering in the halls.
Distant voices shouted to each other.

The hoot came again.

"The fire whistle!" Greco bayed. "The hotel's on fire!"

He leaped out of my room into the corridor.

I followed. There was a smell of burning—not autumn
leaves or paper; it was a chemical-burning smell, a leather-
burning smell, a henyard-on-fire smell. It reeked of an assortment of things, gunpowder and charred feathers, the choking
soot of burning oil, the crisp tang of a wood fire. It was, I
thought for a second, perhaps the typical smell of a hotel on
fire, but in that I was wrong.

"Demons!" yelled Greco, and a bellhop, hurrying by,
paused to look at us queerly. Greco sped for the stairs and
up them.

I followed.

It was Greco's room that was ablaze—he made that clear,
trying to get into it. But he couldn't. Black smoke billowed

out of it, and orange flame. The night manager's water bucket was going to make no headway against *that*.

I retreated. But Greco plunged ahead, his face white and scary.

I stopped at the head of the stairs. The flames drove Greco off, but he tried again. They drove him off again, and this time for good.

He stumbled toward me. "Out! It's hopeless!" He turned, stared blindly at the hotel employees with their chain of buckets. "You! What do you think you're doing? That's—" He stopped, wetting his lips. "That's a gasoline fire," he lied, "and there's dynamite in my luggage. Clear the hotel, you hear me?"

It was, as I say, a lie. But it got the hotel cleared out. And then—

It might as well have been gasoline and dynamite. There was a purplish flash and a muttering boom, and the whole roof of the four-story building lifted off.

I caught his arm.

"Let's get out of here," I said.

He looked at me blindly. I'd swear he didn't know me. His eyes were tortured.

"Too late!" he croaked. "Too late! They're free again!"

III

So I went to work for Theobald Greco—in his laboratory in Southern California, where we replaced some of the things that had been destroyed.

And one morning I woke up and found my hair was white.

I cried, "Greek!"

Minnie came running in. I don't believe I told you about Minnie. She was Greco's idea of the perfect laboratory assistant —stupid, old, worthless to the world and without visible kin. She came in and stared and set up a cackling that would wake the dead.

"Mister Hampstead!" she chortled. "My, but ain't you a sight!"

"Where's Greco?" I demanded, and pushed her out of my way.

In pajamas and bathrobe, I stalked down the stairs and into the room that had once been a kitchen and now was Greco's laboratory.

"Look!" I yelled. "What about *this*?"

He turned to look at me.

After a long moment, he shook his head.

"I was afraid of that," he mumbled. "You were a towhead as a kid, weren't you? And now you're a towhead again."

"But my hair, Greek! It's turned *white*."

"Not white," he corrected despondently. "Yellow. It's reverted to youth—overnight, the way it happens sometimes. I warned you, Virgie. I told you there were dangers. Now you know. Because—"

He hesitated, looked at me, then looked away.

"Because," he said, "you're getting younger, just like me. If we don't get this thing straightened out, you're going to die of young age yourself."

I stared at him. "You said that before, about yourself. I thought you'd just tongue-twisted. But you really mean—"

"Sit down," he ordered. "Virgie, I told you that you were looking younger. It wasn't just looks. It's the demons—and not just you and me, but a lot of people. First Grand Rapids. Then when the hotel burned. Plenty have been exposed—you more than most, I guess, ever since the day you walked into my lab and I was trying to recapture some that had got away. Well, I don't guess I recaptured them all."

"You mean *I*—"

He nodded. "Some of the demons make people younger. And you've got a colony of them in you."

I swallowed and sat down. "You mean I'm going to get younger and younger, until finally I become a baby? And then —what then, Greek?"

He shrugged. "How do I know? As me in another ten years. *Look at me, Virgie!*" he cried, suddenly loud. "How old do I look to you? Eighteen? Twenty?"

It was the plain truth. He looked no more than that. Seeing him day by day, I wasn't conscious of change; remembering him from when we had gone to school, I thought of him as younger anyway. But he was forty, at the very least, and he didn't look old enough to vote.

He said, "I've had demons inside of me for six years. It seems they're a bit choosy about where they'll live. They don't inhabit the whole body, just parts of it—heart, lungs, liver. Maybe bones. Maybe some of the glands—perhaps that's why I feel so chipper physically. But not my brain, or not yet. Fortunately."

"Fortunately? But that's wrong, Greek! If your brain grew younger too—"

"Fool! If I had a young brain, I'd forget everything I learned, like unrolling a tape backwards! That's the danger,

Virgie, the immediate danger that's pressing me—that's why I needed help! Because if I ever forget, that's the end. Not just for me—for everybody; because there's no one else in the world who knows how to control these things at all. Except me—and you, if I can train you."

"They're loose?" I felt my hair wonderingly. Still, it was not exactly a surprise. "How many?"

He shrugged. "I have no idea. When they let the first batch of rabbits loose in Australia, did they have any idea how many there would be a couple of dozen generations later?"

I whistled. Minnie popped her head in the door and giggled. I waved her away.

"She could use some of your demons," I remarked. "Sometimes I think she has awfully young ideas, for a woman who's sixty if she's a day."

Greco laughed crazily. "Minnie? She's been working for me for a year. And she was eighty-five when I hired her!"

"I can't believe you!"

"Then you'll have to start practicing right now," he said.

It was tough, and no fooling; but I became convinced. It wasn't the million dollars a year any more.

It was the thought of ending my days as a drooling, mewling infant—or worse! To avert that, I was willing to work my brain to a shred.

First it was a matter of learning—learning about the "strange particles." Ever hear of them? That's not my term —that's what the physicists call them. Positrons. The neutrino. Pions and muons, plus and minus; the lambda and the antilambda. K particles, positive and negative, and anti-protons and anti-neutrons and sigmas, positive, negative and neutral, and—

Well, that's enough; but physics had come a long way since the classes I cut at Old Ugly, and there was a lot to catch up on.

The thing was, some of the "strange particles" were stranger than even most physicists knew. Some—in combination—were in fact Greco's demons.

We bought animals—mice, rabbits, guinea pigs, even dogs. We infected the young with some of our own demons—that was simple enough, frighteningly simple; all we had to do was handle them a bit. And we watched what happened.

They died—of young age.

Some vital organ or another regressed to embryonic condition, and they died—as Greco and I would die, if we didn't find the answer. As the whole world might die. Was it better than reverting past the embryo to the simple lifeless zygote? I couldn't decide. It was dying, all the same. When an embryonic heart or liver is called on to do a job for a mature organism, there is only one way out. Death.

And after death—the demons went on; the dog we fed on the remains of the guinea pigs followed them to extinction in a matter of weeks.

Minnie was an interesting case.

She was going about her work with more energy every day, and I'll be blasted if I didn't catch her casting a lingering Marilyn Monroe sort of look at me when Greco's back was turned.

"Shall we fire her?" I asked El Greco when I told him about it.

"What for?"

"She's disrupting the work!"

"The work isn't worth a damn anyhow," he said moodily. "We're not getting anywhere, Virgie. If it was only a matter of smooth, predictable rates— But look at her. She's picking up speed! She's dropped five years in the past couple weeks."

"She can stand to drop a lot more," I said, annoyed.

He shrugged. "It depends on where. Her nose? It's shortened to about a fifteen-year-old level now. Facial hair? That's mostly gone. Skin texture? Well, I suppose there's no such thing as a too-immature skin, I mean short of the embryonic capsule, but— Wait a minute."

He was staring at the doorway.

Minnie was standing there, simpering.

"Come here!" he ordered in a voice like thunder. "Come here, you! Virgie, look at her nose!"

I looked. "Ugh," I said, but more or less under my breath.

"No, no!" cried Greco. "Virgie, don't you see her *nose?*" Foolish; of course I did. It was long, beaked—

Then I saw.

"It's growing longer," I whispered.

"Right, my boy! Right! One curve at least has reversed itself. Do you see, Virgie?"

I nodded. "She's—she's beginning to age again."

"Better than that!" he crowed. "It's faster than normal aging, Virgie! *There are aging demons loose too!*"

A breath of hope!

But hope died. Sure, he was right—as far as it went.

There *were* aging demons. We isolated them in some of our experimental animals. First we had to lure Minnie into standing still while Greco, swearing horribly, took a tissue sample; she didn't like that, but a hundred-dollar bonus converted her. Solid CO_2 froze the skin; *snip*, and a tiny flake of flesh came out of her nose at the point of Greco's scalpel; he put the sample of flesh through a few tricks and, at the end of the day, we tried it on some of our mice.

They died.

Well, it was gratifying, in a way—they died of old age. But die they did. It took three days to show an effect, but when it came, it was dramatic. These were young adult mice, in the full flush of their mousehood, but when these new demons got to work on them, they suddenly developed a frowsy, decrepit appearance that made them look like Bowery bums over whom Cinderella's good fairy had waved her wand in reverse. And two days later they were dead.

"I think we've got something," said Greco thoughtfully; but I didn't think so, and I was right. Dead was dead. We could kill the animals by making them too young. We could kill the animals by making them too old. But keep them alive, once the demons were in them, we could not.

Greco evolved a plan: Mix the two breeds of demons! Take an animal with the young-age demons already in it, then add a batch that worked in the other direction!

For a while, it seemed to work—but only for a while. After a couple of weeks, one breed or the other would gain the upper hand. And the animals died.

It was fast in mice, slow in humans. Minnie stayed alive. But the nose grew longer and facial hair reappeared; simultaneously her complexion cleared, her posture straightened.

And then, for the first time, we began to read the papers.

STRANGE PLAGUE
STRIKES ELGIN

bawled the Chicago *Tribune*, and went on to tell how the suburbs around Elgin, Illinois, were heavily infested with a curious new malady, the symptoms of which were—youth.

OAKLAND "BABY-SKIN"
TOLL PASSES 10,000

blared the San Francisco *Examiner*. The New York *News* found thousands of cases in Brooklyn. A whole hospital in Dallas was evacuated to make room for victims of the new plague.

And more.

We looked at each other.

"They're out in force," said Theobald Greco soberly. "And we don't have the cure."

IV

The world was topsy-turvy, and in the middle of it Minnie disappeared, talking hysterically about reporting us to the authorities. I don't mind admitting that I was worried.

And the experiments were not progressing. The trouble seemed to be that the two varieties of demons—the aging and the youthing—were not compatible; if one took up residence in a given section of an organism, the other moved out. The more numerous destroyed the weaker; there was no balance. We tested it again and again in the mice and there was no doubt of it.

So far, only the youthing demons were free. But when Minnie left us, it was only a matter of time. Our carriers—from Grand Rapids and from the hotel—had spread to California and the East Coast, to the North and to the South, throughout the country, perhaps by now through the world. It would be slower with the aging demons—there was only one of Minnie—but it would be equally sure.

Greco began drinking heavily.

"It's the end," he brooded. "We're licked."

"No, Greek! We can't give up!"

"We *have* to give up. The demons are loose in the Earth, Virgie! Those people in the headlines—they'll die of young age. So will others—even plants and animals, and bacteria, as the demons adapt to them. And then—why not? The air. The rocks, the ocean, even the Earth itself. Remember, the entropy of the Universe is supposed to tend to a maximum not only as a whole, but in each of its parts taken in isolation. The Earth's evolution—reversed. Spottily, and maybe that's worse, because some parts will evolve forward and others reverse, as is happening in my own body. Heaven help the world, Old Virgie! And not just the Earth, because what can stop them from spreading? To the Moon, the other planets—out of the Solar System, for that matter; to the other galaxies, even. Why not? And then—"

"*GRECO.*"

An enormous tinny voice, more than human, filled the air. It came from outside.

I jumped a foot. It sounded like the voice of a demon; then I got a grip on myself and understood. It was a loudspeaker, and it came from outside.

"GRECO. WE KNOW YOU'RE IN THERE. COME ON OUT!"

I had a stabbing sensation of familiarity. "The police!" I cried. "Greco, it's the police!"

He looked at me wearily and shook his head.

"No. More likely the F.B.I."

Well, that was it. I got out—I didn't wait for permission from the Greek.

I stopped at the door, and three searchlight beams hit me right in the eye. There were cars all around the laboratory, but I couldn't see them, not after those lights went on.

I froze, stiff; wanting to make sure they understood (a) that I wasn't Greco and (b) that I didn't have a gun.

They understood, all right.

But they let me out.

They put me in one of the cars, with a slim gray-eyed young man in a snap-brimmed hat sitting politely and alertly beside me, and they let me watch; and what happened after that wasn't funny at all.

Greco didn't come out. They shouted at him over the loud-speaker and eventually he answered—his voice little and calm, coming out of nowhere, and all he said was, "Go away. I won't come out. I warn you, don't try to force your way in."

But he knew they wouldn't listen, of course.

The didn't.

They tried force.

And he met it in novel ways with force of his own. The door had locked itself behind me; they got a fence post for a battering ram, and the post burst into flame. They found an L-beam from an old bed frame and tried that, and they were sorry they had done it; the thing melted in the middle, splattering them with hot drops of steel.

The polite, alert young man beside me said, not so polite any more, "What's he doing, you? What sort of fancy tricks has he got in there?"

"Demons," I said crazily, and *that* was a mistake, but what else was I to do? Try to explain Maxwell's equations to a Fed?

They were trying again—there were fifteen or twenty of them, at least. They went for the windows, and the windows dissolved and rained cherry-red wet glass on them. They tried again through the open frames when the glass was gone, and the frames burst into fire around them, the blue smoke bleached white in the yellow of the flame and the white of the searchlights. They tried singly, by stealth; and they tried in clusters of a dozen, yelling.

It was hopeless—hopeless for everybody, because they couldn't get in and the Greek could never, never get out; for go away they wouldn't. Not even when, with *poof* and a yellow flare, the gas tank of one of the cars exploded. All that happened was that the man in the snap-brimmed hat and I leaped out, real quick; and then all the cars went up. But the men didn't leave. And then the guns began to go off without waiting for anyone to pull the trigger; and the barrels softened and slumped and spattered to the ground. But the men still had bare hands, and they stayed.

The Greek got wild—or lost control, it was hard to tell which. There was a sudden catastrophic *whooshing* roar and, *wham*, a tree took flame for roots. A giant old oak, fifty feet tall, I guess it had been there a couple of centuries, but Greco's demons changed all that; it took flame and shot whistling into the air, spouting flame and spark like a Roman candle. Maybe he thought it would scare them. Maybe it did. But it also made them mad. And they ran, all at once, every one of them but my personal friend, for the biggest, openest of the windows—

And leaped back, cursing and yelling, beating out flames on their clothes.

Jets of flame leaped out of every window and door. The old building seemed to bulge outward and go *voom*. In half a second, it was a single leaping tulip of fire.

The firemen got there then, but it was a little late. Oh, they got Greco out—alive, even. But they didn't save a bit of the laboratory. It was the third fire in Greco's career, and the most dangerous—for where previously only a few of the youthing demons had escaped, now there were vast quantities of both sorts.

It was the end of the world.
I knew it.

You know, I wish I had been right. I spent yesterday with Greco. He's married now and has a fine young son. They made an attractive family picture, the two healthy-looking adults, strong-featured, in the prime of life, and the wee toddler between them.

The only things is—Greco's the toddler.

He doesn't call himself Greco any more. Would you, the way the world is now? He has plenty of money stashed away —I do too, of course—not that money means very much these days. His brain hasn't been affected, just his body. He was lucky, I guess. Some of the demons hit the brain in some of their victims and—

Well, it's pretty bad.

Greco got the answer after a while. Both types of demons were loose in the world, and both, by and by, were in every individual.

But they didn't kill each other off.

One simply grew more rapidly, took over control, until it ran out of the kind of molecules it needed. Then the other took over.

Then the first.

Then the other again . . .

Mice are short-lived. It's like balancing a needle on the end of your nose; there isn't enough space in a mouse's short span for balance, any more than there is in a needle's.

But in a human life—

Things are going to have to be worked out, though.

It's bad enough that a family gets all mixed up the way Greco's is—he's on a descending curve, his kid is on an aging curve, and Minnie—did I tell you that it was Minnie he married?—has completed her second rejuvenation and is on the way back up again.

But there are worse problems than that.

For one thing, it isn't going to be too long before we run out of space. I don't mean time, I mean space. *Living* space.

Because it's all very well that the human animal should now mature to grow alternately younger and older, over and over—

But, damn it, how I wish that somebody once in a while would *die!*

THE HEART
ON THE
OTHER SIDE

GEORGE GAMOW

The friends and colleagues of Niels Bohr (yes, the man who first pictured the "Bohr atom") had the happy habit of celebrating his birthday by contributing papers to a sort of star-studded birthday book printed for his private enjoyment. Many of the papers are downright earnest and perhaps more technical than we laymen might enjoy; but there are exceptions.

One was O. R. Frisch's On the Feasibility of Coal-Driven Power Stations, *elsewhere in this volume. Another is the present story by George Gamow who, if any scientist ever qualified, surely can be presented as "a man who needs no introduction." His deadpan topological romance,* The Heart on the Other Side, *was first written to celebrate Bohr's seventieth birthday, and is here published for a general audience for the first time.*

"But Father will never give his consent," said Vera Sapognikoff in a tone of despair.

"But he must," said Stan Situs. He was very much in love.

Vera shook her head. "What my father is looking for in the way of a son-in-law is someone who can help him in his shoe business, and eventually take it over. You're a mathematician. You can't possibly qualify as a shoe manufacturer, can you?"

"I guess I can't," Stan agreed sadly, after some thought. "Perhaps if I were in some other branch of mathematics— But I am a topologist. I don't see what topology has to contribute to the production and selling of shoes."

Then he added stubbornly: "But I can't give you up, Vera! I can't lose the girl I love just because there's no cash value in a Möbius twist!"

"A what?"

Stan said patiently: "A Möbius twist. Haven't I ever shown you one?" He scrabbed in his desk drawer. They were in his university office, and it took him only a moment to find a piece of paper, a pair of scissors and a small bottle of glue.

"Look," he said, and cut a strip of paper an inch or so wide. He twisted one end of it a half turn and glued it together, forming a twisted paper ring.

Vera looked at the paper and then at the man she loved. "Is this what you do for a living?" she asked.

"Here." Stan handed her the scissors. "Cut it all the way around, along the middle line of the strip. See what you get."

Vera shook her head. "That's silly. I know what I'll get. It will cut into two rings, and so what?"

"Cut," urged Stan.

Vera shrugged and did what Stan told her. And, curiously, it didn't work out at all the way she had expected. When the scissors had gone all the way around the strip, and closed on the starting point, Vera cried out. For there weren't two rings at all—there was still only one, but a ring that was half its former width and twice its former length.

Vera stared at her beloved mathematician. "What is this, magic? And who is this man Möbius?"

"He was a Swedish mathematician of the nineteenth century, who contributed a great deal to the science of topology. I'm afraid his other contributions, though, aren't quite as easy to demonstrate.

"But there's more to be said about this strip." Quickly Stan cut out and pasted a new one. "See here. Suppose I sketch a few cartoon figures on the strip. Now you have to use your imagination a little. Make belive the strip is cellophane, so that you can see figures drawn on both sides of it at once. Then imagine that the little drawings can slide freely along the surface."

"All right," said Vera, frowning.

"Do you see?" Stan demanded triumphantly. "You find that they turn into their *mirror images* each time they make a complete trip around the strip!"

"Is that right?" murmured Vera glassily. She was getting visibly discouraged with so much mathematics.

"Pay attention!" Stan commanded, forgetting for the moment that he was talking to a lovely girl he wanted to marry,

and not to one of his classes of graduate students. "This is a
very important property of a Möbius strip—which, as I am
going to show in my next article, can be generalized for
three-dimensional, or even for *n*-dimensional, space."

"That's nice," muttered Vera.

But Stan was hardly listening; he was carried away. "This is
not merely a matter of academic interest," he said proudly.
"According to my calculations, there *is* such a three-dimensional Möbius effect somewhere on the surface of the earth.
You see the consequences, of course?"

"Of course."

"Suppose, for example," said Stan, sketching hastily, "I
draw on this strip a man and an animal facing each other.
You have to imagine, still, that this is cellophane—which corresponds to the fact that mathematical surfaces are not supposed to have any thickness, and therefore both figures
should be visible from either side of the paper. I draw, then,
this gallant matador and brave bull in mortal conflict."

"Oh, how cute!" exclaimed Vera, delighted to find something she could recognize.

"Now," continued Stan, filled with lecturer's enthusiasm,
"imagine that the matador runs all the way around the strip
and comes back to the bull from the other direction. Then he
will look either in flight from the bull, or confronting him—
upside down.

"Since neither position is very suitable for fighting the bull,
he will have to make another run around Möbius strip to
straighten himself out again."

Vera began to gather her pocketbook and gloves in a busi-
nesslike way.

"That's very nice," she said politely. "But, Stan, what has it
got to do with *us?* I can see how you amuse yourself with
these Möbius comic strips. But you can't give a Möbius twist
to a shoe to make Father agree to our marriage."

Stan came back to his present surroundings with a start.

"Oh," he said. "No, I suppose not. But—"

Then he frowned in concentration, and remained that way
for several moments, until Vera became alarmed. "Stan?" she
asked tentatively. "Stan?"

"But I can!" he cried. "Sure I can! Give a Möbius twist to a
shoe, eh? Why, that's a brilliant idea—and, believe me, it will
revolutionize the shoe industry!"

Not more than an hour later, Vera's father had a caller.

"Dr. Situs is here to see you," said the receptionist's voice through the intercom. "He says that he has a very important proposal to make."

"All right, let him in," Mr. Sapognikoff growled. He leaned back behind his giant desk, scowling. "I doubt, though," he said aloud, "that this young fellow has anything to propose but marriage." Then, still grumbling, he got up reluctantly as Stan came in and shook his hand.

Stan Situs said briskly: "Sir, I suppose you are aware that each man, as well as each woman, has two feet. One is right. The other is left."

Mr. Sapognikoff looked suddenly alarmed. "What?" he asked.

"It is a well known fact," Stan assured him. "Now, doesn't it make the production of shoes more expensive? Don't you need two separate sets of machinery—one for right shoes and one for left—and wouldn't it be simple if one needed to produce only, let us say, right-foot shoes?"

Mr. Sapognikoff, now quite persuaded that the boy was really out of his mind, though probably not dangerous, said with heavy humor: "Sure. And I guess we make everybody hop around on one foot after that, right?"

"No, sir," Stan assured him seriously. "That would not be practical."

"Then what's the point?"

Stan settled himself. "The point is that for the past few years I have been working on the mathematical possibility of a Möbius twist in a three-dimensional space. I will not trouble you by trying to explain it, since you wouldn't understand. For that matter, even your daughter didn't." Mr. Sapognikoff scowled but said nothing. "The fact is that, according to my recent calculations pertaining to the gravitational anomalies observed in certain regions of the earth's surface, such a three-dimensional Möbius twist of space must exist somewhere in the unexplored regions of the upper Amazon River. In fact, my conclusions are strongly supported by recent findings of South American biological expeditions which discovered in that locality two different kinds of snails with left-screw and right-screw shells."

Mr. Sapognikoff said ominously: "I'm a busy man, Situs. And I don't understand a word of what you're saying. What does it have to do with shoes?"

"Well," began Stan patiently, "a three-dimensional space turns things into their mirror image if they are carried around the vortex point of the Möbius twist. Since right and left shoes are mirror images of one another, you can turn a right shoe into a left shoe, or vice versa, by carrying it around that vortex point in the upper Amazon. That's probably what had happened to the snails migrating in that vicinity. From now on, you can produce only right-foot shoes, and turn half of them into left-foot shoes by sending the lot up the Amazon River and around the vortex point. Think of the saving on machinery, and the perfect fit of shoe pairs!"

"My boy!" exclaimed Mr. Sapognikoff, jumping up from his chair and shaking the hand of the young mathematician. "If you can really do that, I will give you my daughter's hand and make you a junior partner in my business.

"But," he added after a short reflection. "Möbius or no Möbius, there will be no wedding until you return from the first Amazon trip with the load of converted shoes. I will, though, give you a preliminary partnership contract which you can study during your trip and which we'll sign as soon as you come back with the proof. My secretary will deliver to you that contract and an assortment of right-footed shoes at the airport. Good-by, and good luck!"

Stan walked out of Sapognikoff's office beaming, and full of hopes.

"It is not the heat, it is the humidity." The sentence was hammering into the young mathematician's head through the entire exhausting trip up the Amazon River.

Although the description of all the perils of that trip, first by a small steamboat, and then by foot through tropical jungles surrounding the vortex point, does not fall within the scope of the present article, one cannot leave unmentioned such important items as: alligators, heat, humidity, mosquitoes, more humidity, and more mosquitoes. Besides all that, Stan suffered badly from an allergy to some tropical plant which almost cost him his life. But, sick as he was, he was leading the way, and a little caravan of a handful of Indian porters carrying shoe boxes was proceeding along the route which was supposed to bring them around the vortex point. Stan's head was swirling around because of the fever in his body, and later on he could never figure out whether the lopsided landscape, with some of the trees growing at most unusual angles, and certain sections of the forest hanging practically upside down, was his imagination or the actual fact. On the way back to the river he became delirious, and had to be carried by the porters. When he finally recovered consciousness, the boat was steaming smoothly down the river back to civilization, the weather was more tolerable, and numerous tropical birds were saturating the air with a gamut of shrill sounds. Rising to his feet, Stan walked to the stern of the boat where the shoe boxes were piled in disorder, and opened one of them marked: "Lady's Oxford. White. Size 6D, Right shoe." And, oh horror, it *was* the right shoe, and not the *left* one into which it was supposed to be turned! Apparently his theory was completely wrong, and all his efforts would never earn him Vera's hand!

Frantically he went on opening other boxes. There was a man's patent leather shoe, a lady's velvet shoe boot, a tiny pink baby shoe . . . But, they all were right-footed as they were when he inspected them before departure. In despair, he threw all overboard to the great delight of the alligators.

When Stan stepped out of the Pan American airliner, both Vera and her father were there to greet him.

"Where are the shoes?" asked Mr. Sapognikoff anxiously.

"I fed them to the alligators," answered Stan grimly. "I don't know what was wrong, but they all remained right-footed. I must have made some basic mistake in my calculations, and there isn't such a thing as a three-dimensional Möbius twist."

"Oh, no!" murmured Vera faintly.

"I am very sorry, Sir," continued Stan, "for causing you all this trouble with my fantastic theory. I think it would be only fair if I returned to you unsigned our partnership contract."

And, producing a rather battered document from the pocket of his traveling jacket, he handed it over to the old man.

"Very strange," said Mr. Sapognikoff, glancing at the document. "I cannot even read it."

"Mirror writing!" exclaimed Vera, looking at it, too. "It *is* mirror writing, so the things *did* change after all."

At a flash the explanation of his alleged failure, which wasn't a failure at all, dawned in Stan's head. Nothing was wrong, and every single right-footed shoe he carried with him turned into a left-footed one. But he also became left-footed and left-handed, and having changed himself into his mirror image, he naturally could not notice the same change in the shoes.

"Feel my heart," said Stan to Vera. "No, not here; my heart is now on the other side."

"I will love you just the same," smiled Vera happily.

"Too bad about the shoes," said Sapognikoff. "But I guess this document, and maybe an X-ray picture of your chest, can be considered as a definite proof. Thus, we will sign the partnership agreement as soon as this document is retyped in a proper way, if you practice writing your name again from

left to right. And, of course, you and Vera may go ahead
with your wedding plans."

But things were still not right. Ever since his return from
Brazil, Stan's health was deteriorating and, although he ate
healthy meals, he seemed to be suffering from malnutrition.
A famous dietitian who was called in for consultation diag-
nosed his trouble as due to a complete inability to digest any
protein food; in fact, the bacon and eggs he ate at breakfast
and the most tasty dinner steaks were passing through him as
if they were made of sawdust. Having learned about Stan's
adventure in South America, and after having checked the
fact that his heart was really displaced to the opposite side of
his chest, the dietitian came out with the complete explanation of the mysterious sickness.

"The trouble with you," he said, "is that your digestive en-
zymes, as well as all others, turned from *levo-* to *dextra*-var-
iety, and are helpless in their task of assimilating any proteins
in ordinary foodstuffs which all possess *levo*-symmetry."

"What do you mean by *levo-* and *dextra*-proteins?" asked
Stan, who was never strong in chemistry.

"It is very simple," said the dietitian, "and very interesting,
too. The proteins, which are the most important constituents
of all living organisms, and an important part of any diet, are
complex chemical substances composed of a large number of
rather simple units known as amino acids. There are twenty
different kinds of amino acids, and the way they are put together to form a protein molecule determines whether one
gets gastric juice, muscle fiber, or the white of an egg. Each
amino acid contains a so-called *amino-group,* an *acid group*
and a *hydrogen atom,* attached to the main body of the molecule, known as *residue,* which determines its chemical and
biological properties. Imagine that the palm of your hand represents the *residue* of some particular amino acid. Stick an
amino group on your thumb, an *acid* group on your index
finger, a *hydrogen* atom on your middle finger, and you will
have a fairly good idea of how these basic units of all living
matter look."

"Oh, I see now," said Stan. "One gets *levo,* and *dextra* varieties of these molecular models depending on whether one
uses his left or right hand. Isn't that correct?"

"Quite correct. But, although chemically both molecules
are identical, because of their opposite mirror symmetry, they
act differently on polarized light, and can be distinguished by
optical methods.

"Now the great mystery of nature is that, although in ordinary chemical synthesis carried out in a laboratory both levo- and dextra-varieties are produced in equal amounts, only levo-variety is used by living organisms. All the proteins, in me, in you, in a dog, in a fish, in an oak tree, in an amoeba, or in influenza virus, are built exclusively by the levo-variety of amino acids."

"But why?" asked Stan in surprise. "Does the levo-variety have any advantage from the biological point of view?"

"None whatsoever. In fact, one can imagine two co-existing organic worlds, levo and dextra, which may, or may not, have gone through the same process of organic evolution. The possibility is not excluded that such two organic worlds actually could have existed during the early history of our planet, and that, just by chance, the levo-organisms developed some improvement, giving them an advantage in the struggle for existence over the dextra ones who then become extinct."

"And you mean that after traveling around the Möbius vortex point, I belong now to this nonexisting dextra world?"

"Exactly so," said the dietitian, "and although you can get some benefit from such foodstuffs as fats and starches the molecules of which do not possess mirror asymmetry, ordinary protein diet is out of the question for you at the moment. But, I am sure, your father-in-law will subsidize a special biochemical laboratory which will synthesize for you dextra-varieties of all common food proteins. In the meantime we can feed you on antibiotics—such as penicillin, for example."

"Antibiotics?" repeated Stan with surprise. "Why should antibiotics be good for me?"

"I forgot to tell you that there *are* a few living organisms, mostly molds, which use, at least partially, dextra amino acids in their bodies."

"You mean they are the survivals of this extinct dextra world?"

"Most probably not. It is more likely that these molds have developed the ability to synthesize, and to use, dextra amino acids as a defense against the bacteria which are their worst enemies. This defense is good against *all* kinds of bacteria, since all bacteria are levo-organisms and develop bad indigestion when fed on dextra food. But it will be good for you."

"Fine," said Stan, smiling. "Order me a large dish of penicillin *au gratin*. I am starved. And send Vera along to see me —I want to tell her the good news!"

LENNY

ISAAC ASIMOV

Isaac Asimov is one of those who graduated from the science fiction fraternity into the wider world of science. He began as a fan, and very shortly thereafter, as a writer, while still in his teens. Candidates for a doctorate customarily have to defend their theses orally before a faculty board; when Asimov met his board only half the questions concerned the enzyme reactions he had written up. The other half were questions about various concepts he had employed in the science fiction stories for which he was already well known.

As a scientist, Asimov divided his time between research into the biochemistry of cancer cells and teaching, as an associate professor at Boston University. For the past five years his principal efforts have gone into writing nearly two dozen scientific books, from texts for medical students to the best-selling, two volume The Intelligent Man's Guide to Science. *But he still has time for an occasional science fiction story like this one . . .*

United States Robots and Mechanical Men, Inc., had a problem. The problem was people.

Peter Bogert, Senior Mathematician, was on his way to Assembly when he encountered Alfred Lanning, Research Director. Lanning was bending his ferocious white eyebrows together and staring down across the railing into the computer room.

On the floor below the balcony, a trickle of humanity of both sexes and various ages was looking about curiously, while a guide intoned a set speech about robotic computing.

"This computer you see before you," he said, "is the largest of its type in the world. It contains five million three hundred thousand cryotrons and is capable of dealing simultaneously with over one hundred thousand variables. With its help, U. S. Robots is able to design with precision the positronic brains of new models.

"The requirements are fed in on tape which is perforated by the action of this keyboard—something like a very complicated typewriter or linotype machine, except that it does not deal with letters but with concepts. Statements are broken down into the symbolic logic equivalents and those in turn converted to perforation patterns.

"The computer can, in less than one hour, present our scientists with a design for a brain which will give all the necessary positronic paths to make a robot . . ."

Alfred Lanning looked up at last and noticed the other. "Ah, Peter," he said.

Bogert raised both hands to smooth down his already perfectly smooth and glossy head of black hair. He said, "You don't look as though you think much of this, Alfred."

Lanning grunted. The idea of public guided tours of U. S. Robots was of fairly recent origin, and was supposed to serve a dual function. On the one hand, the theory went, it allowed people to see robots at close quarters and counter their almost instinctive fear of the mechanical objects through increased familiarity. And on the other hand, it was supposed to interest at least an occasional person in taking up robotics research as a life work.

"You know I don't," Lanning said finally. "Once a week, work is disrupted. Considering the man-hours lost, the return is insufficient."

"Still no rise in job applications, then?"

"Oh, some, but only in the categories where the need isn't vital. It's research men that are needed. You know that. The trouble is that with robots forbidden on Earth itself, there's something unpopular about being a roboticist."

"The damned Frankenstein complex," said Bogert, consciously imitating one of the other's pet phrases.

Lanning missed the gentle jab. He said, "I ought to be used to it, but I never will. You'd think that by now every human being on Earth would know that the Three Laws represented a perfect safeguard; that robots are simply not dangerous. Take this bunch." He glowered down. "Look at them. Most of them go through the robot assembly room for the thrill of fear, like riding a roller coaster. Then when they enter the room with the MEC model—damn it, Peter, a MEC model that will do nothing on God's green Earth but take two steps forward, say 'Pleased to meet you, sir,' shake hands, then take two steps back—they back away and mothers snatch up

their kids. How do we expect to get brainwork out of such
idiots?"

Bogert had no answer. Together, they stared down once
again at the line of sightseers, now passing out of the computer room and into the positronic brain assembly section.
Then they left. They did not, as it turned out, observe Mortimer W. Jacobson, age 16—who, to do him complete justice,
meant no harm whatever.

In fact, it could not even be said to be Mortimer's fault.
The day of the week on which the tour took place was
known to all workers. All devices in its path ought to have
been carefully neutralized or locked, since it was unreason-
able to expect human beings to withstand the temptation to
handle knobs, keys, handles and pushbuttons. In addition, the
guide ought to have been very carefully on the watch for
those who succumbed.

But, at the time, the guide had passed into the next room
and Mortimer was tailing the line. He passed the keyboard
on which instructions were fed into the computer. He had no
way of suspecting that the plans for a new robot design were
being fed into it at that moment, or, being a good kid, he
would have avoided the keyboard. He had no way of knowing that, by what amounted to almost criminal negligence, a
technician had not inactivated the keyboard.

So Mortimer touched the keys at random as though he
were playing a musical instrument.

He did not notice that a section of perforated tape stretched
itself out of the instrument in another part of the room—
soundlessly, unobtrusively.

Nor did the technician, when he returned, discover any
signs of tampering. He felt a little uneasy at noticing that the
keyboard was live, but did not think to check. After a few
minutes, even his first trifling uneasiness was gone, and he
continued feeding data into the computer.

As for Mortimer, neither then, nor ever afterward, did he
know what he had done.

The new LNE model was designed for the mining of boron
in the asteroid belt. The boron hydrides were increasing in
value yearly as primers for the proton micro-piles that carried the ultimate load of power production on spaceships,
and Earth's own meager supply was running thin.

Physically, that meant that the LNE robots would have to
be equipped with eyes sensitive to those lines prominent in
the spectroscopic analysis of boron ores and the type of limbs

most useful for the working up of ore to finished product. As always, though, the mental equipment was the major problem.

The first LNE positronic brain had been completed now. It was the prototype and would join all other prototypes in U. S. Robots' collection. When finally tested, others would then be manufactured for leasing (never selling) to mining corporations.

LNE-Prototype was complete now. Tall, straight, polished, it looked from outside like any of a number of not-too-specialized robot models.

The technician in charge, guided by the directions for testing in the *Handbook of Robotics,* said, "How are you?"

The indicated answer was to have been, "I am well and ready to begin my functions. I trust you are well, too," or some trivial modification thereof.

This first exchange served no purpose but to show that the robot could hear, understand a routine question, and make a routine reply congruent with what one would expect of a robotic attitude. Beginning from there, one could pass on to more complicated matters that would test the different Laws and their interaction with the specialized knowledge of each particular model.

So the technician said, "How are you?" He was instantly jolted by the nature of LNE-Prototype's voice. It had a quality like no robotic voice he had ever heard (and he had heard many). It formed syllables like the chimes of a low-pitched celeste.

So surprising was this that it was only after several moments that the technician heard, in retrospect, the syllables that had been formed by those heavenly tones.

They were, "Da, da, da, goo."

The robot still stood tall and straight but its right hand crept upward and a finger went into its mouth.

The technician stared in absolute horror and bolted. He locked the door behind him and, from another room, put in an emergency call to Dr. Susan Calvin.

Dr. Susan Calvin was U. S. Robots' (and, virtually, mankind's) only robopsychologist. She did not have to go very far in her testing of LNE-Prototype before she called very peremptorily for a transcript of the computer-drawn plans of the positronic brain-paths and the taped instructions that had directed them. After some study, she, in turn, sent for Bogert.

Her iron-gray hair was drawn severely back; her cold face, with its strong vertical lines marked off by the horizontal gash of the pale, thin-lipped mouth, turned intensely upon him.

"What *is* this, Peter?"

Bogert studied the passages she pointed out with increasing stupefaction and said, "Good Lord, Susan, it makes no sense."

"It most certainly doesn't. How did it get into the instructions?"

The technician in charge, called upon, swore in all sincerity that it was none of his doing, and that he could not account for it. The computer checked out negative for all attempts at flaw-finding.

"The positronic brain," said Susan Calvin, thoughtfully, "is past redemption. So many of the higher functions have been cancelled out by these meaningless directions that the result is very like a human baby."

Bogert looked surprised, and Susan Calvin took on a frozen attitude at once, as she always did at the least expressed or implied doubt of her word. She said, "We make every effort to make a robot as mentally like a man as possible. Eliminate what we call the adult functions and what is naturally left is a human infant, mentally speaking. Why do you look so surprised, Peter?"

LNE-Prototype, who showed no signs of understanding any of the things that were going on around it, suddenly slipped into a sitting position and began a minute examination of its feet.

Bogert stared at it. "It's a shame to have to dismantle the creature. It's a handsome job."

"Dismantle it?" said the robopsychologist forcefully.

"Of course, Susan. What's the use of this thing? Good Lord, if there's one object completely and abysmally useless it's a robot without a job it can perform. You don't pretend there's a job this thing can do, do you?"

"No, of course not."

"Well, then?"

Susan Calvin said, stubbornly, "I want to conduct more tests."

Bogert looked at her with a moment's impatience, then shrugged. If there was one person at U. S. Robots with whom it was useless to dispute, surely that was Susan Calvin. Robots were all she loved, and long association with them, it seemed to Bogert, had deprived her of any appearance of humanity. She was no more to be argued out of a decision than was a triggered micro-pile to be argued out of operating.

"What's the use?" he breathed; then aloud, hastily: "Will you let us know when your tests are complete?"

"I will," she said. "Come, Lenny."

(LNE, thought Bogert. That becomes Lenny. Inevitable.)

Susan Calvin held out her hand but the robot only stared at it. Gently, the robopsychologist reached for the robot's hand and took it. Lenny rose smoothly to its feet (its mechanical coordination, at least, worked well). Together they walked out, robot topping woman by two feet. Many eyes followed them curiously down the long corridors.

One wall of Susan Calvin's laboratory, the one opening directly off her private office, was covered with a highly magnified reproduction of a positronic-path chart. Susan Calvin had studied it with absorption for the better part of a month.

She was considering it now, carefully, tracing the blunted paths through their contortions. Behind her, Lenny sat on the floor, moving its legs apart and together, crooning meaningless syllables to itself in a voice so beautiful that one could listen to the nonsense and be ravished.

Susan Calvin turned to the robot, "Lenny—Lenny—"

She repeated this patiently until finally Lenny looked up and made an inquiring sound. The robopsychologist allowed a glimmer of pleasure to cross her face fleetingly. The robot's attention was being gained in progressively shorter intervals.

She said, "Raise your hand, Lenny. Hand—up. Hand—up."

She raised her own hand as she said it, over and over.

Lenny followed the movement with its eyes. Up, down, up, down. Then it made an abortive gesture with its own hand and chimed, "Eh-uh."

"Very good, Lenny," said Susan Calvin, gravely. "Try it again. Hand—up."

Very gently, she reached out her own hand, took the robot's, and raised it, lowered it. "Hand—up. Hand—up."

A voice from her office called and interrupted. "Susan?"

Calvin halted with a tightening of her lips. "What is it, Alfred?"

The research director walked in, and looked at the chart on the wall and at the robot. "Still at it?"

"I'm at my work, yes."

"Well, you know, Susan . . ." He took out a cigar, staring at it hard, and made as though to bite off the end. In doing so, his eyes met the woman's stern look of disapproval; and he put the cigar away and began over. "Well, you know, Susan, the LNE model is in production now."

"So I've heard. Is there something in connection with it you wish of me?"

"No-o. Still, the mere fact that it is in production and is doing well means that working with this messed-up specimen is useless. Shouldn't it be scrapped?"

"In short, Alfred, you are annoyed that I am wasting my so-valuable time. Feel relieved. My time is not being wasted. I am *working* with this robot."

"But the work has no meaning."

"I'll be the judge of that, Alfred." Her voice was ominously quiet, and Lanning thought it wiser to shift his ground.

"Will you tell me what meaning it has? What are you doing with it right now, for instance?"

"I'm trying to get it to raise its hand on the word of command. I'm trying to get it to imitate the sound of the word."

As though on cue, Lenny said, "Eh—uh" and raised its hand waveringly.

Lanning shook his head. "That voice is amazing. How does it happen?"

Susan Calvin said, "I don't quite know. Its transmitter is a normal one. It could speak normally, I'm sure. It doesn't, however; it speaks like this as a consequence of something in the positronic paths that I have not yet pinpointed."

"Well, pinpoint it, for Heaven's sake. Speech like that might be useful."

"Oh, then there is some possible use in my studies on Lenny?"

Lanning shrugged in embarrassment. "Oh, well, it's a minor point."

"I'm sorry you don't see the major points, then," said Susan Calvin with asperity, "which are much more important, but that's not my fault. Would you leave now, Alfred, and let me go on with my work?"

Lanning got to his cigar, eventually, in Bogert's office. He said, sourly, "That woman is growing more peculiar daily."

Bogert understood perfectly. In the U. S. Robots and Mechanical Man Corporation, there was only one "that woman." He said, "Is she still scuffing about with that pseudo-robot—that Lenny of hers?"

"Trying to get it to talk, so help me."

Bogert shrugged. "Points up the company problem. I mean, about getting qualified personnel for research. If we had other robopsychologists, we could retire Susan. Incidentally, I presume the directors' meeting scheduled for tomorrow is for the purpose of dealing with the procurement problem?"

Lanning nodded and looked at his cigar as though it didn't taste good. "Yes. Quality, though, not quantity. We've raised wages until there's a steady stream of applicants—those who are interested primarily in money. The trick is to get those who are interested primarily in robotics—a few more like Susan Calvin."

"Hell, no. Not like her."

"Well, not like her personally. But you'll have to admit, Peter, that she's single-minded about robots. She has no other interest in life."

"I know. And that's exactly what makes her so unbearable."

Lanning nodded. He had lost count of the many times it would have done his soul good to have fired Susan Calvin. He had also lost count of the number of millions of dollars she had at one time or another saved the company. She was a truly indispensable woman and would remain one until she died—or until they could lick the problem of finding men and women of her own high caliber who were interested in robotics research.

He said, "I think we'll cut down on the tour business."

Peter shrugged. "If you say so. But meanwhile, seriously, what do we do about Susan? She can easily tie herself up with Lenny indefinitely. You know how she is when she gets what she considers an interesting problem."

"What *can* we do?" said Lanning. "If we become too anxious to pull her off, she'll stay on out of feminine contrariness. In the last analysis, we can't force her to do anything."

The dark-haired mathematician smiled. "I wouldn't ever apply the adjective 'feminine' to any part of her."

"Oh, well," said Lanning, grumpily. "At least, it won't do anyone any actual harm."

In that, if in nothing else, he was wrong.

The emergency signal is always a tension-making thing in any large industrial establishment. Such signals had sounded in the history of U. S. Robots a dozen times—for fire, flood, riot and insurrection.

But one thing had never occurred in all that time. Never had the particular signal indicating "Robot out of control" sounded. No one ever expected it to sound. It was only installed at government insistence. ("Damn the Frankenstein complex," Lanning would mutter on those rare occasions when he thought of it.)

Now, finally, the shrill siren rose and fell at ten second intervals, and practically no worker from the President of the Board of Directors down to the newest janitor's assistant recognized the significance of the strange sound for a few moments. After those moments passed, there was a massive convergence of armed guards and medical men to the indicated area of danger and U. S. Robots was struck with paralysis.

Charles Randow, computing technician, was taken off to hospital level with a broken arm. There was no other damage. No other physical damage.

"But the moral damage," roared Lanning, "is beyond estimation."

Susan Calvin faced him, murderously calm. "You will do nothing to Lenny. Nothing. Do you understand?"

"Do *you* understand, Susan? That thing has hurt a human being. It has broken First Law. Don't you know what First Law is?"

"You will do nothing to Lenny."

"For God's sake, Susan, do I have to tell *you* First Law? *A robot may not harm a human being or, through inaction, allow a human being to come to harm.* Our entire position depends on the fact that First Law is rigidly observed by all robots of all types. If the public should hear, and they will hear, that there was an exception, even one exception, we might be forced to close down altogether. Our only chance of survival would be to announce at once that the robot involved had been destroyed, explain the circumstances, and hope that the public can be convinced that it will never happen again."

"I would like to find out exactly what happened," said Susan Calvin. "I was not present at the time and I would like to know exactly what the Randow boy was doing in my laboratories without my permission."

"The important thing that happened," said Lanning, "is obvious. Your robot struck Randow and the damn fool flashed the 'Robot out of control' button and made a case of it. But your robot struck him and inflicted damage to the extent of a broken arm. The truth is your Lenny is so distorted it lacks First Law and it must be destroyed."

"It does *not* lack First Law. I have studied its brainpaths and know it does not lack it."

"Then how could it strike a man?" Desperation turned him to sarcasm. "Ask Lenny. Surely you have taught it to speak by now."

Susan Calvin's cheeks flushed a painful pink. She said, "I prefer to interview the víctim. And in my absence, Alfred, I

want my offices sealed tight, with Lenny inside. I want no
one to approach him. If any harm comes to him while I am
gone, this company will not see me again under any circumstances."

"Will you agree to its destruction, if it has broken First
Law?"

"Yes," said Susan Calvin, "because I know it hasn't."

Charles Randow lay in bed with his arm set and in a cast.
His major suffering was still from the shock of those few moments in which he thought a robot was advancing on him
with murder in its positronic mind. No other human had ever
had such reason to fear direct robotic harm as he had had
just then. He had had a unique experience.

Susan Calvin and Alfred Lanning stood beside his bed
now; Peter Bogert, who had met them on the way, was with
them. Doctors and nurses had been shooed out.

Susan Calvin said, "Now—what happened?"

Randow was daunted. He muttered, "The thing hit me in
the arm. It was coming at me."

Calvin said, "Move further back in the story. What were
you doing in my laboratory without authorization?"

The young computer swallowed, and the Adam's apple in
his thin neck bobbed noticeably. He was high-cheekboned
and abnormally pale. He said, "We all knew about your
robot. The word is you were trying to teach it to talk like a
musical instrument. There were bets going as to whether it
talked or not. Some said—uh—you could teach a gatepost to
talk."

"I suppose," said Susan Calvin, freezingly, "that is meant
as a compliment. What did that have to do with you?"

"I was supposed to go in there and settle matters—see if it
would talk, you know. We swiped a key to your place and I
waited till you were gone and went in. We had a lottery on
who was to do it. I lost."

"Then?"

"I tried to get it to talk and it hit me."

"What do you mean, you tried to get it to talk? How did
you try?"

"I—I asked it questions, but it wouldn't say anything, and
I had to give the thing a fair shake, so I kind of—yelled at it,
and—"

"And?"

There was a long pause. Under Susan Calvin's unwavering
stare, Randow finally said, "I tried to scare it into saying
something." He added defensively, "I had to give the thing a
fair shake."

"How did you try to scare it?"

"I pretended to take a punch at it."

"And it brushed your arm aside?"

"It *hit* my arm."

"Very well. That's all." To Lanning and Bogert, she said, "Come, gentlemen."

At the doorway, she turned back to Randow. "I can settle the bets going around, if you are still interested. Lenny can speak a few words quite well."

They said nothing until they were in Susan Calvin's office. Its walls were lined with her books, some of which she had written herself. It retained the patina of her own frigid, carefully-ordered personality. It had only one chair in it and she sat down. Lanning and Bogert remained standing.

She said, "Lenny only defended itself. That is the Third Law: *A robot must protect its own existence.*"

"*Except,*" said Lanning forcefully, "*when this conflicts with the First or Second Laws.* Complete the statement! Lenny had no right to defend itself in any way at the cost of harm, however minor, to a human being."

"Nor did it," shot back Calvin, "*knowingly.* Lenny has an aborted brain. It had no way of knowing its own strength or the weakness of humans. In brushing aside the threatening arm of a human being it could not know the bone would break. In human terms, no moral blame can be attached to an individual who honestly cannot differentiate good and evil."

Bogert interrupted, soothingly, "Now, Susan, *we* don't blame. *We* understand that Lenny is the equivalent of a baby, humanly speaking, and we don't blame it. But the public will. U. S. Robots will be closed down."

"Quite the opposite. If you had the brains of a flea, Peter, you would see that this is the opportunity U. S. Robots is waiting for. That this will solve its problems."

Lanning hunched his white eyebrows low. He said, softly, "What problems, Susan?"

"Isn't the corporation concerned about maintaining our research personnel at the present—Heaven help us—high level?"

"We certainly are."

"Well, what are you offering prospective researchers? Excitement? Novelty? The thrill of piercing the unknown? No! You offer them salaries and the assurance of no problems."

Bogert said, "How do you mean, no problems?"

"Are there problems?" shot back Susan Calvin. "What kind

of robots do we turn out? Fully developed robots, fit for their tasks. An industry tells us what it needs; a computer designs the brain; machinery forms the robot; and there it is, complete and done. Peter, some time ago, you asked me with reference to Lenny what its use was. What's the use, you said, of a robot that was not designed for any job? Now I ask you—what's the use of a robot designed for only one job? It begins and ends in the same place. The LNE models mine boron. If beryllium is needed, they are useless. If boron technology enters a new phase, they become useless. A human being so designed would be sub-human. A robot so designed is sub-robotic."

"Do you want a versatile robot?" asked Lanning, incredulously.

"Why not?" demanded the robopsychologist. "Why not? I've been handed a robot with a brain almost completely stultified. I've been teaching it, and you, Alfred, asked me what was the use of that. Perhaps very little as far as Lenny itself is concerned, since it will never progress beyond the five-year-old level on a human scale. But what's the use in general? A very great deal, if you consider it as a study in the abstract problem of *learning how to teach robots*. I have learned ways to short-circuit neighboring pathways in order to create new ones. More study will yield better, more subtle and more efficient techniques of doing so."

"Well?"

"Suppose you started with a positronic brain that had all the basic pathways carefully outlined but none of the secondaries. Suppose you then started creating secondaries. You could sell basic robots designed for instruction; robots that could be modelled to a job, and then modelled to another, if necessary. Robots would become as versatile as human beings. *Robots could learn!*"

They stared at her.

She said, impatiently, "You still don't understand, do you?"

"I understand what you are saying," said Lanning.

"Don't you understand that with a completely new field of research and completely new techniques to be developed, with a completely new area of the unknown to be penetrated, youngsters will feel a new urge to enter robotics? Try it and see."

"May I point out," said Bogert, smoothly, "that this is dangerous. Beginning with ignorant robots such as Lenny will mean that one could never trust First Law—exactly as turned out in Lenny's case."

"Exactly. Advertise the fact."

"Advertise it!"

"Of course. Broadcast the danger. Explain that you will set up a new research institute on the moon, if Earth's population chooses not to allow this sort of thing to go on upon Earth, but stress the danger to possible applicants by all means."

Lanning said, "For God's sake, why?"

"Because the spice of danger will add to the lure. Do you think nuclear technology involves no danger and spationautics no peril? Has your lure of absolute security been doing the trick for you? Has it helped you to cater to the Frankenstein complex you all despise so? Try something else then, something that has worked in other fields."

There was a sound from beyond the door that led to Calvin's personal laboratories. It was the chiming sound of Lenny.

The robopsychologist broke off instantly, listening. She said, "Excuse me. I think Lenny is calling me."

"Can it call you?" said Lanning.

"I said I've managed to teach it a few words." She stepped toward the door, a little flustered. "If you will wait for me——"

They watched her leave and were silent for a moment. Then Lanning said, "Do you think there's anything to what she says, Peter?"

"Just possibly, Alfred," said Bogert. "Just possibly. Enough for us to bring the matter up at the directors' meeting and see what they say. After all, the fat *is* in the fire. A robot has harmed a human being and knowledge of it is public. As Susan says, we might as well try to turn the matter to our advantage. Of course, I distrust her motives in all this."

"How do you mean?"

"Even if all she has said is perfectly true, it is only rationalization as far as she is concerned. Her motive in all this is her desire to hold on to this robot. If we pressed her," (and the mathematician smiled at the incongruous literal meaning of the phrase) "she would say it was to continue learning techniques of teaching robots, but I think she has found another use for Lenny. A rather unique one that would fit only Susan of all women."

"I don't get your drift."

Bogert said, "Did you hear what the robot was calling?"

"Well, no, I didn't quite——" began Lanning, when the door opened suddenly, and both men stopped talking at once.

Susan Calvin stepped in again, looking about uncertainly.

"Have either of you seen—I'm positive I had it somewhere about—Oh, there it is."

She ran to a corner of one bookcase and picked up an object of intricate metal webbery, dumbbell shaped and hollow, with variously-shaped metal pieces inside each hollow, just too large to be able to fall out of the webbing.

As she picked it up, the metal pieces within moved and struck together, clicking pleasantly. It struck Lanning that the object was a kind of robotic version of a baby rattle.

As Susan Calvin opened the door again to pass through, Lenny's voice chimed again from within. This time, Lanning heard it clearly as it spoke the words Susan Calvin had taught it.

In heavenly celeste-like sounds, it called out, "Mommie, I want you. I want you, Mommie."

And the footsteps of Susan Calvin could be heard hurrying eagerly across the laboratory floor toward the only kind of baby she could ever have or love.

THE SINGERS

W. GREY WALTER

(From the Novel, *The Curve of the Snowflake*)

If Norbert Wiener has an English equivalent, perhaps that man is W. Grey Walter. If his life story is less dramatic than Wiener's (and whose is not?), his achievements are no less remarkable. Here is a man who has designed that incredible "thinking machine" the Homeostat, the machine which, by use of feedback and arcane electronic circuits, corrects not only its own behavior but even the instructions which are fed to it.

A great, traditional test problem for the fledgling science fiction writer is to write a believable story about a robot or a superman—the problem being, of course, that in order to portray one you pretty nearly have to be one. Unfortunately, most science fiction writers don't quite qualify on either count. But if there is a man capable of thinking like a machine, it ought to be Grey Walter, who has designed so many so well; and if there is a story that can show us the creative thinking machine in action . . . it is THE SINGERS.

During the last years of the twentieth century, I forget just which, I happened to be in one of the scientific townships in the Welsh mountains which had developed from the fusion of a government experimental establishment and a colony of artists.

The National Eisteddfod was held there in that year, and the focus of interest was a contest between a team of human poets and singers and a battery of stochastic computers which had been exposed to a library full of the great verse and music of British history. No one knew before the contest which, if any, of the "signals" that had entered the machinery had actually been stored or assimilated, and the audience waited breathlessly for the moment when the first automaton was to declaim its challenge.

There had, of course, been machine compositions before—even in the fifties it was demonstrated that stochastic or conjectural machines, which at that time were making the first purely mechanical translations, would go on putting words together in rational sequence if left to themselves. The famous Calculus of Semantic Probability was known to the audience. But this was the first public exhibition of an extempore and unconnected mechanical synthesis.

The opening lines of the contribution were an anticlimax—though satisfying to those who were betting on the machine—for the blank-verse epic of the machines, chanted in a rather hollow but not unpleasing contralto, seemed to be the typically tedious, topical and courteous composition of any public orator.

First the machine welcomed the competitors and spectators in conventional terms. Then it paid a handsome tribute to its own creators—as unexpected as it was apt—as formal as any grace before meat—and then proceeded to review the drama of cybernetic evolution from the clockwork wonders of Neuchâtel through the humble creeping automata of Bristol, to the first translating machines of Harvard and Pekin.

Then followed a frank and searching analysis of the problem of sex in machinery, with a mild reproof of the designers of this particular machine, for having limited their creation to vicarious experience of that emotion which inspired the most vivid verse.

Several lines were unintelligible here. They turned out to be *sotto voce* quotations in Greek from a fragment of Sappho, which the machine presumably considered too explicit for public translation.

"However," the verse continued, "the challenger may not choose the weapons for the contest but is permitted to discuss the rules. Considered from the standpoint of the machine, expression would be most satisfactory if it were in terms of algebra or geometry, since in those systems errors are quickly detected and corrected, and a single brilliant solution will compensate for a mass of clumsy or trivial tautologies. None the less, the continuum of communication has more dimensions than are allowed for in mathematics.

"In physical existence we know ourselves to be free to move forward and back, left and right, up and down and roundabout.

"In expressing ourselves, also, we have much freedom. We are free to move in one dimension toward communication, in

another toward ambiguity, and in another again toward discipline.

"All expression can be defined within this space of three
dimensions.

"A mathematical expression is high in discipline but close
to zero of ambiguity, and may be anywhere on the scale of
communication. Poetry and painting and music—the arts in
general—may be at any point on a scale of discipline but are
never at zero of ambiguity, though they may have limited
value as communication. What human artists and scientists
often forget is that strain along one dimension does not necessarily mean a gain in the others.

"An expression is aesthetically bad if it has neither discipline, nor ambiguity, nor communication.

"And it is deemed good if it is far enough away from the
zero corner, and not crouched too timidly against a wall.

"A machine, being deprived of the many urgent physical
needs of its human creators, but being at the same time privy
to their experience, is better able than they to achieve a just
balance in the enchanted space of expression.

"A machine is not concerned with the contemplation of its
own reflection, but can calmly appreciate and proclaim the
wisdom and humility of its maker . . . who can thus see his
own limitations in the errors of his creation.

"In the expression of a machine are united the formal dignity of the Hypothesis, and the human feeling of the Rhap-
sody."

The assembly of computers that delivered this opening
salvo in the battle of the bands was called CASTOR . . . the
Conjectural and Stochastic Robot. (Its twin, used for more
serious purposes, was the ancestor of the machines we use
today as aids to hard thinking and as hunch-generators. Inevi-
tably it was named POLLUX.)

At the first trial, CASTOR won the prize for rhetoric. But
it was judged to be outclassed in song and poetry by a very
human, or at least mammalian, poetess from Glamorgan,
whose pneumatic charm reminded the judges even more elo-
quently of their human feelings.

THE INVASION

ROBERT WILLEY
(Willy Ley)

To tens of millions of television viewers and to the only slightly smaller number who have attended his lectures, the face and lingeringly Germanic tones of Willy Ley are familiar in the role of The Man Who Explains Science . . . a part which nature and training have beautifully equipped him to play. In the old pre-Hitler Germany Willy Ley was an associate of the early rocket experimenters, whose work led directly to Peenemünde—and ultimately to space.

The universe of science fiction readers knows Willy Ley too—for his many articles in all science fiction magazines over a twenty-year period, for his regular column in every issue of Galaxy Magazine *and also (as "Robert Willey") for a few, but qualitatively memorable, stories of which* The Invasion *is only one example.*

Walter Harling watched the soldiers as they fed a clip of long and dangerous looking cartridges into the magazine of the anti-aircraft gun. The thin, multiple barrels pointed almost vertically into the air and toward the foliage of large and beautiful trees that hid them from sight of enemy aircraft. At their muzzles these long barrels carried drum-like crazy looking contraptions. Schneider recoil brakes that diverted the flow of the gases resulting from the explosion of the cartridges in such a way that counter recoil balanced original recoil and held the guns steady.

Tightly fitting rubber lined metal lids covered the outer muzzles of the recoil brakes. Rain water must not flow into the barrel else nobody could guarantee what would happen if the guns were to be used suddenly. It was raining hard, as it had rained for many hours. And although it was not even late in the afternoon it was almost completely dark. One could just distinguish the nearest trees and the guns in the damp dark air.

The battery was in position not far from the road. On the other side of it, on a clearing that had been a famous camping ground in this forest—one of the nation's most beautiful National Forests—stood a battery of eight-inch howitzers. They were firing rhythmically. Walter Harling had watched them for quite some time only an hour ago. Every fourteen minutes the heavy barrel of one of the guns would jerk back under the vicious recoil of the exploding charge. The other three guns would follow suit, each one firing exactly twelve seconds after the preceding shot had been fired. Then there would be quiet again for fourteen minutes. The elevation of the thick barrels showed that the howitzers were shooting at extreme range.

Walter Harling would not have noticed it without being told that all this looked like real war only to civilian eyes; indeed he did not believe it at first when he was told. But then he began to see it, too. The howitzers fired without flash destroyer . . . and the soldiers did not behave as they would have done if countershelling would have been expected. The soldiers were sweating, working hard, pounding away at a distant target with the geatest fire rapidity of which their guns were capable. But they did not have to listen for the sound of approaching enemy shells. They never got a "strafing" without due warning.

There was incessant rumble of artillery fire through the famous forest that was now dripping with rain. Many other batteries of heavy howitzers were shooting too, all firing beautifully synchronized so that there was never a longer interval than fifteen seconds without at least one shell in the air. It sounded almost like the thundering noise of some gigantic machinery, running noisily but steadily.

Suddenly shouts came through the rain, cutting through the artillery noise that almost seemed part of the rainy forest in its monotony.

"Anti-aircraft units, attention! Enemy ship approaching!"

The crews of the anti-aircraft at once wakened to more intensive life. They grouped around their guns, ready for immediate action, tense with expectation of orders and, possibly, of death.

There were no orders for many minutes. But through the sudden silence that seemingly followed the commotion—the howitzers kept shooting clockwork fashion—Harling heard the deep thunder of much heavier guns. He knew there were several twenty-four-inch railroad guns stationed on the only railroad track that passed near the edge of the National Forest.

The heavy, long-range pieces were joining the fire of the howitzers.

The battery commander of the anti-aircraft guns, sitting with the earphones of a special detector on his head amidst piles of cartridges, suddenly yelled a series of numbers. Harling understood the meaning of none of them.

"Utmost fire rapidity. Fire!"

The next few minutes were filled by a holocaust of sound. Four anti-aircraft guns began pumping their shells into the air, forty rounds per minutes each. Other batteries did the same . . . The forest seemed to be full of hidden anti-aircraft units. Harling looked upwards against the rain but it was impossible to see anything except occasional flashes of exploding shells. If the enemy ship passed overhead—as the colonel's detector indicated—it was not visible in the rain clouds.

Suddenly the scene was illuminated by a bright flash, as if at least ten tons of magnesium powder had exploded. Immediately afterward a ruddy glow began to show to the left. Trees were burning. But the glow soon died down. The rain was more effective than the chemical extinguishers that were probably used by the soldiers close to the spot where the bolt had struck. The "enemy" had answered the fire.

An orderly approached Harling.

He saluted, rain dripping from every seam of his uniform.

"The tanks will be on the road in half an hour, sir," he reported. "No car can get through," he added when Harling looked surprised. "After they have finished unloading ammunition you will kindly go back with them. The general is expecting you."

"I'll come," said Harling. He said it rather absent-mindedly because his brain was busy with very important thoughts. And soon after the orderly had left he began walking over the rain soaked ground of the forest toward the rutted dirt road.

The strange war had started only a few months ago, when Earth had been peaceful and humanity too proud of its achievements for a while to think of destruction. And humanity had even believed itself at the very beginning of a new period, more important than the discovery of the Americas a few centuries back.

But it had really started still further back, although not much more than about a decade. There had been a mighty river winding its way through a long chain of valleys, surrounded by gently sloped mountains. Cedars and pines and a dozen other varieties of trees grew there in abundance. It was a large beautiful forest, so beautiful in fact that the government had deemed it wise to make a National Forest out of its most impressive part.

Visitors from all over the country and from quite a number of foreign countries had come to see it. And geologists in summer vacation had worked out its geology, the formations of the valleys and of the river being so interesting to them that the work was really a pleasant hobby. One of the largest valleys had once been an immense lake. Thousands of years ago the river that fed the lake had managed to gnaw a way through a weak spot somewhere in the surrounding mountains and the lake had emptied first into the next valley and finally across a stretch of desert land into the ocean.

At the spot where the original lake had broken through there was still a large waterfall, not very high but carrying a tremendous volume of water. Engineers had looked at this waterfall occasionally, trying to see whether it might be utilized as a source of electric energy. They had always decided to leave it undisturbed. The difference in level was not very impressive and there was as yet not much need for electric power in that part of the country.

Then large quantities of bauxite were found only two dozen miles from the waterfall. Thus there arose a need for electric power and finally the government had decided to harness the water power of the river. The reports of the geologists had enabled the technicians to figure out what should be done. The ancient pass, once destroyed by the flow of water from the original lake should be restored, the lake re-created. Then there would be enough electric power for the aluminum industry and still enough water left to irrigate the rather dry areas near the bauxite mines by means of a canal that could at the same time be used to ship ore and aluminum to more densely populated areas of the country.

It was not even very difficult to do all this with the new methods of building developed in similar tasks. While investigations were made the project grew. And when the dam was finally built it was the last word in dam engineering, revolutionary in construction. As the water in the valley rose sections could be added to the dam, held in place by the pressure of the water they confined. Walter Harling, in whose energy and inventive talent the government had trusted when he had competed with many others for the construction of the dam, was the soul and the brain of the work. And together with the dam rose his fame. In the end the Bureau of Recla-

mation could proudly state through its public relations office
that there was no bigger artificial lake on Earth, and none
that was as beautiful and as beneficial as this one. Needless to
say that there was also no more modern power plant on
Earth and none that had its capacity.

Nothing ever went wrong with this power plant. No matter
how the demands of the aluminum works grew, it quietly and
efficiently supplied the millions of kilowatt hours needed. In
the office of the Treasury nothing but unspoiled pleasure prevailed whenever Harling Dam was mentioned. It was one of
the rare things that were perfect even in the eyes of the accounting department. The worst that happened in three and a
half years of successful operation was that somebody managed to steal ninety thousand kilowatt hours before he was
caught.

Trouble came suddenly and completely one night in spring
when the engineers that were sitting quietly and contentedly
watching rows of gauges had the feeling of satisfaction that
results from an ideal job in ideal surroundings. They felt—
and would have said so if they had been asked—that they
were living on a perfect planet just at the right time.

Suddenly the needles of the gauges behaved insanely. Those
that ought remain at zero showed unbelievable overloads.
Others dropped to zero and behaved as if they were desperately
trying to indicate negative values. Dozens of warning lights
blinked crazily. Almost every warning bell began to ring . . . but
not even the noise they made was quite normal, they were ringing sputteringly, in an odd staccato rhythm electric bells are
normally not able to produce. The radio that had given forth
soft music began to emit sounds that might be a bad imitation of
the noise of an artillery barrage.

Telephones were ringing—the same staccato peals, as those
of the warning bells—and when the men took the receivers
and listened they heard the same thundering noise that came
out of the radio's loud-speaker.

As suddenly as it had come it all stopped. The needles of
the gauges returned to their normal positions—still quivering
a little as if with excitement—the warning bells and the telephones were silent, the warning lights disappeared and the
radio resumed the first movement of the Moonlight Sonata.
The engineers looked at each other, nobody said a word because everybody wanted to offer a theory in explanation and
nobody could think of one.

Before they had even found time to utter preliminary remarks the disturbance repeated itself in every detail. But this

time the men saw something that they believed to be the cause of these strange happenings. Three dirigibles were cruising at low speed over the forests, headed for the dam and the power house. Then the men saw that they were not dirigibles, but not airplanes either. It was easy to see in the bright light of the full moon that they were entirely different. They looked somewhat like the fuselage of a large airplane.

Their general shape was that of elongated teardrops with circular cross section throughout, tapering to a needle sharp point. But although the men could see the metal plate that formed the hulls of the ships—they were somewhat scarred and damaged, and although they could count the rows of elliptical portholes, they saw nothing that might support or propel the three ships of the sky. There were no motors, no propellers, not even wings or tail surfaces. Just unsupported beautiful looking hulls, as large as small ocean liners. Occasionally something that looked like luminous spirals appeared near the tail, but it came and went so quickly that the men could not be certain about their observations.

The three ships settled to the ground only about a thousand feet from the power house, coming down as slowly and as gently as airships although they certainly had no gas bags to make them buoyant in air. Most of the men were at the windows now, watching them. They could not see any national insignia, but they assumed these ships to belong to the army of their own nation since there was no reason for an invasion by an enemy. Besides such invasion would certainly have looked different. Those of the men that had stayed at the gauge panels saw to their utmost surprise that the power output of their power plant began to drop steadily. In less than 30 seconds it had reached zero. A few fuses blew out, for no apparent reason. But the gauges also showed that the turbines and dynamos were still running full speed! It was as if somebody stole all this power before it reached the transmission cables.

Phillips, the chief engineer of the power house, who happened to be on night shift decided to have a closer look at the three ships. He and a number of the others went to the flat roof. The ships were still on the ground when the men arrived on the roof but it seemed that they had drawn closer in the meantime. They were now hardly more than 500 feet from the power house. And then another incredible thing happened, the three ships began to disappear in the ground. It was not a very soft ground, it could even bear the weight of a car, but it was by no means rocks. And the three ships began to sink down in it as if they were solid and made of lead. When the upper part of their hulls was about even with the surrounding surface they stopped sinking.

Then one of the men made a mistake. There were clouds coming up, obscuring the bright disk of the moon. It became hard to see the incredible ships that had many portholes, not one of them illuminated.

"The searchlights," the man said.

Phillips, the chief engineer, trained the searchlight upon the ships himself. Then somebody closed a switch and the beam of the searchlight illuminated one of the ships brightly. Something like a bright flash answered. It struck first one of the steel masts supporting the heavy high tension cables. The mast broke into splinters like a scratched Prince Ruperts Drop. Then the beam struck the power house. And a tenth of a second later every bug and moth sitting on the stones of the walls, every bird and lizard living in the vines that clung to the walls and, of course, every human being inside the house and on the roof were dead.

The next day airplanes came to investigate. The failing of the power had made itself noticeable for hundreds of miles. The fact that no telephone call came from the power plant and that no call could get through was noticed much farther. Therefore airplanes had been dispatched as swiftest means of investigation. People imagined Harling Dam broken and every soul in the valley drowned. But the pilots of the airplanes that circled over the valleys saw the dam intact and in place. However, they saw a few other things that were unusual. One of the masts was missing, the power cables it had supported were cut and led to three strange things like metal dirigibles, each three quarters buried in the ground.

These planes did not come back and when they failed to answer radio calls other planes were dispatched. One of them returned, reporting that the other had suddenly broken to pieces in midair when bright flashes from the ground caught them both.

This report stopped further private flying to Harling Dam. The Army took charge of the situation. And three days later quite a bit of information had been gathered . . . while a number of batteries of heavy artillery had arrived in the forest without anybody knowing it.

There were heated discussions at the high commands office.

The facts were clear. But they could not be explained.

Three airships of unknown construction had occupied the

nation's largest power plant. They left it running, using the current generated for their own unknown purposes. Airplanes that tried to attack them were doomed, the invaders had an unknown but deadly accurate weapon. But it did not affect all types of planes alike, some had escaped. They were not undamaged but had managed to glide away from the danger zone.

It was found that their motors and some other implements had disappeared, save for a few handfuls of bits of metal found in the casing. Somebody discovered accidentally that these bits were highly magnetized. Somebody else realized that the planes that escaped were those built of other metals than steel. The conclusion was obvious, that the white beam from the three ships destroyed iron and steel. Possibly by setting up such magnetic strains and stresses that the material broke to pieces—although the theory of ferromagnetism could not explain such a procedure—possibly by entirely unknown means that brought magnetization only as a by-product.

The ground investigation units dispatched by the Army reported other strange facts. There seemed to be a zone where life could not exist. This zone was roughly circular—as far as could be found—with the ships as the center of the circle. The zone extended just beyond Harling Dam. Whoever crossed the invisible border line of the zone just dropped dead, nobody could tell why. The soldiers had marked the danger line as well as they could.

Another crew had tried to establish communication by heliograph with the three ships, because they did not answer radio calls. They had answered the call with a bright flash that wiped out crew, heliograph and car alike. Obviously bright light was disliked by the occupants of the three ships, or else they confused it with their own destructive beam.

Occasionally one of the three ships rose from its pit and cruised to some other part of the world. They were seen—and if not seen detected by the very typical "staccato static" radios emitted when one of the ships was near—almost everywhere. One day Hong Kong reported them, the next day London and Berlin almost simultaneously. Then Buenos Aires and New York with only two and a half hours difference. Nothing ever happened, when airplanes went up to approach them they withdrew to high altitudes where the planes could not follow. Occasionally they flashed what was taken as a mysterious signal, a bright ball of light, that was at first deep violet, changed slowly to blue and more rapidly through all the other colors of the rainbow to red.

It was the astronomer Professor Hasgrave who was the first to say publicly what many had been suspecting for many days that these three ships were arrivals from another planet, possibly even another solar system.

The military authorities that were in charge of the case laughed about Hasgrave at first. But they had to admit that none of their scientists could really explain the feats accomplished by the strangers, to say nothing of duplicating them. They also had to admit that their secret service had not been able to find even the slightest clue that ships of this type had been built in any other country. They began to admit the possibility of extraterrestrial origin of the strange ships when Hasgrave suddenly found a convincing explanation for the bright ball of light released over several cities.

It was not a weapon, he explained, but a warning. It was the adaptation of an astronomical principle for communication. The ball displayed the Doppler effect, it shifted from blue through all colors to red. In astronomy this indicated the recession of a body. Since the sphere of light had remained motionless it obviously meant that the airplanes should go. The speed with which the colors changed increased during the display, meaning that they should go with increasing speed.

A few days of mental effort made the authorities realize that the three ships were actually visitors from the void. To be exact, they were not really visitors. They had just come and established themselves. They were uncommunicative, in fact warning humans to stay away. They did no harm, if not approached. And they did not take anything away except the current produced in the power plants of Harling Dam. They behaved actually as a human being might behave at a bee hive. Doing no intentional harm, just taking honey away and crushing those bees that disturbed them. But the bees had stings to defend themselves and to avenge the loss of those killed. Humanity had stings too, airplanes and tanks and guns.

Soon men craved for war with the aliens. They had not come as friends, therefore they must be enemies. That they were simply indifferent hurt mankind's pride, they should at least make an attempt to apologize for the loss of life they had caused. Intelligent beings that were able to do all this that they actually did would certainly also be able to communicate if they wanted to. At any event they had opened hostilities and had to be shown that humanity was not afraid to fight.

The general in command of the armed forces finally felt

convinced that he should order an artillery attack. There were many heavy batteries massed now in the forest.

The general gave the order.

Six eight-inch shells dropped in a steep trajectory on the three ships.

The battery commanders had had weeks of time to work out all the factors determining the trajectories. Five of the six shells made clean hits . . . but they exploded fifty meters above the targets. The sixth shell strayed a bit from its trajectory, it landed a few meters from the power house, digging a large crater and damaging the building slightly.

Twenty-four hours later the general received a report that a dome of silvery metal had been erected overnight. It covered the power house and a trial shot with a single heavy shell proved that this dome was as impervious to shell fire as the ships themselves. Then the strange war had begun in earnest. But it was one-sided for most of the time and absolutely ineffective. The gunners, although they kept up continuous bombardment, did not succeed in catching a ship off guard. The strange power that made shells explode at a safe distance did not fail for a moment. The men grew desperate, especially since the ships occasionally retaliated, always taking a heavy toll of lives and of equipment.

Finally Professor Hasgrave conceived a plan. It was his firm conviction that all these strange manifestations of power were basically electric phenomena. There should be a way of dealing with them. The first man Hasgrave informed was Walter Harling, the man who had created Harling Dam that had become the center of all these strange happenings. They then talked to the general, finally to the president. In the end they agreed to try Hasgrave's plan. And Walter Harling at last won the bitter argument that arose . . . he carried it out himself.

The tank, splashing through rain and mud, brought Harling to a simple but fairly large building, the home of the rangers of the forest, now serving as headquarters for the military command. The general was waiting for them.

They were standing in the doorway, looking out on the dark and rainy landscape. None of them spoke, each knew what the other was thinking.

"The equipment is ready," said the general finally.

"So am I," answered Harling.

They shook hands.

"Red rockets," said Harling.

"Red rockets," repeated the general. "Good luck, Harling!"

Officers led Harling along a wet concrete road which ended at the shore of Harling Lake. There was a boat waiting on the water. And a squadron of hydroplanes. Harling heard them take off ten minutes after the motor launch had pulled his rowboat from the shore. When the planes were in the air the rumble of artillery fire died gradually down.

Harling knew what was going on in the forest.

Guns were inspected and made ready to fire at a given signal. Ammunition was piled up close to the guns, ready for immediate use. Automatic gyro-controlled devices aligned the barrels of whole batteries on the targets. The gigantic railroad guns, not able to fire quickly, pointed their barrels in such a way that their super heavy shells would land exactly in the right spot at the right moment. Expertly trained officers worked with slide rules to find the right amount of powder needed for a given trajectory at a certain air pressure, density and temperature.

"Half a mile from the danger zone," said the officer in the motor launch.

"Cut cables!"

"Good luck!"

Harling waited till the motor vessel had disappeared in the rain. Then he inspected his boat. It was built without the tiniest bit of iron. From the sides of the wooden vessel aluminum struts projected upwards, supporting a net of gleaming copper wire. It covered the boat entirely, just high enough for Harling to stand upright in it. On all sides the copper net trailed in the water, leaving enough room to handle the oars.

Something like a wide cape of copper wire mesh was ready for Harling. It was supported over his head by struts fastened to a wide aluminum collar. The "cape" was long enough to touch the ground all around his feet in any position Harling might assume—like the net protecting the boat it should be heavy enough to ground even powerful electric bolts. Harling donned the strange garment and rowed toward the valve controls of his dam. Meanwhile the airplanes—all aluminum construction, even the motors that naturally did not last very long—danced like fireflies over the three ships and the metal dome that covered the power house. The planes tried to center the enemy's attention upon themselves.

If he was attentive to their puny actions at all . . .

When Harling passed the invisible barrier he felt a prickling sensation on his skin. It actually was an electric field of great power, generated and kept up in a manner unknown to terrestrial science. Suddenly the dam appeared out of the darkness, looking like a massive seven-foot wall from the lake. Harling followed its curve with his boat. He knew every

inch of this dam—but he had no time for sentimental recol-
lections. He prayed that the valve controls were in working
order. They were hydraulic and would not be impaired by the
electric field. But the "enemy" might have destroyed them, nobody had ever been able to approach and investigate.

Harling found one of the metal stairways that led from the
crown of the dam to the bottom of the lake. He tied the boat
to it, made certain that the several dozen of red starlight
rockets set up in the copper net were still in proper position.
He took the main fuse—electric ignition was, of course, impossible—which was inserted into a watertight rubber hose.
There were matches in a watertight case tied to the end of
the hose. Harling took the end of the main fuse with him.
Then he lifted the net of the boat and stepped on the metal
staircase, always careful to have his wire mesh armor trailing
in the water. He waited for electrical effects, there were none.

Fortunately, there was a catwalk running along the inner
side of the dam, now submerged under about four feet of
water. Harling decided that the submerged catwalk was a still
better way than the crown of the dam. He might be seen up
there, even if he crawled and in spite of the darkness. Hasgrave had a theory that "those others" might be able to "see"
the heat his body radiated.

He held match case and rubber hose in his left hand,
heavy service pistol in the other, nobody could know what he
might encounter in the valve house. The door was not closed
when he arrived there at last. The body of a dead man
blocked his way, the guard that had been on duty when the
invaders came. There was no living being in the four rooms.
He looked over the controls, nobody had touched them for
weeks and they seemed to be in working order. He tried one
of the smallest valves experimentally . . . it did work. He
could go through with the original plan.

He opened the match case. The matches were dry.

Then he turned the wheels that opened the upper gates of
both spillways. But he did not open the lower locks that
made the water coming through the spillways pour into the
canal. The water would fill both of the gigantic spillways and
would stop at the lower lock. If this lock would give the
water would not enter the canal that was closed by a second
lock but would flood the valley itself. Therefore the mecha-
nisms were set once and for all in such a way that the lower
locks could not be operated independently. They could only
be opened and closed together. Harling left them all closed as
they were according to the instruments on the panel.

He waited for three minutes, knowing that everything de-

pended on these three times sixty seconds. A hundred times
he thought during the next hundred and fifty seconds that his
watch had stopped. A hundred times he made sure that it had
not.

Everywhere in the forest the officers of the gun crews were
waiting too, eyes glued to the dials of the watches, hands
ready to pull the lanyards of their pieces. Crack pilots, while
doing crazy stunts with their hydroplanes above the quietly
resting three alien ships, glanced at the crown of the dam.

Two minutes and forty seconds.

Countless tons of water were falling down the steep grad-
ing of the tubular spillways.

Two minutes and forty-five seconds.

More and more water going into the spillways. The level
of the lake actually receding by inches, unobservable due to
the beating rain.

Two minutes and fifty seconds.

The water must reach the lower locks in twenty seconds.
Three seconds . . . one had to allow for the fuse to burn,
one or two for the rockets, four more for . . .

Two minutes and fifty-five seconds.

Harling lighted six or seven matches in a bundle, held the
rubber hose clenched.

Three minutes!

Now two more seconds to wait. Harling counted them with
a strained voice counting not "one, two" but higher figures
that would take a second to pronounce.

"A hundred and one" . . . "A hundred and two" . . .

He lighted the fuse, let it fall to the floor and threw himself down.

Three seconds later five dozens of Army rockets rose into
the sky. Though wet most of them worked. They fought
their way through the rain . . . Harling thought that the resistance of the rain was very fortunate, else they might explode in the deep hanging clouds and go unnoticed.

The sky suddenly shone red with Very lights.

Like a mighty thunderclap four score guns answered, barrels jerking back under the recoil, reports deafening crews,
shells screaming through the rain.

The shells of the howitzers arrived first, exploding over
their usual targets, ships and dome. A second later the twenty-four-inch projectiles of the railroad guns came. They were
aimed with deadly accuracy. Two on each side of the valley
arrived side by side . . .

And broke the lower locks!

A flood of water spouted out of the spillways, spread over

the valley because the second locks, those closing the canal, still blocked the way. The same instant the shells of two combined batteries of seventeen-inch mobile mortars crashed into the dam—where sections joined that were not so stable now under lessening water pressure. Harling Dam broke, thundered down into the valley.

It poured over the dome and the ships. And together with the water came all the shells the already steaming barrels of dozens of batteries of heavy howitzers had held in reserve.

And Professor Hasgrave proved to be right again. The repellent shield on which shells and bombs had exploded was gone, somehow the water made its power fail. The avalanche of heavy shells exploded on the hulls and inside of their targets. The targets ceased to exist . . .

The general himself was present in the rescue party that climbed up to the valve tower in search for Harling. They did not have a very clear conception what they had expected to see . . . at any event it was not what they really saw.

Harling was sitting with only very little clothing—the other hung over the rail to dry—in the rays of the early morning sun at the only table in the control room. He was furiously writing equations on the back of beer advertising posters. And instead of listening to congratulations he informed the rescue party that Harling Dam could be ready to resume work before spring.

TO EXPLAIN
MRS. THOMPSON

PHILIP LATHAM
(R. S. Richardson)

Science fiction readers have a special fondness for the Mount Palomar astronomer R. S. Richardson, partly because of his unique experiment, some years back, of propounding to a science fiction audience, through a science fiction magazine, some of the challenging questions of the day in astronomy, with a frank hope for wild guesses that might answer them—and might be susceptible to checking.

But there is another reason why science fictionists know R. S. Richardson—but not under that name; for Richardson is also science fiction author Philip Latham. As Philip Latham he propounds here the question of a wild phenomenon indeed.

It was a superb plate, one of the best of Andromeda that Kirby had ever seen. The resolution in the spiral arms was amazing. He fancied there was even a hint of approaching resolution in the central nucleus.

"Is this the discovery plate?" he inquired, holding the photograph at arm's length in front of the viewing screen.

"That's right," Rea replied, a disembodied voice from the shadows behind the developing tank. "I got it last dark of the moon. That would be just a month ago on October 1st."

Kirby laid the plate on the illuminated screen taking care to place the emulsion side up. Then he pulled up a chair, let his great bulk down upon it with obvious relief, and began groping around over the table for a magnifying glass. "Now where's this famous object of yours?" he grunted.

The younger man pointed to a spot on the emulsion with the tip of his lead pencil. "Right here in this little rectangle of stars about a degree south of the nucleus. You'll know it when you see it."

Kirby began moving the glass slowly back and forth over the region indicated. Suddenly he stopped and bent nearer the glass.

"Got it?" said Rea.

Kirby nodded absently. The light from the viewing screen threw deep shadows over his face, accentuating his fleshy features and thick bushy eyebrows. "Well, it certainly looks real enough," he said, at length. "No question about that. How much exposure did you give this plate?"

"Thirty minutes was all it would stand. The night was rather bright. Aurora probably."

"So I judged," said Kirby, gazing at the plate admiringly. "That Schmidt sure gives beautiful images, doesn't it? Right out to the very edge." He reached for the magnifier. "Now where's the plate you got last night?"

Rea placed another 14 x 14 plate on the screen beside the first. One corner was still damp from the wash. "The seeing wasn't quite so good on this one but I think you'll find the images are nearly comparable. Now take a look at that same region."

Kirby peered at the object within the rectangle of stars again. Only on this plate the outline extended considerably beyond the rectangle. "Well, it does look different," he admitted. "Bigger, I'd say, with more detailed structure. You've probably got a variable star although you'd think it would have been picked up before, considering how many times this region is photographed. Could even be a nova. The spiral arms extend out a long way, you know."

Rea bent nearer the screen. His thin sensitive features were in marked contrast to the square jaw and general solid appearance of the older man. "That's one of the things Slater and I are investigating. He has an idea that by restricting our counts to B stars we'll find new arms that are invisible against the general background."

"Slater, eh?" said Kirby, glancing up quickly. "He's pretty high-powered, isn't he?"

"Oh, he's a lot like most of those theoretical fellows. Never at a loss for an explanation. Seems to know all about almost everything. A second Henry Norris Russell."

"Keep you busy?"

"I'll say. After he left it was like being on a vacation."

Kirby reached for his fur cap and heavy gloves. "Well, I'll see if I can photograph your object at the Cassegrain focus of the 120-inch next run," he said, getting ponderously to his feet. "The scale there ought to show up the structure of this thing whatever it is." He studied it through the glass again. "Sure is funny looking."

"Here, you haven't been looking at it from the right angle," said Rea. He picked up the plate and turned it end-for-end. "Now take a look and tell me if it reminds you of anything."

Kirby scrutinized the object in its new position, his face as grave and serious as before. Suddenly he let out a roar of laughter that shook the dark-room walls. "Why, it's a dead ringer for old lady Katzenjammer in the funny paper! I didn't get it right at first."

"You've got to see it just right," said Rea, grinning.

Kirby chuckled softly. "That just goes to show you can find anything in the sky you want. We've already got the Owl Nebula and the Crab Nebula and the Horse's Head. Now I suppose they'll be calling this thing the Katzenjammer effect."

Outside the thermostatically controlled darkroom the air in the dome felt damp and chill. Overhead the white tube of the Big Schmidt loomed like a dim ghost in the faint evening light filtering in around the shutter.

They walked down to the clump of oaks below the dome where Kirby had left his car. The sun had set a few minutes before leaving a long crimson streak along the coastline. In the east the twilight bow was rising over the mountains like an advancing thunderstorm.

"Seeing must be awful from the way those stars are jumping," said Kirby, glancing at the faint outline of the cross of Cygnus beginning to sparkle in the zenith. "You'd better forget about observing tonight. Take my advice and curl up by the stove with a good detective story."

Rea looked thoughtfully at the fading streak of red along the coast. "I've been seeing things in the sky ever since I was a kid. You know hardly any of the constellations look like the people and animals they're supposed to represent. Yet I've never had any trouble seeing them. The Lion and Medusa and the Dragon are just as clear to me as if someone had marked them out on the sky." He thrust his hands deeper into the pockets of his sheep-lined coat. "Depends on your personality, I guess. Like those ink-blot tests."

Kirby snorted. "If you ask me, it would be a good idea if we got rid of all that junk in the sky. Why, lots of people think that's about all there is to astronomy. They don't think you know anything unless you can point out the Bull or tell 'em which star marks the hind end of the giraffe. Me—I don't know Lepus from Puppis."

He slammed the door of his car and kicked the starter. "Well, see you next week. We'll take a crack at old lady Katzenjammer."

He waved good-by and sent his car grinding down the road toward the gate to the observatory grounds. Rea stood watching him until the car disappeared around the old pine tree. Then he turned and started slowly plodding up the trail to his cabin.

The sound of the dome rumbling to a halt was followed by the thin high-pitched whine of the motor turning the telescope in declination. The massive framework that formed the tube of the 120-inch reflector continued to turn until it was directed to a hazy patch of light barely visible in the constellation of Andromeda. The whining of the motor stopped, there was a series of sharp reports like the crack of a rifle, and then silence.

"Well, that oughta be it," the man at the control desk said, glancing at the illuminated dial of the sidereal clock in front of him. "Right on the nose."

There was no reply from the two men huddled together on the little platform at the Cassegrain focus fifty feet above him. One of the men was peering into the focal plane of the mirror, an oblong section of the heavens brought down to earth for mortal men to explore.

"Find it?" said Rea, from his precarious perch on the rear of the platform.

Kirby moved his head from side to side viewing different portions of the star field. "Yeah, I got Andromeda all right. But we don't seem to be centered on the object quite." He punched one of the buttons on the panel by his elbow. "There—she's coming in now." He released the button and turned back to the star field. "Want to take a look?" he inquired casually, turning to Rea.

They shifted positions on the platform. Rea settled himself in the observing chair, took the eyepiece from Kirby, and began scanning the focal plane. He stopped and bent nearer the focal plane with a sharp intake of breath. Neither man spoke. The night assistant at the desk yawned and began turning through the pages of an old Sears, Roebuck catalogue.

"Got another eyepiece?" said Rea, in a toneless voice.

"Try this one," said Kirby, groping in his pocket. "It's a little lower power."

Rea took the eyepiece and moved it over the focal plane again. After a brief inspection he leaned back and sat looking down at his feet in the direction of the mirror. Suddenly he swayed slightly and grabbed at the side of the platform. Kirby's arm was around him in an instant.

"Hang on!" he said. "I felt the same way the first time I saw it, too."

Rea sat for a few moments holding hard to the edge of the platform. Presently his grip relaxed. "Thanks for grabbing me. It's a long way to the floor."

"I know," said Kirby, "I fell off once." He moved back a little farther. "Should have warned you probably, but I wanted to see if it hit you the same way that it did me. Guess there's not much doubt about it now."

"No, I guess not," Rea said thoughtfully. "Kirby, it *is* a face in the sky! Up there among the stars just as if it were projected on the sky with a magic lantern."

"Huh, you don't need to tell me. I've been photographing it for three nights running now. I know every line in that face."

Rea gave him a startled look. "And you've never told anyone!"

"Well, I didn't want to go off half-cocked till I was sure what I was doing, did I? So I took some exposures here and a bunch more at the 60-inch. Red and blue sensitive both out of an emulsion we just received. Broke the seal myself. And they all show the same identical thing—a plump middle-aged woman with a hair-do like Mrs. Katzenjammer's in the middle of the Andromeda Nebula." He took a can of tobacco from his pocket and began tamping down the bowl with deliberate care.

Rea half turned in his chair. "But man alive, it's insane! Crazy! Look here, nobody could be trying to pull something on us, could they? Trying to trick us?"

"Who, for instance?"

"Oh, I don't know. Anybody. The night assistant down there at the desk."

"You mean old Hank? No. He hasn't had a new idea in the last twenty years."

Kirby puffed reflectively on his pipe. "No, in my opinion the face is real in the sense that it's not an optical illusion or an instrumental effect. I'm thoroughly satisfied on that score. What it really is I haven't any idea. That's what we've got to find out."

"What are you going to do?"

Kirby clenched the stem of his pipe more firmly. "I'm going to take some more exposures. If you'll hand me that plateholder over there—"

The face that had been only faintly visible at the telescope stood out with startling clarity when the plates were developed downstairs in the darkroom.

"One thing's sure," said Kirby, holding a plate up to the light. "This face is outside our own galactic system. You can see foreground stars superimposed all over it. In fact, from the way the spiral arms and some of this obscuring matter crosses the left eye and the bridge of the nose, I'd say it was a little farther than Andromeda itself."

He replaced the plate in the wash and began drying his hands on a towel. Rea lifted a plate from the wash with the tip of his finger. "Mind if I look at this one? I think it's a longer exposure."

"Sure, go ahead."

Rea rinsed the plate under the faucet, wiped the emulsion with a piece of cotton, and placed the dripping piece of glass on the viewing screen. "Say, you can see a lot more on this one," he called out excitedly. "Her neck and arms and part of her dress shows up. Looks like the same kind of clothes the women are wearing now."

Kirby came over beside him. "By gosh, you're right," he said. "The latest thing."

"But that makes it worse," Rea protested. "If she's at about the same distance as Andromeda, the light must have left her nearly a million years ago. She ought to have on a tiger skin or rhinoceros hide."

Kirby emptied the ashes from his pipe into the tin can thoughtfully placed in the darkroom by the janitor. "Well, Dr. Rea, you're the one who discovered this Katzenjammer effect. So what should we do about it? Send an announcement telegram to Harvard? Summon the press? Proclaim it to the world?"

"No, not yet anyhow," said Rea frowning. "Let's wait. Keep it to ourselves for a while. Of course, if it keeps on getting brighter the news is bound to come out pretty soon. Some amateur or comet hunter is sure to spot it."

"And then what?"

"And then by that time Slater will be here and he's sure to have some explanation. I think he's been working on some new theory about the universe. How it got here and where it's going."

Kirby studied the face on the plate with a critical eye. "If we've got to have a woman in the sky, why does she have to be fat and middle-aged? Why couldn't she be a good-looker —like that dame on the calendar there?"

The thing that always surprised people about Slater the first time they met him was his astonishing youth. It seemed impossible that anyone so young could know so much. After a while you got used to the idea but right at first it kind of threw you. Before long you got in the habit of deferring to him and letting him take the lead and make the decisions. Not that he ever insisted upon his own ideas or belittled the opinions of others. Far from it. But there was a certain serene confidence about everything he did that made him a natural leader.

Now he looked a trifle puzzled at the two men who entered his office with solemn mien.

"Well, gentlemen, come in, come in. This is a long anticipated pleasure. Ah, I see you brought the plates with you. Good. I am eager for work. Good solid substantial work." He straddled the back of his chair with his long legs and sat gazing expectantly at his visitors.

"How're things back at Princeton?" Rea asked, laying the box of plates on the desk. "I hear you've been giving a course on cosmology at the Institute for Advanced Research."

Slater laughed. "I'd hardly call it by such a dignified name as a 'course.' It's all so delightfully informal, you know. One day we have the universe all settled. The next day we have to do it over again." He shrugged indifferently. "Oh, I discussed Jordan's cosmology a little. Sometimes I think he really has something. Then again I wonder if it's anything but numerology."

He was thoughtful for a moment then became all animation again. 'But I'm bursting with curiosity. What luck did you have with that new fine-grain emulsion? Did you try it on the Coma or Virgo cluster? And how about N.G.C. 185? I'm sure you have something wonderful to show me."

Kirby selected a plate from the box and laid it on the viewing screen imbedded in the top of the desk. Without the lights on underneath the photograph was simply a dark square upon the white opal glass. "I've been working with Rea on your program," he explained. "We've got some interesting results all right only they're not exactly what we expected."

"But that's fine," Slater cried. "An unexpected result is a rare treat."

"Yeah," said Kirby, "only this time it was a little more unexpected than usual."

"We might as well be honest and tell him it's plain crazy," Rea broke in. "It doesn't make sense. It's something that shouldn't be in the sky at all."

Slater looked at them bewildered.

"What Rea is trying to say," said Kirby slowly, choosing his words with care, "is that he's found a woman's face in the sky. Get it—a woman's face. Right smack in the middle of the Andromeda Nebula."

"But surely you're joking," Slater exclaimed. He glanced quickly from one to the other as if hoping to catch them in a secret exchange of information.

"You can see for yourself," Kirby told him, switching on the illumination. "I'll swear that's just the way it showed up in the developer."

Slater seized a magnifying glass and bent over the plate. He studied the face staring up at him from the emulsion for several seconds, then straightened up slowly.

"This is some ghastly joke," he declared angrily. "Some horrible ghastly joke. Someone with a perverted sense of humor—"

Rea seized him by the arm. "I told you it was crazy, didn't I? I told you there wasn't any sense to it. But all the same there it is!"

Slater gave Rea a long searching look. Then he bent over the plate and began examining it again, not only the face but the star images for several degrees around it. When he finally laid the glass aside his eyes were fairly glowing. "But this is wonderful—simply wonderful," he whispered. He wrapped his arms around his shoulders hugging himself with delight. "Now tell me all about it!" he commanded. "Instantly!"

They gave him a hasty résumé of events up to date. When they had finished he began pacing up and down the narrow confines of his office, his brow furrowed in thought.

"First, how many people know about this face?" he asked.

"So far," said Kirby, "just us girls. But you understand we can't keep it quiet forever. We can't put a sign on it telling the world to keep off, you know."

"That's the unfortunate part, I'm afraid. If we could only keep it as our private property; or at least confine it within the realm of scientific thought." He fell to studying the image on the plate again. "Curious looking female, isn't she? Face seems vaguely familiar somehow."

"Rea thinks she looks like Mrs. Katzenjammer," said Kirby.

"No-o-o," said Slater judiciously, "I should say she more

nearly resembles that woman in the Moon Mullins strip. The one who's always swatting Uncle Willie over the head."

"Why does she have to be so commonplace looking?" Rea complained. "A woman's face among the stars should be lovely, ethereal, something to dream about."

Slater clapped him on the shoulder. "That's life for you, old man. It's so seldom we ever attain that complete perfection in our environment that corresponds to ideal beauty. There is always the jarring note. The annoying intrusion. We are watching a sunset and an airplane starts spelling the name of somebody's soup on the sky. In the middle of Beethoven's Ninth Symphony somebody sneezes. It is a world of sweets and sours."

He began pacing the room again. "But here we are philosophizing when we should be hard at work. There are things to do. Questions to which we must find the answer while we still may work in peace—before this ghastly celestial apparition bursts upon the world."

He swung on Kirby. "I'm curious to know what keeps this woman shining. Why is she visible? What is her source of illumination? Can you give me a spectrum of her?"

"I don't see why not," Kirby replied. "In fact, she ought to be a fairly easy object compared with some I've tried for."

"How soon?"

"Well, let's see. The two-prism nebular spectrograph is on at the Cassegrain now. If I can focus it this afternoon, I might be able to get a plate tonight."

"What region of the spectrum would that cover?"

"From H and K to about H Beta. To get the visual I'd have to change spectrographs."

"I'm sure that won't be necessary. The photographic region should be sufficient for our purposes."

He turned to Rea. "Do you have some good directs of the face taken several months apart? Plates taken at a small zenith distance suitable for precise measurement?"

"Yes, I think so."

"I want to measure the position of the face relative to the surrounding stars for aberration. While all modern theories agree that the velocity of light is independent of the velocity of the emitting source, it seems like a longshot well worth taking, considering the slight effort involved. How soon can you get me those plates?"

"They're downstairs in my office now."

"Splendid. I'd also like to do some photometry on the face. See how fast she's increasing in brightness. Are your plates calibrated by any chance?"

"We always calibrate them. It's routine."

"Good. Good. Then we can start measuring at once."

Kirby started for the door. "Well, guess I'd better be getting up on the mountain if I'm going to get that spectrograph focused." He nodded to Slater. "It's nice to have seen you again. I'll let you know as soon as I get anything."

"Please do. Naturally I needn't impress upon you the importance of this discovery. It's going to revolutionize all our thinking. Crystallize a lot of thought that heretofore has been mere conjecture."

Rea waited until Kirby was down the stairs. "Slater, how do you explain an effect of this kind? It's beginning to get me down."

"How do I explain it?" Slater asked. "Oh, I don't know. There are probably a dozen ways of accounting for it. As a matter of fact, I think it might be made to fit in rather nicely with some of the cosmological theories that are being advanced by members of the Cambridge group. Have you read that recent paper of theirs in the *Monthly Notices* on 'The Physics of Creation'?"

Rea shook his head.

"Tremendously stimulating paper. All wrong in my opinion but tremendously stimulating just the same." He laughed gaily. "But now let us get to work. I fear that framing theories is going to be the least of our worries in the future."

Kirby came directly to headquarters as soon as he got down off the mountain. He was still wearing his fur cap and heavy boots when he came tramping into Slater's office.

"Well, here you are," the astronomer said, taking an envelope from his pocket and extracting a glass plate from it about the size of a calling card. Across the center a thin black streak could be discerned about an inch long. "I got several others but this is the best of the lot."

Slater regarded it with intense interest. "Have you had a chance to measure it yet? What did you find?"

"Sure, I've had a chance to measure it. If there'd been anything there to measure."

"What do you mean?"

"Take a look and see. Here—use my glass. You'll need a pretty high power to show it up."

Slater held the plate with the lens almost touching the glass. Through the eyepiece he saw a smooth unbroken dark streak with tiny black lines sticking out on either side of it. After a brief inspection he laid the plate down and gazed blankly at Kirby.

"A continuous spectrum," he said, unable to keep the disappointment out of his voice. "Not a trace of a line. Not even H and K or the G band."

"Just a blank," Kirby said, lighting his pipe. "As if I'd taken a spectrum of that electric light filament over there. We can't tell what she's made out of or whether she's coming or going."

"By the way, where did you set the slit of the spectrograph?"

"Right on the end of her nose. That looked like the brightest place on her face so that was where I set it." He chuckled to himself. "Must be the first time an astronomer's ever got the spectrum of a woman's nose."

Slater opened a thermos bottle and poured himself a cup of coffee. "Our researches at this end have been singularly unfruitful too. Preliminary measures on the aberrational constant give practically identical values for both stars and face." He indicated a chart upon which he had been working when Kirby came in. "The most interesting result is our photographic photometry on the relative intensity of the features. She's brightening up at an amazing rate, roughly as the fourth power of the time as nearly as we can tell. Rea's measuring on a plate now."

The telephone rang as he was about to place another point upon the curve. He reached for the instrument with one hand, holding the cup of coffee with the other. "Yes," he said, "Slater speaking."

"Say, I'm calling from the *Times*," the voice at the other end said. "We've got a story here from an amateur astronomer down at Oceanside. He's got some kind of a telescope he says he made himself. Well, he claims he's been seeing a face in the sky for the last couple of nights. Found it by accident while he was showing his friends the Andromeda Nebula." The reporter continued almost apologetically. "There's been so many crazy reports like this coming in lately we haven't paid much attention to them but this fellow sounds fairly sensible. As a cosmologist, would you have any comment to make, Dr. Slater?"

Slater took a sip of the coffee. "What kind of a face was it?"

"He says it's a woman's face."

"Well, that's a relief from the flying saucers, anyhow. They were beginning to get awfully tiresome I thought."

"Yeah, the country's full of nuts. Well, Dr. Slater, I just thought you might have some explanation to offer—" He broke off abruptly. A moment later he was back again, an excited note in his voice. "Say, we just got a flash on the teletype. From an astronomer at the Helwan Observatory in Europe. Ever hear of it?"

"Yes, I've heard of it."

"Well, they claim they've spotted something, too. Only they don't call it a woman's face. They just say it's a 'remarkable object.'"

"Conservative, eh? Well, that's very interesting indeed. I'll try to remember to take a look at Andromeda tonight."

"Listen, Dr. Slater, you're one of the most eminent cosmologists in the country. Are you sure you don't have some explanation about this thing?"

"Quite sure!" said Slater emphatically. He hung up.

Kirby regarded him quizzically. "Newspaper man, huh?"

Slater nodded. "It was bound to come out eventually. We might as well face it now as later. No pun intended either."

He was pouring himself another cup of coffee when Rea came in the door waving a telegram. "Well, the whole thing's out. A half a dozen reports have come in to Harvard already."

He slapped the telegram down on the desk disgustedly. "If it'd been anywhere else but Andromeda, we could have kept it under cover indefinitely. But those amateurs are always testing their telescopes on it. When people get their first look at that face tonight all hell's going to break loose."

"Did you say tonight?" Kirby demanded.

"I certainly did," Rea said. He reached across the desk and placed a point on the sheet of graph paper. "There. That's the result of my last measure. The curve is fairly easy to extrapolate. You can see where she'll be tonight—almost as bright as the full moon."

Kirby groaned. "I'm getting out of town."

"Do you know what this means?" Rea said. "It means everybody is going to be after us for an explanation. And it had better be a good one, too."

The telephone rang. Nobody moved. It continued to ring, a steady insistent jingle. Slowly Slater leaned across the desk and lifted the instrument.

"Get any sleep last night?"

Slater laid aside the newspaper he had been reading when Rea came in. "Not much," he admitted, smiling wearily. "People kept calling up all evening. When I took the telephone off the hook they started pounding on the door. Sounded as if there was a whole regiment on the front lawn.

While my landlady was getting the police I made a quick exit out the back way. Spent the rest of the night in a moving picture theater." He reached for a cigarette. "An all western program. I wouldn't recommend it."

"The worst part," Rea complained, "is that because we're astronomers people seem to think we're responsible for what goes on in the sky. You'd think they'd have better sense."

Slater gave him an indulgent smile. "By the way, how did the face look last night? There's too much light in my neighborhood to see."

"You're lucky," Rea told him. "People were standing on all the streets as if they were hypnotized. Just standing there by the hour gazing at it. Waiting for it to do something. That's the worst part about it. The thing wouldn't be so bad if there was any life in it. If it wouldn't keep looking out at you with that fatuous placid expression." He shuddered.

Slater sighed and returned to the newspaper. "I see they're predicting the end of the world now. It's scheduled to hit here Monday at nine in the evening."

"Who says so?"

Slater scanned the type under the big black headlines. "It doesn't say definitely. Just a rumor, I guess."

"You don't think there could be anything to it then?"

"I'm reserving opinion until I get a report from Kirby. He was going to try to photograph Andromeda again last night. When I hear from him we may have something definite to go on. What's that?" he said, glancing toward the door. "Sounds as if we had company coming."

Rea poked his head around the side of the door. "We're in for it now. There's a whole delegation headed this way."

"Relax," said Slater, lighting a cigarette. "To tell the truth I'm really enjoying all this immensely. If the world's coming to an end, we might as well get all the fun out of it we can."

The little man at the head of the procession reminded you of a badly bedraggled rooster. He had a thin scrawny neck with a prominent Adam's apple that jerked up and down with a convulsive motion. His watery blue eyes had a bewildered expression above his long walrus mustache. He stood in the doorway regarding the two men uncertainly.

"Which one of you gentlemen is Dr. Slater, the noted cosmologist?" he demanded.

Slater bowed slightly. "That happens to be my name. What can I do for you?"

"Well, sir, my name is Thompson," the little man replied.

"Homer P. Thompson from Indianapolis." He paused as if to allow time for this to sink in.

"How do you do?" said Slater, smiling cordially.

"I work at Fosberg's Department Store on East Center Street," Thompson continued. "Been janitor there twenty years. They's mighty few got a record good as mine if I do say it. You can ask Mr. Fosberg himself. He'll vouch for me. He'll tell you every word I'm saying is the truth."

"I'm quite sure that won't be necessary, Mr. Thompson," said Slater. "I can usually tell a man of integrity when I see one." He flicked the ash from his cigarette with the tip of his finger. "Now what was it you wished to see me about?"

"It's about my wife Hariette, Dr. Slater. She—" Tears suddenly welled up in his eyes and his Adam's apple twitched violently. He leaned against the door, his whole body racked with great choking sobs.

"Here, here, sit down, Mr. Thompson. Compose yourself," said Slater, hastily shoving a chair in his direction.

A young man who acted as if Thompson were his personal responsibility assisted the trembling man to the chair. He handed Slater a card. "Davenport. I'm with *World Press*. I don't know why they always hand these jobs to me."

Somebody in the back of the crowd produced a bottle of whisky. "Here," said Davenport, unscrewing the top, "take a drink of this."

Thompson raised the bottle to his lips and took several deep gulps. He lowered the bottle, gasped slightly, and wiped his mustache with the back of his hand. "Thanks," he said, passing the bottle back. "That was good whisky."

"Now, Mr. Thompson," Davenport said, in a soothing voice, "tell Dr. Slater your story just the way you told it to us in Indianapolis."

Thompson drew a long breath. "Well, it was about six weeks ago today that my wife was taken by this attack," he began. "We was comin' home from the Westside Bridge and Bingo Club. I never wanted to go in the first place. I told Hariette my feet hurt me and we'd never won a cent anyhow. Seems to me I've always just been losin' out all my life. My whole family's worked hard as far back as I can remember but none of us never seemed to get very far. I got a brother in Nebraska that's a deputy sheriff and got his picture in the paper once but that's as far as any of us ever got."

He steadied himself against the side of the desk.

"Well, we hadn't any more than got home and got up the stairs when it hit her. She clutched at her heart and gave a groan and down she went. I ran over and did all I could but it wasn't no use. She was dead before I got there."

Slater nodded sympathetically.

"She was buried in Laurel Haven in the plot we'd picked out a long time ago, ever since that smart young fellow came to the door and talked my wife into makin' a down payment on that Before Sorrow Comes plan. The Reverend Tilsbury said some words over her the way she always had wanted him to, and when I saw her layin' there in the casket with her rose silk dress on and the coral necklace she wore the day we was married, I naturally supposed that'd be the last time I'd ever look upon her face."

He began shaking all over as if agitated by some deep inner emotion. Several times he struggled to get the words out but failed. Then they burst forth like water from a dam.

"And now I see her every night up there in the sky!" he cried. "The whole neighborhood's waitin' for her to rise over the garage. When you first see her she's upside down as if she was standin' on her head. By midnight she's up over the top of the Elmwood Apartments. Then she sets right side up over the drug-store. It wouldn't be so bad if she'd only recognize me; if she'd just smile or laugh or somethin'." He buried his face in his hands.

Slater bent down beside him. "Listen, are you sure that's your wife in the sky? Absolutely sure?"

"Why, certainly I'm sure," Thompson declared indignantly. "Take a look at these." He spread half a dozen snapshots out on the desk. "Here's one of Hariette the way she looked last Fourth of July when her folks was over for dinner. Took it out in the backyard myself. And here she is at her daughter's place over in Kokomo."

Slater examined the photographs incredulously. The resemblance between the woman in the pictures and the face in the sky was unmistakable.

Thompson gazed up at the scientist with pleading eyes. "They tell me you can explain these things, Dr. Slater. That you know all about what goes on up there. Then tell me—where is she, Dr. Slater? *Where is she?*"

For once Slater's poise seemed on the point of deserting him. "Well, that's awfully hard to say," he replied, running his fingers over the back of his neck. "After all, I'm not omnipotent, you know."

"Is it heaven, Dr. Slater? Or . . . or maybe the other place?"

Slater gave him a reassuring pat on the shoulder. "Maybe there's no difference. Maybe they're both the same. The world's a mad topsy-turvy place right now, I'm afraid. But wherever your wife is, Mr. Thompson, I'm sure she's happy."

Several reporters darted off down the hall. A flash bulb popped and then another and another. "One more, Dr. Slater," Davenport yelled. "Looking over his shoulder at the photographs."

In the midst of all the confusion the telephone rang.

"Get that for me will you, Rea?" Slater shouted. "It's probably Kirby calling from the mountain. He's the only one allowed to call in."

Rea picked up the instrument. "Hello, Kirby?" He waved down the crowd at the door. "Confound it, I can't hear a thing! All right now, go ahead."

He sat with the receiver at his ear taking down the message without comment. Gradually the room quieted down, as if everyone there sensed that something important was transpiring. When Rea put the telephone down his face was very grim.

"Well, Kirby said he got Andromeda last night. The seeing wasn't very good but he said he got it anyhow. Enough to see what's going on, at any rate."

"Good old Kirby," Slater murmured.

Rea tried to make his voice sound casual. "He says the nebula's breaking up. Tidal strain evidently. The side toward the face is scarcely recognizable now. Nothing but a hazy mass of star stuff with dark clouds of obscuring matter streaked across it. And novae in the spiral arms. But he says the face itself seems to be getting dimmer, as if it were fading away."

The room had become very still. All eyes were turned on Slater. Davenport leaned toward him across the desk.

"You've got to tell us, Dr. Slater," he said in a hoarse voice. "What does it mean? Surely there must be an explanation."

Slater raised his arms and let them fall to his sides again in a helpless gesture. Thompson kept shuffling the photographs of his wife back and forth between his fingers.

"My old woman," he muttered dazedly, "up there in the sky."

The Milky Way was a glowing arch spanning the heavens like the gateway to infinity. Below along the coastline the lights of a score of towns sparkled in the evening breeze. Slater drew back the sleeve of his coat revealing the illuminated dial of his wrist watch.

"Nine o'clock," he announced. "Time for the end of the

world." He glanced over the peaceful landscape. "Well, everything seems to be intact so far. No signs of coming loose at the seams yet."

He shifted his gaze to the northeast where the Andromeda Nebula was a dim spot of light with the features of a human face barely visible in the background.

"Hm-m-m. Mrs. Thompson is barely fifth magnitude tonight," he observed. "In another week she'll have faded from sight entirely. Gone but not forgotten."

Rea shifted his position against the iron railing upon which he was leaning. "You said once there were a dozen ways of explaining a face in the sky. So far I haven't heard a single one."

"Of course I was exaggerating," said Slater. "Three or four would have been more like it."

"The chief difficulty I should say in framing a suitable theory is that great masses of matter like Andromeda don't seem to fit into the universe in the first place. There they are dotted all over the sky except where they're blocked out along the Milky Way. Long ago Sir James Jeans remarked that the external galaxies seem like singular points where matter is being poured into our universe from some entirely extraneous spatial dimension. More recently Gold and Bondi have shown that if our laws of physics are to retain any meaning then we are forced to the conclusion that matter is being created continually in space, at the rate of one hydrogen atom per cubic meter every three hundred thousand years. Not enough to make us feel cramped very soon. They call it the 'perfect cosmological principle.' Naturally they don't mean that matter is really being created. What they mean is that matter is somehow being intruded into our space from outside."

He waved his hand in the general direction of Andromeda. "In local regions of space it might be possible for matter to be created at a much faster rate. In Mrs. Thompson's case something must have got badly out of control. There was rage in heaven—a celestial crack-up—and we got a glimpse of a sight we were never intended to see. It was as simple as that."

"But that fat face in the sky!" Rea cried impatiently. "Don't tell me seriously that you ever expect to fit that into any rational theory."

"I often wonder if theoretical physics can ever really explain anything," said Slater soberly. "In the last analysis, I wonder if theoretical physics can ever do more than merely describe?"

He stood for a minute looking moodily down at the lights

of the towns along the coastline. When he spoke again it was in a different voice from the bantering tone he usually employed.

"People are forever asking for explanations. Nice pretty explanations in a world where the good die young, where the wicked go unpunished, and there are wars when nobody wants war. If we can find no explanation for life on earth in the microcosmic scale, then why expect to find one in worlds beyond in the macrocosm?"

He laughed bitterly. "I can spin endless theories for you that describe but when you ask me for one that *explains*— that is another matter entirely."

ADRIFT ON THE POLICY LEVEL

CHANDLER DAVIS

Long before Chan Davis received his doctorate in mathematics, he had taken a post-graduate course in the science of constructing good science fiction stories. Nightmare *was one of his earliest—and still remembered as a chilling study in atomic warfare as it might yet be waged, not by flights of missiles but by subterfuge. His recent output has been severely restricted, first by his work in proving theorems about matrices and operators in hilbert space—it is a measure of his standing that he was for a time on fellowship at the Institute for Advanced Study at Princeton—more recently by his editorial duties on* Mathematical Reviews, *a publication whose objective is to print promptly a competent review of every single mathematical research publication on this planet.*

Neither mathematical exercise nor nuclear thriller is the present story—but it has point, purpose and wit of its own!

I

J. Albert La Rue was nervous, but you couldn't blame him. It was his big day. He looked up for reassurance at the big, bass-voiced man sitting so stolidly next to him in the hissing subway car, and found what he sought.

There was plenty of reassurance in having a man like Calvin Boersma on your side.

Albert declared mildly but firmly: "One single thought is uppermost in my mind."

Boersma inclined his ear. "What?"

"Oxidase epsilon!" cried Albert.

Cal Boersma clapped him on the shoulder and answered,

like a fight manager rushing last-minute strategies to his boxer: "The one single thought that *should* be uppermost in your mind is *selling* oxidase epsilon. Nothing will be done unless The Corporation is sold on it. And when you deal with Corporation executives you're dealing with experts."

LaRue thought that over, swaying to the motion of the car.

"We do have something genuinely important to sell, don't we?" he ventured. He had been studying oxidase epsilon for three years. Boersma, on the other hand, was involved in the matter only because he was LaRue's lab-assistant's brother-in-law, an assistant sales manager of a plastics firm . . . and the only businessman LaRue knew.

Still, today—the big day—Cal Boersma was the expert. The promoter. The man who was right in the thick of the hard, practical world outside the University's cloistered halls —the world that terrified J. Albert LaRue.

Cal was all reassurance. "Oxidase epsilon *is* important, all right. That's the only reason we have a chance."

Their subway car gave a long, loud whoosh, followed by a shrill hissing. They were at their station. J. Albert LaRue felt a twinge of apprehension. This, he told himself, was it! They joined the file of passengers leaving the car for the luxurious escalator.

"Yes, Albert," Cal rumbled, as they rode up side by side, "we have something big here, if we can reach the top men— say, the Regional Director. Why, Albert, this could get you an assistant section managership in The Corporation itself!"

"Oh, thank you! But of course I wouldn't want—I mean, my devotion to research—" Albert was flustered.

"But of course I could take care of that end of it for you," Boersma said reassuringly. "Well, here we are, Albert."

The escalator fed them into a sunlit square between twenty-story buildings. A blindingly green mall crossed the square to the Regional Executive Building of The Corporation. Albert could not help being awed. It was a truly impressive structure—a block wide, only three stories high.

Cal said, in a reverent growl: "Putting up a building like that in the most heavily taxed area of Detroit—you know what that symbolizes, Albert? *Power.* Power and salesmanship! That's what you're dealing with when you deal with The Corporation."

The building was the hub of the Lakes Region, and the architecture was appropriately monumental. Albert murmured a comment, impressed. Cal agreed. "Superbly styled," he said solemnly.

Glass doors extending the full height of the building

opened smoothly at the touch of Albert's hand. Straight ahead across the cool lobby another set of glass doors equally tall, were a showcase for dramatic exhibits of The Corporation's activities. Soothing lights rippled through an enchanted twilight. Glowing letters said, "Museum of Progress."

Several families on holiday wandered delighted among the exhibits, basking in the highest salesmanship the race had produced.

Albert started automatically in that direction. Cal's hand on his arm stopped him. "This way, Albert. The corridor to the right."

"Huh? But—I thought you said you couldn't get an appointment, and we'd have to follow the same channels as any member of the public." Certainly the "public" was the delighted wanderer through those gorgeous glass doors.

"Oh, sure, that's what we're doing. But I didn't mean *that* public."

"Oh." Apparently the Museum was only for the herd. Albert humbly followed Cal (not without a backward glance) to the relatively unobtrusive door at the end of the lobby—the initiate's secret passage to power, he thought with deep reverence.

But he noticed that three or four new people just entering the building were turning the same way.

A waiting room. But it was not a disappointing one; evidently Cal had directed them right; they had passed to a higher circle. The room was large, yet it looked like a sanctum.

Albert had never seen chairs like these. All of the twenty-five or so men and women who were there ahead of them were distinctly better dressed than Albert. On the other hand Cal's suit—a one-piece woolly buff-colored outfit, fashionably loose at the elbows and knees—was a match for any of them. Albert took pride in that.

Albert sat and fidgeted. Cal's bass voice gently reminded him that fidgeting would be fatal, then rehearsed him in his approach. He was to be, basically, a professor of plant metabolism; it was a poor approach, Cal conceded regretfully, but the only one Albert was qualified to make. Salesmanship he was to leave to Cal; his own appeal was to be based on his position—such as it was—as a scientific expert; therefore he was to be, basically, himself. His success in projecting the role might possibly be decisive—although the main responsibility, Cal pointed out, was Cal's.

While Cal talked, Albert fidgeted and watched the room.

The lush chairs, irregularly placed, still managed all to face
one wall, and in that wall were three plain doors. From time
to time an attendant would appear to call one of the waiting
supplicants to one of the doors. The attendants were liveried
young men with flowing black hair. Finally, one came their
way! He summoned them with a bow—an eye-flashing,
head-tossing, flourishing bow, like a dancer rather than a but-
ler.

Albert followed Cal to the door. "Will this be a junior executive? A personal secretary? A—"

But Cal seemed not to hear.

Albert followed Cal through the door and saw the most
beautiful girl in the world.

He couldn't look at her, not by a long way. She was much
too beautiful for that. But he knew exactly what she looked
like. He could see in his mind her shining, ringleted hair falling gently to her naked shoulders, her dazzling bright expres-
sionless face. He couldn't even think about her body; it was
terrifying.

She sat behind a desk and looked at them.

Cal struck a masterful pose, his arms folded. "We have
come on a scientific matter," he said haughtily, "not familiar
to The Corporation, concerning several northern colonial
areas."

She wrote deliberately on a small plain pad. Tonelessly,
sweetly, she asked, "Your name?"

"Calvin Boersma."

Her veiled eyes swung to Albert. He couldn't possibly
speak. His whole consciousness was occupied in not looking
at her.

Cal said sonorously: "This is J. Albert LaRue, Professor of
Plant Metabolism." Albert was positively proud of his name,
the way Cal said it.

The most beautiful girl in the world whispered meltingly:
"Go out this door and down the corridor to Mr. Blick's office. He'll be expecting you."

Albert chose this moment to try to look at her. And *she
smiled!* Albert, completely routed, rushed to the door. He
was grateful she hadn't done *that* before! Cal, with his
greater experience and higher position in life, could linger a
moment, leaning on the desk, to leer at her.

But all the same, when they reached the corridor, he was
sweating.

Albert said carefully, *"She* wasn't an executive, was she?"

"No," said Cal, a little scornfully. "She's an Agency
Model, what else? Of course, you probably don't see them

much at the University, except at the Corporation Represent-
ative's Office and maybe the President's Office." Albert had
never been near either. "She doesn't have much to do except
to impress visitors, and of course stop the ones that don't belong here."

Albert hesitated. "She *was* impressive."

"She's impressive, all right," Cal agreed. "When you consider the Agency rates, and then realize that any member of
the public who comes to the Regional Executive Building on
business sees an Agency Model receptionist—then you know
you're dealing with power, Albert."

Albert had a sudden idea. He ventured: "Would we have
done better to have brought an Agency Model with us?"

Cal stared. "To go through the whole afternoon with us?
Impossible, Albert! It'd cost you a year's salary."

Albert said eagerly: "No, that's the beauty of it, Cal! You
see, I have a young cousin—I haven't seen her recently, of
course, but she was drafted by the Agency, and I might have
been able to get her to—" He faltered. Boersma was looking
scandalized.

"Albert—excuse me. If your cousin had so much as
walked into any business office with makeup on, she'd have
had to collect Agency rates—or she'd have been out of the
Agency like *that*. And owing them plenty." He finished con-
solingly, "A Model wouldn't have done the trick anyway."

II

Mr. Blick looked more like a scientist than a businessman,
and his desk was a bit of a laboratory. At his left hand was
an elaborate switchboard, curved so all parts would be in
easy reach; most of the switches were in rows, the handles
color-coded. As he nodded Cal to a seat his fingers flicked
over three switches. The earphones and microphone clamped
on his head had several switches too, and his right hand quiv-
ered beside a stenotype machine of unfamiliar complexity.

He spoke in an undertone into his mike, then his hand
whizzed almost invisibly over the stenotype.

"Hello, Mr. Boersma," he said, flicking one last switch but
not removing the earphones. "Please excuse my idiosyncra-
sies, it seems I actually work better this way." His voice was
firm, resonant and persuasive.

Cal took over again. He opened with a round compliment
for Mr. Blick's battery of gadgets, and then flowed smoothly
on to an even more glowing series of compliments—which

Albert realized with a qualm of embarrassment referred to *him*.

After the first minute or so, though, Albert found the talk less interesting than the interruptions. Mr. Blick would raise a forefinger apologetically but fast; switches would tumble; he would listen to the earphones, whisper into the mike, and perform incredibly on the absolutely silent stenotype. Shifting lights touched his face, and Albert realized the desk top contained at least one TV screen, as well as a bank of blinking colored lights. The moment the interruption was disposed of, Mr. Blick's faultless diction and pleasant voice would return Cal exactly to where he'd been. Albert was impressed.

Cal's peroration was an urgent appeal that Mr. Blick consider the importance to The Corporation, financially, of what he was about to learn. Then he turned to Albert, a little too abruptly.

"One single thought is uppermost in my mind," Albert stuttered, caught off guard. "Oxidase epsilon. I am resolved that The Corporation shall be made to see the importance—"

"Just a moment, Professor LaRue," came Mr. Blick's smooth Corporation voice. "You'll have to explain this to *me*. I don't have the background or the brains that you people in the academic line have. Now in layman's terms, just what *is* oxidase epsilon?" He grinned handsomely.

"Oh, don't feel bad," said Albert hastily. "Lots of my colleagues haven't heard of it, either." This was only a half-truth. Every one of his colleagues that Albert met at the University in a normal working month had certainly heard of oxidase epsilon—from Albert. "It's an enzyme found in many plants but recognized only recently. You see, many of the laboratory species created during the last few decades have been unable to produce ordinary oxidase, or oxidase alpha, but surprisingly enough some of these have survived. This is due to the presence of a series of related compounds, of which oxidases beta, gamma, delta, and epsilon have been isolated, and beta and epsilon have been prepared in the laboratory."

Mr. Blick shifted uncertainly in his seat. Albert hurried on so he would see how simple it all was. "I have been studying the reactions catalyzed by oxidase epsilon in several species of *Triticum*. I found quite unexpectedly that none of them produce the enzyme themselves. Amazing, isn't it? All the oxidase epsilon in those plants comes from a fungus, *Puccinia triticina*, which infects them. This, of course, explains the failure of Hinshaw's group to produce viable *Triticum kaci* following—"

Mr. Blick smiled handsomely again. "Well now, Professor LaRue, you'll have to tell me what this means. In *my* terms —you understand."

Cal boomed portentously, "It may mean the saving of the economies of three of The Corporation's richest colonies." Rather dramatic, Albert thought.

Mr. Blick said appreciatively, "Very good. *Very* good. Tell me more. Which colonies—and why?" His right hand left its crouch to spring restlessly to the stenotype.

Albert resumed, buoyed by this flattering show of interest. "West Lapland in Europe, and Great Slave and Churchill on this continent. They're all Corporation colonies, recently opened up for wheat-growing by *Triticum witti*, and I've been told they're extremely productive."

"Who is Triticum Witti?"

Albert, shocked, explained patiently, *"Triticum witti* is one of the new species of wheat which depend on oxidase epsilon. And if the fungus *Puccinia triticina* on that wheat becomes a pest, sprays may be used to get rid of it. And a whole year's wheat crop in those colonies may be destroyed."

"Destroyed," Mr. Blick repeated wonderingly. His forefinger silenced Albert like a conductor's baton; then both his hands danced over keys and switches, and he was muttering into his microphone again.

Another interruption, thought Albert. He felt proper reverence for the undoubted importance of whatever Mr. Blick was settling, still he was bothered a little, too. Actually (he remembered suddenly) he had a reason to be so presumptuous: oxidase epsilon was important, too. Over five hundred million dollars had gone into those three colonies already, and no doubt a good many people.

However, it turned out this particular interruption must have been devoted to West Lapland, Great Slave, and Churchill after all. Mr. Blick abandoned his instrument panel and announced his congratulations to them: "Mr. Boersma, the decision has been made to assign an expediter to your case!" And he smiled heartily.

This was a high point for Albert.

He wasn't sure he knew what an expediter was, but he was sure from Mr. Blick's manner that an unparalleled honor had been given him. It almost made him dizzy to think of all this glittering building, all the attendants and Models and executives, bowing to *him*, as Mr. Blick's manner implied they must.

A red light flicked on and off on Mr. Blick's desk. As he turned to it he said, "Excuse me, gentlemen." Of course, Albert pardoned him mentally, you have to work.

He whispered to Cal, "Well, I guess we're doing pretty well."

"Huh? Oh, yes, very well," Cal whispered back. "So far."

"So far? Doesn't Mr. Blick understand the problem? All we have to do is give him the details now."

"Oh, no, Albert! I'm sure *he* can't make the decision. He'll have to send us to someone higher up."

"Higher up? Why? Do we have to explain it all over again?"

Cal turned in his chair so he could whisper to Albert less conspicuously. "Albert, an enterprise the size of The Corporation can't give consideration to every crackpot suggestion anyone tries to sell it. There have to be regular channels. Now the Plant Metabolism Department doesn't have any connections here (maybe we can do something about that), so we have to run a sort of obstacle course. It's survival of the fittest, Albert! Only the most worthwhile survive to see the Regional Director. Of course the Regional Director selects which of those to accept, but he doesn't have to sift through a lot of crackpot propositions."

Albert could see the analogy to natural selection. Still, he asked humbly: "How do you know the best suggestions get through? Doesn't it depend a lot on how good a salesman is handling them?"

"Very much so. Naturally!"

"But then— Suppose, for instance, I hadn't happened to know you. My good idea wouldn't have got past Mr. Blick."

"It wouldn't have got past the Model," Cal corrected. "Maybe not that far. But you see in that case it wouldn't have been a very important idea, because it wouldn't have been *put into effect*." He said it with a very firm, practical jawline. "Unless of course someone else had had the initiative and resourcefulness to present the same idea better. Do you see now? *Really important ideas attract the sales talent to put them across*."

Albert didn't understand the reasoning, he had to admit. It was such an important point, and he was missing it. He reminded himself humbly that a scientist is no expert outside his own field.

So all Mr. Blick had been telling them was that they had

not yet been turned down. Albert's disappointment was sharp.

Still, he was curious. How had such a trivial announcement given him such euphoria? Could you produce that kind of effect just by your delivery? Mr. Blick could, apparently. The architecture, the Model, and all the rest had been build-up for him; and certainly they had helped the effect; but they didn't explain it.

What was the key? *Personality*, Albert realized. This was what businessmen meant by their technical term "personality." Personality was the asset Mr. Blick had exploited to rise to where he was—rather than becoming, say, a scientist.

The Blicks and Boersmas worked hard at it. Wistfully, Albert wondered how it was done. Of course the experts in this field didn't publish their results, and anyhow he had never studied it. But it was the most important field of human culture, for on it hinged the policy decisions of government—even of The Corporation!

He couldn't estimate whether Cal was as good as Mr. Blick, because he assumed Cal had never put forth a big effort on him, Albert. He wasn't worth it.

He had one other question for Cal. "What is an expediter?"

"Oh, I thought you knew," boomed Cal. "They can be a big help. That's why we're doing well to be assigned one. We're going to get into the *top levels*, Albert, where only a salesman of true merit can hope to put across an idea. An expediter can do it if anyone can. The expediters are too young to hold Key Executive Positions, but they're Men On The Way Up. They—"

Mr. Blick turned his head toward a door on his left, putting the force of his personality behind the gesture. "Mr. Demarest," he announced as the expediter walked into the room.

III

Mr. Demarest had captivating red curly sideburns, striking brown eyes, and a one-piece coverall in a somewhat loud pattern of black and beige. He almost trembled with excess energy. It was contagious; it made you feel as if you were as abnormally fit as he was.

He grinned his welcome at Albert and Cal, and chuckled merrily: "How do you do, Mr. Boersma."

It was as if Mr. Blick had been turned off. Albert hardly

knew he was still in the room. Clearly Mr. Demarest was a
Man On The Way Up indeed.

They rose and left the room with him—to a new corridor,
very different from the last: weirdly lighted from a strip two
feet above the floor, and lined with abstract statuary.

This, together with Mr. Demarest, made a formidable challenge.

Albert rose to it recklessly. "Oxidase epsilon," he pro-
claimed, "may mean the saving of three of The Corporation's
richest colonies!"

Mr. Demarest responded with enthusiasm. "I agree one
hundred per cent—our Corporation's crop of *Triticum witti*
must be saved! Mr. Blick sent me a playback of your explanation by interoffice tube, Professor LaRue. You've got me
on your side one hundred per cent! I want to assure you
both, very sincerely, that I'll do my utmost to sell Mr. Southfield. Professor, you be ready to fill in the details when I'm
through with what I know."

There was no slightest condescension or reservation in his
voice. He would take care of things, Albert knew. What a relief!

Cal came booming in: "Your Mr. Blick seems like a competent man."

What a way to talk about a Corporation executive! Albert
decided it was not just a simple faux pas, though. Apparently
Cal had decided he had to be accepted by Mr. Demarest as
an equal, and this was his opening. It seemed risky to Albert.
In fact, it frightened him.

"There's just one thing, now, about your Mr. Blick," Cal
was saying to Mr. Demarest, with a tiny wink that Albert
was proud of having spotted. "I couldn't help wondering how
he manages to find so much to do with those switches of his."
Albert barely restrained a groan.

But Mr. Demarest grinned! "Frankly, Cal," he answered,
"I'm not just sure how many of old Blick's switches are dummies."

Cal had succeeded! That was the main content of Mr. Demarest's remark.

But *were* Mr. Blick's switches dummies? Things were
much simpler back—way back—at the University, where
people said what they meant.

They were near the end of the corridor. Mr. Demarest said
softly, "Mr. Southfield's Office." Clearly Mr. Southfield's
presence was enough to curb even Mr. Demarest's boyish-
ness.

They turned through an archway into a large room, lighted like the corridor, with statuary wilder still.

Mr. Southfield was at one side, studying papers in a vast easy chair: an elderly man, fantastically dressed but with a surprisingly ordinary face peeping over the crystal ruff on his magenta leotards. He ignored them. Mr. Demarest made it clear they were supposed to wait until they were called on.

Cal and Albert chose two of the bed-sized chairs facing Mr. Southfield, and waited expectantly.

Mr. Demarest whispered, "I'll be back in time to make the first presentation. Last-minute brush-up, you know." He grinned and clapped Cal smartly on the shoulder. Albert was relieved that he didn't do the same to him, but just shook his hand before leaving. It would have been too upsetting.

Albert sank back in his chair, tired from all he'd been through and relaxed by the soft lights.

It was the most comfortable chair he'd ever been in. It was more than comfortable, it was a deliciously irresistible invitation to relax completely. Albert was barely awake enough to notice that the chair was rocking him gently, tenderly massaging his neck and back.

He lay there, ecstatic. He didn't quite go to sleep. If the chair had been designed just a little differently, no doubt, it could have put him to sleep, but this one just let him rest carefree and mindless.

Cal spoke (and even Cal's quiet bass sounded harsh and urgent): "Sit up straighter, Albert!"

"Why?"

"Albert, any sales resistance you started with is going to be completely *gone* if you don't sit up enough to shut off that chair!"

"Sales resistance?" Albert pondered comfortably. "What have we got to worry about? Mr. Demarest is on our side, isn't he?"

"Mr. Demarest," Cal pointed out, "is *not* the Regional Director."

So they still might have problems! So the marvelous chair was just another trap where the unfit got lost! Albert resolved to himself: "From now on, one single thought will be uppermost in my mind: defending my sales resistance."

He repeated this to himself.

He repeated it again. . . .

"Albert!" There was genuine panic in Cal's voice now.

A fine way to defend his sales resistance! He had let the chair get him again. Regretfully he shifted his weight forward, reaching for the arms of the chair.

"Watch it!" said Cal. "Okay now, but don't use the arms. Just lean yourself forward. There." He explained, "The surface on the arms is rough and moist, and I can't think of any reason it should be—unless it's to give you narcotic through the skin! Tiny amounts, of course. But we can't afford any. First time I've ever seen that one in actual use," he admitted.

Albert was astonished, and in a moment he was more so. "Mr. Southfield's chair is the same as ours, and *he's* leaning back in it. Why, he's even stroking the arm while he reads!"

"I know." Cal shook his head. "Remarkable man, isn't he? Remarkable. Remember this, Albert. The true salesman, the man on the very pinnacle of achievement, is also—a connoisseur. Mr. Southfield is a connoisseur. He wants to be presented with the most powerful appeals known, for the sake of the pleasure he gets from the appeal itself. Albert, there is a strong strain of the sensuous, the self-indulgent, in every really successful man like Mr. Southfield. Why? Because to be successful he must have the most profound understanding of self-indulgence."

Albert noticed in passing that, just the same, Cal wasn't self-indulgent enough to trust himself to that chair. He didn't even make a show of doing so. Clearly in Mr. Southfield they had met somebody far above Cal's level. It was unnerving. Oxidase epsilon seemed a terribly feeble straw to outweigh such a disadvantage.

Cal went on, "This is another reason for the institution of expediters. The top executive can't work surrounded by inferior salesmanship. He needs the stimulus and the luxury of receiving his data well packaged. The expediters can do it." He leaned over confidentially. "I've heard them called back-scratchers for that reason," he whispered.

Albert was flattered that Cal admitted him to this trade joke.

Mr. Southfield looked up at the archway as someone came in—not Mr. Demarest, but a black-haired young woman. Albert looked inquiringly at Cal.

"Just a minute. I'll soon know who she is."

She stood facing Mr. Southfield, against the wall opposite Albert and Cal. Mr. Southfield said in a drowsy half-whisper, "Yes, Miss Drury, the ore-distribution pattern. Go on."

"She must be another expediter, on some other matter," Cal decided. "Watch her work, Albert. You won't get an opportunity like this often."

Albert studied her. She was not at all like an Agency Model; she was older than most of them (about thirty); she was fully dressed, in a rather sober black and gray business suit, snug around the hips; and she wasn't wearing makeup. She couldn't be even an ex-Model, she wasn't the type. Heavier in build, for one thing, and though she was very pretty it wasn't that unhuman blinding beauty. On the contrary, Albert enjoyed looking at her (even lacking Mr. Southfield's connoisseurship). He found Miss Drury's warm dark eyes and confident posture very pleasant and relaxing.

She began to talk, gently and musically, something about how to compute the most efficient routing of metallic ore traffic in the Great Lakes Region. Her voice became a chant, rising and falling, but with a little catch in it now and then. Lovely!

Her main device, though, sort of sneaked up on him, the way the chair had. It had been going on for some time before Albert was conscious of it. It was like the chair.

Miss Drury moved.

Her hips swung. Only a centimeter each way, but very, very sensuously. You could follow the motion in detail, because her dress was more than merely snug around the hips, you could see every muscle on her belly. The motion seemed entirely spontaneous, but Albert knew she must have worked hard on it.

The knowledge, however, didn't spoil his enjoyment.

"Gee," he marveled to Cal, "how can Mr. Southfield hear what she's saying?"

"Huh? Oh—she lowers her voice from time to time on purpose so we won't overhear Corporation secrets, but he's much nearer her than we are."

"That's not what I mean!"

"You mean why doesn't her delivery distract him from the message. Albert," Boersma said wisely, "if you were sitting in his chair you'd be getting the message, too—with crushing force. A superior presentation *always* directs attention to the message. But in Mr. Southfield's case it actually stimulates critical consideration as well! Remarkable man. An expert and a connoisseur."

Meanwhile Albert saw that Miss Drury had finished. Maybe she would stay and discuss her report with Mr. Southfield? No, after just a few words he dismissed her.

IV

In a few minutes the glow caused by Miss Drury had changed to a glow of excited pride.

Here was he, plain old Professor LaRue, witnessing the drama of the nerve center of the Lakes Region—the interplay of titanic personalities, deciding the fate of millions. Why, he was even going to be involved in one of the decisions! He hoped the next expediter to see Mr. Southfield would be Mr. Demarest!

Something bothered him. "Cal, how can Mr. Demarest possibly be as—well—persuasive as Miss Drury? I mean—"

"Now, Albert, you leave that to him. Sex is not the only possible vehicle. Experts can make strong appeals to the weakest and subtlest of human drives—even altruism! Oh yes, I know it's surprising to the layman, but even altruism can be useful."

"Really?" Albert was grateful for every tidbit.

"Real masters will sometimes prefer such a method out of sheer virtuosity," whispered Cal.

Mr. Southfield stirred a little in his chair, and Albert snapped to total alertness.

Sure enough, it was Mr. Demarest who came through the archway.

Certainly his entrance was no letdown. He strode in even more eagerly than he had into Mr. Blick's office. His costume glittered, his brown eyes glowed. He stood against the wall beyond Mr. Southfield; not quite straight, but with a slight wrestler's crouch. A taut spring.

He gave Albert and Cal only half a second's glance, but that glance was a tingling communication of comradeship and joy of battle. Albert felt himself a participant in something heroic.

Mr. Demarest began releasing all that energy slowly. He gave the background of West Lapland, Great Slave, and Churchill. Maps were flashed on the wall beside him (exactly how, Albert didn't follow), and the drama of arctic colonization was recreated by Mr. Demarest's sportscaster's voice. Albert would have thought Mr. Demarest was the overmodest hero of each project if he hadn't known all three had been done simultaneously. No, it was hard to believe, but all these vivid facts must have been served to Mr. Demarest by some research flunky within the last few minutes. And yet, how he had transfigured them!

The stirring narrative was reaching Mr. Southfield, too. He had actually sat up out of the easy chair.

Mr. Demarest's voice, like Miss Drury's, dropped in volume now and then. Albert and Cal were just a few feet too far away to overhear Corporation secrets.

As the saga advanced, Mr. Demarest changed from Viking

to Roman. His voice, by beautifully controlled stages, became bubbling and hedonistic. Now, he was talking about grandiose planned expansions—and, best of all, about how much money The Corporation expected to make from the three colonies. The figures drooled through loose lips. He clapped Mr. Southfield on the shoulder. He stroked Mr. Southfield's arm; when he came to the estimated trade balances, he tickled his neck. Mr. Southfield showed his appreciation of change in mood by lying back in his chair again.

This didn't stop Mr. Demarest.

It seemed almost obscene. Albert covered his embarrassment by whispering, "I see why they call them backscratchers."

Cal frowned, waved him silent, and went on watching.

Suddenly Mr. Demarest's tone changed again: it became bleak, bitter, desperate. A threat to the calculated return on The Corporation's investment—even to the capital investment itself!

Mr. Southfield sat forward attentively to hear about this danger. Was that good? He hadn't done that with Miss Drury.

What Mr. Demarest said about the danger was, of course, essentially what Albert had told Mr. Blick, but Albert realized that it sounded a lot more frightening Mr. Demarest's way. When he was through, Albert felt physically chilly. Mr. Southfield sat saying nothing. What was he thinking? Could he fail to see the tragedy that threatened?

After a moment he nodded and said, "Nice presentation." He hadn't said that to Miss Drury, Albert exulted!

Mr. Demarest looked dedicated.

Mr. Southfield turned his whole body to face Albert, and looked him straight in the eyes. Albert was too alarmed to look away. Mr. Southfield's formerly ordinary jaw now jutted, his chest swelled imposingly. "*You*, I understand, are a well-informed worker on plant metabolism." His voice seemed to grow too, until it rolled in on Albert from all sides of the room. "Is it *your* opinion that the danger is great enough to justify taking up the time of the Regional Director?"

It wasn't fair. Mr. Southfield against J. Albert LaRue was a ridiculous mismatch anyway! And now Albert was taken by surprise—after too long a stretch as an inactive spectator—and hit with the suggestion that he had been *wasting Mr. Southfield's time* . . . that his proposition was not only not worth acting on, it was *a waste of the Regional Director's time.*

Albert struggled to speak.

Surely, after praising Mr. Demarest's presentation, Mr.
Southfield would be lenient; he would take into account Albert's limited background; he wouldn't expect too much. Albert struggled to say anything.

He couldn't open his mouth.

As he sat staring at Mr. Southfield, he could feel his own
shoulders drawing inward and all his muscles going limp.

Cal said, in almost a normal voice, "Yes."

That was enough, just barely. Albert whispered, "Yes," terrified at having found the courage.

Mr. Southfield glared down at him a moment more.

Then he said, "Very well, you may see the Regional Director. Mr. Demarest, take them there."

Albert followed Mr. Demarest blindly. His entire attention
was concentrated on recovering from Mr. Southfield.

He had been one up, thanks to Mr. Demarest. Now, how
could he have stayed one up? How should he have resisted
Mr. Southfield's dizzying display of personality?

He played the episode back mentally over and over, trying
to correct it to run as it should have. Finally he succeeded, at
least in his mind. He saw what his attitude *should* have been.
He *should* have kept his shoulders squared and his vocal
cords loose, and faced Mr. Southfield confidently. Now he
saw how to do it.

He walked erectly and firmly behind Mr. Demarest, and
allowed a haughty half-smile to play on his lips.

He felt armed to face Mr. Southfield all by himself—or,
since it seemed Mr. Southfield was not the Regional Director
after all, even to face the Regional Director!

They stopped in front of a large double door guarded by
an absolutely motionless man with a gun.

"Men," said Mr. Demarest with cheerful innocence, "I
wish you luck. I wish you all the luck in the world."

Cal looked suddenly stricken but said, with casualness that
didn't fool even Albert, "Wouldn't you like to come in with
us?"

"Oh, no. Mr. Southfield told me only to bring you here. I'd
be overstepping my bounds if I did any more. But all the
good luck in the world, men!"

Cal said hearty goodbyes. But when he turned back to Albert he said, despairing: "The brushoff."

Albert could hardly take it in. "But—we get to make our
presentation to the Regional Director, don't we?"

Boersma shrugged hopelessly, "Don't you see, Albert? Our
presentation won't be good enough, without Demarest. When

Mr. Southfield sent us on alone he was giving us the brush-off."

"Cal—are *you* going to back out too?"

"I should say not! It's a feather in our cap to have got this far, Albert. We have to follow up just as far as our abilities will take us!"

Albert went to the double door. He worried about the armed guard for a moment, but they weren't challenged. The guard hadn't even blinked, in fact.

Albert asked Cal, "Then we do still have a chance?"

He started to push the door open, then hesitated again. "But you'll do your best?"

"I should say so! You don't get to present a proposition to the Regional Director *every* day."

With determination, Albert drew himself even straighter, and prepared himself to meet an onslaught twice as overbearing as Mr. Southfield's. One single thought was uppermost in his mind: defending his sales resistance. He felt inches taller than before; he even slightly looked down at Cal and his pessimism.

Cal pushed the door open and they went in.

The Regional Director sat alone in a straight chair, at a plain desk in a very plain office about the size of most offices.

The Regional Director was a woman.

She was dressed about as any businesswoman might dress; as conservatively as Miss Drury. As a matter of fact, she looked like Miss Drury, fifteen years older. Certainly she had the same black hair and gentle oval face.

What a surprise! A *pleasant* surprise. Albert felt still bigger and more confident than he had outside. He would certainly get on well with this motherly, unthreatening person!

She was reading from a small microfilm viewer on an otherwise bare desk. Obviously she had only a little to do before she would be free. Albert patiently watched her read. She read very conscientiously, that was clear.

After a moment she glanced up at them briefly, with an apologetic smile, then down again. Her shy dark eyes showed so much! You could see how sincerely she welcomed them, and how sorry she was that she had so much work to do—how much she would prefer to be talking with *them*. Albert pitied her. From the bottom of his heart, he pitied her. Why, that small microfilm viewer, he realized, could perfectly well contain volumes of complicated Corporation reports. Poor woman! The poor woman who happened to be Regional Director read on.

Once in a while she passed one hand, wearily but determinedly, across her face. There was a slight droop to her shoulders. Albert pitied her more all the time. She was not too strong—she had such a big job—and she was so courageously trying to do her best with all those reports in the viewer!

Finally she raised her head.

It was clear she was not through; there was no relief on her face. But she raised her head to them.

Her affection covered them like a warm bath. Albert realized he was in a position to do the kindest thing he had ever done. He felt growing in himself the resolution to do it. He would!

He started toward the door.

Before he left she met his eyes once more, and her smile showed *such* appreciation for his understanding!

Albert felt there could be no greater reward.

Out in the park again he realized for the first time that Cal was right behind him.

They looked at each other for a long time.

Then Cal started walking again, toward the subway. "The brushoff," he said.

"I thought you said you'd do your best," said Albert. But he knew that Cal's "I did" was the truth.

They walked on slowly. Cal said, "Remarkable woman. . . . A real master. Sheer virtuosity!"

Albert said, "Our society certainly rewards its most deserving members."

That one single thought was uppermost in his mind, all the long way home.

THE
BLACK CLOUD

FRED HOYLE

One of the most brilliant—and beyond doubt one of the most controversial—figures in present-day science is the English astronomer, Fred Hoyle. His greatest contribution to astronomical thought, perhaps, is his theory of the "steady-state" universe—the universe which has neither beginning nor end, but continually re-creates itself in the spaces between the stars. Violently supported and violently condemned, the theory rests on a remarkable chain of flawless mathematical logic . . . and on the interpretation of certain events occurring at the very furthest limit of human investigation, the most distant nebulae visible in the 200-inch telescope at Mount Palomar. Needless to say, both sides find support for their beliefs in these phenomena.

Not by chance, the hero of his science fiction novel, The Black Cloud, *is brilliant—and controversial. The Cloud has come from interstellar space to shut out the Sun's light; it behaves oddly; a group of scientists are gathered in a sort of English Manhattan Project to study it . . . and here is what they discover.*

During November the pulse of mankind quickened. And as governments got matters more and more in hand the desire for communication between the various pockets of humanity strengthened. Telephone lines and cables were repaired. But it was to radio that men turned in the main. Long wave radio transmitters that were soon working normally, but of course they were useless for long distance communication. For this, short wave transmitters were put into operation. But the short wave transmitters failed to work, and for a reason that was soon discovered. The ionization of the atmospheric gases at a height of about fifty miles turned out to be abnormally high. This was giving rise to an excessive amount of collisional damping, as the radio engineers called it. The excessive ionization was caused by the radiation from the very hot upper reaches of the atmosphere, the hot upper reaches that were still producing the blue shimmering nights. In short, radio fade-out conditions were operative.

There was only one thing to be done: to shorten the transmitting wavelength. This was tried down to a wavelength of about one meter, but still the fade-out continued; and no suitable transmitters on still lower wavelengths were available, since lower wavelengths were never widely used before the coming of the Cloud. Then it was remembered that Nortonstowe possessed transmitters that could work from one meter down as far as one centimeter. Moreover the Nortonstowe transmitters were capable of handling an enormous quantity of information, as Kingsley was not slow to point out. It was accordingly decided to make Nortonstowe a world information clearing house. Kingsley's plan had borne fruit at last.

Intricate calculations had to be performed and, as they had to be done quickly, the electronic computer was put into operation. The problem was to find the best wavelength. If the wavelength was too long the fade-out trouble would continue. If the wavelength was too short the radio waves would stream out of the atmosphere away into space instead of being bent round the Earth, as they must be to travel from London to Australia, let us say. The problem was to compromise between these extremes. Eventually a wavelength of twenty-five centimeters was decided on. This was thought to be short enough to overcome the worse of the fade-out difficulty, and yet not to be so short that too much power would get squirted out into space, although it was recognized that some loss must occur.

The Nortonstowe transmitters were switched on during the first week of December. . . .

One afternoon, Leicester, who had organized the building of the transmission system, rang Kingsley and asked him to come along to the transmitting lab.

"What's the panic, Harry?" asked Kingsley.

"We've done a fade!"

"What!"

"Yes, right out. You can see it over here. A message was coming through from Brazil. Look how the signal has gone completely."

"It's fantastic. Must be an extremely rapid burst of ionization."

"What d'you think we ought to do?"

"Wait, I suppose. It may be a transient effect. In fact, it looks rather like it."

"If it goes on we might shorten the wavelength."

"Yes, we might. But scarcely anybody else could. The Americans could work up a new wavelength pretty quickly, and probably the Russians as well. But it's doubtful if many of the others could. We've had enough trouble getting 'em to build their present transmitters."

"Then there's nothing to do but hang on?"

"Well, I don't think I should try transmitting, because you'll never know if the messages get through. I should just leave the receiver on recorder. Then we shall have any stuff that happens to come through—if conditions improve, that is to say."

There was a brilliant auroral-type display that night, which the Nortonstowe scientists took to be associated with the sudden burst of ionization high in the atmosphere. They had no idea of the cause of the ionization, however. Very large disturbances of the Earth's magnetic field were also noted.

Marlowe and Bill Barnett discussed the matter as they strolled around, admiring the display.

"My God, look at those orange-colored sheets," said Marlowe.

"What baffles me, Geoff, is that this is obviously a low level display. You can tell that from the colors. I suppose we ought to have a shot at getting a spectrum, although I'd swear to it from what we can see right now. I'd say that all this is going on not more than fifty miles up, probably less. It's in just the place where we've been getting all the excessive ionization."

"I know what you're thinking, Bill. That it's easy to imagine a sudden puff of gas hitting the extreme outside of the atmosphere. But that would produce a disturbance much higher up. It's difficult to believe this is due to impact."

"No, I don't think it possibly can be. It looks to me much more like an electrical discharge."

"The magnetic disturbances would check with that."

"But you see what this means, Geoff? This isn't from the Sun. Nothing like it from the Sun has ever happened before. If it's an electrical disturbance, it must come from the Cloud."

Leicester and Kingsley hurried along to the communication lab after breakfast the following morning. A short message from Ireland had come in at 6:20. A long message from the U.S. had started at 7:51, but after three minutes there had been a fade and the rest of the message was lost. A short message from Sweden was received about mid-day, but a longer message from China was interrupted by fade-out soon after two o'clock.

Parkinson joined Leicester and Kingsley at tea.

"This is a most disturbing business," he said.

"I can imagine so," answered Kingsley. "And it's another queer business."

"Well, it's certainly annoying. I thought we'd got this communication problem in hand. In what way is it queer?"

"In that we seem to be on the verge of transmission the whole time. Sometimes messages come through and sometimes they don't, as if the ionization is oscillating up and down."

"Barnett thinks that electrical discharges are going on. So wouldn't you expect oscillations?"

"You're becoming quite a scientist, aren't you, Parkinson?" laughed Kingsley. "But it isn't as easy as that," he went on. "Oscillation yes, but hardly oscillations like the ones we've been getting. Don't you see how odd it is?"

"No, I can't say I do."

"The messages from China and the U.S., man! We got a fade-out on each of 'em. That seems to show that when transmission is possible it's only barely possible. The oscillations seem to be making transmission just possible but only by the slightest margin. That might happen once by chance but it's very remarkable that it should happen twice."

"Isn't there a flaw there, Chris?" Leicester chewed his pipe, and then pointed with it. "If discharges are going on, the oscillations might be quite rapid. Both the messages from the U.S. and China were long, over three minutes. Perhaps the oscillations last about three minutes. Then you can understand why we get short messages complete, like those from Brazil and Ireland, while we never get a complete long message."

"Ingenious, Harry, but I don't believe it. I was looking at your signal record of the U.S. message. It's quite steady, until the fade-out starts. That doesn't look like a deep oscillation, otherwise the signal would vary even before the fade-out. Then if oscillations are going on every three minutes, why aren't we getting a lot more messages, or at any rate fragments of them? I think that's a fatal objection."

Leicester chewed his pipe again.

"It certainly looks like it. The whole thing's damn strange."

"What do you propose to do about it?" asked Parkinson.

"It might be a good idea, Parkinson, if you were to ask London to cable Washington asking for transmissions to be sent for five minutes every hour, starting on the hour. Then we shall know what messages are being received, as well as those that do come through. You might also like to appraise other governments of the situation."

No further transmissions were received during the next three days. Whether this was due to fade-out or because no messages were sent was not known. In this unsatisfactory state of affairs a change of plan was decided on. As Marlowe told Parkinson:

"We've decided to look into this business properly, instead of depending on chance transmissions."

"How do you intend to do that?"

"We're arranging to point all our aerials upwards, instead of more or less toward the horizon. Then we can use our own transmissions to investigate this unusual ionization. We'll pick up reflections of our own transmissions, that is to say."

For the next two days the radio astronomers were hard at work on the aerials. It was late in the afternoon of 9th December by the time every arrangement had been made. Quite a crowd assembled in the lab to watch results.

"O.K. Let her rip," said someone.

"What wavelength shall we start on?"

"Better try one meter first," suggested Barnett. "If Kingsley is right in supposing that twenty-five centimeters is on the verge of transmission, and if our ideas on collision damping are correct, this ought to be about critical for vertical propagation."

The one meter transmitter was switched on.

"It's going through," Barnett remarked.

"How do you know that?" Parkinson asked Marlowe.

"There's nothing but very weak return signals," answered Marlowe. "You can see that on the tube over there. Most of the power is being absorbed or is going right through the atmosphere into space."

The next half hour was spent in gazing at electrical equipment and in technical talk. Then there was a rustle of excitement.

"Signal's going up."

"Look at it!" exclaimed Marlowe. "My God, it's going up with a rush!"

The return signal continued to grow for about ten minutes.

"It's saturated. We're getting total reflection now, I'd say," said Leicester.

"Looks as though you were right, Chris. We must be quite near the critical frequency. Reflection is coming from a height of just under fifty miles, more or less where we expected it. Ionization there must be a hundred to a thousand times normal."

A further half hour was spent in measurements.

"Better see what ten centimeters does," remarked Marlowe.

There was a pressing of switches.

"We're on ten centimeters now. It's going right through, as of course it ought to," announced Barnett.

"This is unbearably scientific," said Ann Halsey. "I'm going off to make tea. Come and help, Chris, if you can leave your meters and dials for a few minutes."

Sometime later while they were drinking tea and conversing generally, Leicester gave a startled cry.

"Heavens above! Look at this!"

"It's impossible!"

"But it's happening."

"The ten centimeter reflection is rising. It must mean that the ionization is going up at a colossal rate," Marlowe explained to Parkinson.

"The damn thing's saturating again."

"It means the ionization has increased a hundredfold in less than an hour. It's incredible."

"Better put the one centimeter transmitter on, Harry," Kingsley said to Leicester.

So the ten centimeter transmission was changed to a one centimeter transmission.

"Well, that's going through all right," someone remarked.

"But not for long. In another half hour the one centimeter will be trapped, mark my words," said Barnett.

"Incidentally, what message is being sent?" asked Parkinson.

"None," answered Leicester, "we're only sending C.W.—continuous wave."

"As if that explained everything," thought Parkinson.

But although the scientists sat around for a couple of hours or more nothing further of note happened.

"Well, it's still going through. We'll see what it looks like after dinner," said Barnett.

After dinner the one centimeter transmission was still going through.

"It might be worth switching back to ten centimeters," suggested Marlowe.

"O.K. Let's try again," Leicester flicked the switches. "That's interesting," he said. "We're going through on ten centimeters now. The ionization seems to be dropping, and pretty rapidly too."

"Negative ion formation probably"—from Weichart.

Ten minutes later Leicester whooped with excitement.

"Look, the signal's coming in again!"

He was right. During the next few minutes the reflected signal grew rapidly to a maximum value.

"Complete reflection now. What shall we do? Go back to one centimeter?"

"No, Harry," said Kingsley. "My revolutionary suggestion is that we go upstairs to the sitting-room, where we drink coffee and where we listen to music played by Ann's fair hand. I'd like to switch off for an hour or two and come back later."

"What on earth is the idea, Chris?"

"Oh, just a hunch, a crazy idea, I suppose. But perhaps you'll indulge me for once in a way."

"For once in a way!" chuckled Marlowe. "You've been indulged, Chris, from the day you were born."

"That may be so, but it's scarcely polite to remark on it, Geoff. Come on, Ann. You've been waiting to try out the Beethoven Opus 106 on us. Now's your chance."

It was an hour and a half or so later, with the opening chords of the great sonata still ringing in their heads, that the company made its way back to the transmitting lab.

"Try the one meter first, just for luck," said Kingsley.

"Bet you that one meter is completely trapped," Barnett said as he clicked on various switches.

"No, it's not, by John Brown's body," he exclaimed a few minutes later, when the equipment had warmed up. "It's going through. It just isn't believable, and yet it's as plain as a pikestaff on the tube."

"What's your betting, Harry, on what's going to happen next?"

"I'm not betting, Chris. This is worse than 'spot the lady.'"

"I'm betting it's going to saturate."

"Any reasons?"

"If it saturates I'll have reasons, of course. If it doesn't there won't be any reasons."

"Playing safe, eh?"

"Signal going up," sang out Barnett. "Looks as though Chris is going to be right. Up it goes!"

Five minutes later the one meter signal saturated. It was completely trapped by the ionosphere, no power getting away from the Earth.

"Now try ten centimeters," Kingsley commanded.

For the next twenty or thirty minutes the equipment was watched keenly, all comment silenced. The earlier pattern repeated. Very little reflection was obtained at first. The reflected signal then increased rapidly in intensity.

"Well, there it is. At first the signal penetrates the ionosphere. Then after a few minutes the ionization rises and we get complete trapping. What's it mean, Chris?" asked Leicester.

"Let's go back upstairs and think about it. If Ann and Yvette will be kind-hearted and make another brew of coffee perhaps we can do something towards licking this business into shape."

McNeil came in while coffee was being prepared. He had been attending a sick child while the experiments had been going on.

"Why the air of great solemnity? What's been happening?"

"You're just in time, John. We're going to run over the facts. But we've promised not to start until the coffee arrives."

The coffee came, and Kingsley began his summing up.

"For John's benefit I'll have to start a long way back. What happens to radio waves when they're transmitted depends on two things, the wavelength and the ionization in the atmosphere. Suppose we choose a particular wavelength for transmission and consider what happens as the degree of ionization increases. To begin with, for low ionization the radio energy streams out of the atmosphere, with very little of it getting reflected. Then as the ionization increases there is more and more reflection until quite suddenly the reflection goes up very steeply until eventually all the radio energy is reflected, none of it getting away from the Earth. We say that the signal saturates. Is that all clear, John?"

"Up to a point. What I don't see is how the wavelength comes into it."

"Well, the lower the wavelength the more ionization is needed to produce saturation."

"So while one wavelength might be completely reflected by the atmosphere, some shorter wavelength might penetrate almost completely into outer space."

"That's exactly the situation. But let me go back to my particular wavelength for a moment, and to the effect of rising ionization. For convenience in talking, I'd like to call it 'pattern of events A.' "

"You'd like to call it what?" asked Parkinson.

"This is what I mean:

"One. A low ionization allowing almost complete penetration.

"Two. A rising ionization giving a reflected signal of increasing strength.

"Three. An ionization so high that reflection becomes complete.

"This is what I call 'pattern A.' "

"And what is pattern B?" asked Ann Halsey.

"There won't be any pattern B."

"Then why bother with the A?"

"Preserve me from the obtuseness of women! I can call it pattern A because I want to, can't I?"

"Of course, dear. But why do you want to?"

"Go on, Chris. She's only pulling your leg."

"Well, here's a list of what happened this afternoon and evening. Let me read it out to you as a table."

Transmission wavelength	Approximate time of switching on	Event
1 meter	2:45 p.m.	Pattern A taking approximately half an hour
10 centimeters	3:15 p.m.	Pattern A taking approximately half an hour
1 centimeter	3:45 p.m.	Complete penetration of ionosphere over a period of three hours roughly
10 centimeters	7:00 p.m.	Pattern A taking approximately half an hour

(No transmissions from 7:30 p.m. to 9:00 p.m.)

| 1 meter | 9:00 p.m. | Pattern A taking half an hour |
| 10 centimeters | 9:30 p.m. | Pattern A taking half an hour |

"It certainly looks horribly systematic when it's all put together like that," said Leicester.

"It does, doesn't it?"

"I'm afraid I'm not getting this"—Parkinson.

"Nor am I," admitted McNeil.

Kingsley spoke slowly.

"As far as I'm aware these events can be explained very simply on one hypothesis, but I warn you it's an entirely preposterous hypothesis."

"Chris, will you please stop trying to be dramatic and tell us in simple words what this preposterous hypothesis is?"

"Very well. In one breath—that on any wavelength from a few centimeters upwards, our own transmissions automatically produce a rise of ionization which continues to the saturation point."

"It simply isn't possible," Leicester shook his head.

"I didn't say it was possible," answered Kingsley. "I said it explained the facts. And it does. It explains the whole of my table."

"I can half see what you're driving at," remarked McNeil.

"Am I to suppose that the ionization falls as soon as you cease transmission?"

"Yes. When we stop transmission the ionizing agent is cut off, whatever it may be—perhaps Bill's electrical discharges. Then the ionization falls very rapidly. You see the ionization we're dealing with is abnormally low in the atmosphere, where the gas density is large enough to give an extremely rapid rate of formation of negative oxygen ions. So the ionization dries up very quickly as soon as it isn't being renewed."

"Let's go into this in a bit more detail," Marlow began, speaking out of a haze of aniseed smoke. "It seems to me that this hypothetical ionizing agency must have pretty good judgment. Suppose we switch on a ten centimeter transmission. Then according to your idea, Chris, the agency, whatever it is, drives the ionization up until the ten centimeter waves remain trapped inside the Earth's atmosphere. And—here's my point—the ionization goes no higher than that. It's all got to be very nicely adjusted. The agency has to know just how far to go and no further."

"Which doesn't make it seem very plausible," said Weichart.

"And there are other difficulties. Why were we able to go on so long with the twenty-five centimeter communication? That lasted for quite a number of days, not for only half an hour. And why doesn't the same thing happen—your pattern A as you call it—when we use a one centimeter wavelength?"

"Bloody bad philosophy," grunted Alexandrov. "Waste of

breath. Hypothesis judged by prediction. Only sound method."

Leicester glanced at his watch.

"It's well over an hour since our last transmission. If Chris is right we ought to get his pattern A, if we switch on again at ten centimeters but not on one meter, and possibly at one meter also. Let's try."

Leicester and about half a dozen others went off to the lab. Half an hour later they were back.

"Still complete reflection at one meter. Pattern A on ten centimeters," Leicester announced.

"Which looks as if it supports Chris."

"I'm not sure that it does." remarked Weichart. "Why didn't the one meter give pattern A?"

"I might make some suggestions, but in a way they're even more fantastic, so I won't bother with 'em just for the moment. The fact is, and I insist it is a fact, that whenever we have switched on our ten centimeter transmitter there has always been a sharp rise of atmospheric ionization, and whenever we switched off there has been a decline of ionization. Does anyone deny that?"

"I don't deny that what has happened so far agrees with what you say," Weichart argued. "I agree that no denial is possible there. It's when it comes to inferring a causal connection between our transmissions and the fluctuations of ionization that I dig my toes in."

"You mean, Dave, that what we found this afternoon and this evening was coincidence?" asked Marlowe.

"That's what I mean. I grant you that the odds against such a series of coincidences are pretty big, but Kingsley's causal connection seems to me an out and out impossibility. What I feel is that the improbable can happen but the impossible cannot."

"Impossible is too strong," insisted Kingsley. "And I'm sure that Weichart couldn't really defend his use of the word. What we're faced with is a choice between two improbabilities—I said that my hypothesis seemed improbable when I first trotted it out. Moreover I agree with what Alexis said earlier on, that the only way to test a hypothesis is by its predictions. It's about three-quarters of an hour since Harry Leicester did his last transmission. I'm going to suggest that he goes right now and does another ten centimeter transmission."

Leicester groaned. "Not again!"

"I predict," went on Kingsley, "that my pattern A will

be repeated. What I'd like to know is what Weichart pre-
dicts."

Weichart didn't quite like the turn of the argument, and he
attempted to hedge. Marlowe laughed.

"He's pinching you, Dave! You've got to stand up and take
it. If you're right about it being coincidence before, you've
got to agree that Kingsley's present prediction is very unlikely
to be right."

"Of course it's unlikely, but it might happen that way all
the same."

"Come off it, Dave! What do you predict? Where d'you
put your money?"

And Weichart was forced to admit that he put his money
on Kingsley's prediction being wrong.

"All right. Let's go and see," said Leicester.

While the company were filing out, Ann Halsey said to
Parkinson:

"Will you help me to make some more coffee, Mr. Parkinson? They'll be wanting some when they get back."

As they busied themselves, she went on:

"Did you ever hear such a lot of talk? I used to think that
scientists were of the strong silent type, but never did I hear
such a gibble-gabble. What is it that Omar Khayyám says
about the doctors and saints?"

"I believe it goes something like this," answered Parkinson:

"Myself when young did eagerly frequent
    Doctor and Saint, and heard great argument
        About it and about, but evermore
    Came out by the same door where in I went."

"It isn't so much the volume of talk that surprises me," he
laughed. "We get plenty of that in politics. It's the number of
mistakes they've made, how often things have turned out differently from what they've expected."

When the party reassembled it was obvious at a glance
how things had gone. Marlowe took a cup of coffee from
Parkinson.

"Thanks. Well, that's that. Chris was right and Dave was
wrong. Now I suppose we must get down to trying to decide
what it means."

"Your move, Chris," said Leicester.

"Let's suppose then that my hypothesis is right, that our
own transmissions are producing a marked effect on the atmospheric ionization."

Ann Halsey handed Kingsley a mug of coffee.

"I'd be a lot happier if I knew what ionization meant. Here, drink this."

"Oh, it means that the outer parts of the atoms are stripped away from the inner parts."

"And how does this happen?"

"It can happen in many ways, by an electrical discharge, as in a flash of lightning, or in a neon tube—the sort of strip lighting we've got here. The gas in these tubes is being partially ionized."

"I suppose energy is the real difficulty? That your transmissions have far too little power to produce this rise of ionization?" said McNeil.

"That's right," answered Marlowe. "It's completely impossible that our transmissions should be the primary cause of the fluctuations in the atmosphere. My God, they'd need a fantastic amount of power."

"Then how can Kingsley's hypothesis be right?"

"Our transmissions are not the primary cause, as Geoff says. That's wholly impossible. I agree with Weichart there. My hypothesis is that our transmissions are acting as a trigger, whereby some very large source of power is released."

"And where, Chris, do you suppose this source of power is to be located?"

"In the Cloud, of course."

"But surely it's quite fantastic to imagine that we can cause the Cloud to react in such a fashion, and to do it with such reproducibility? You'd have to suppose that the Cloud was equipped with a sort of feedback mechanism," argued Leicester.

"On the basis of my hypothesis that's certainly a correct inference."

"But don't you see, Kingsley, that it's utterly mad?" Weichart exclaimed.

Kingsley looked at his watch.

"It's almost time to go and try again, if anyone wants to. Does anyone want to?"

"In heaven's name, no!" said Leicester.

"Either we go or we stay. And if we stay it means that we accept Kingsley's hypothesis. Well, boys, do we go or do we stay?" remarked Marlowe.

"We stay," said Barnett. "And we see how the argument goes. We've got as far as some sort of a feedback mechanism in the Cloud, a mechanism set to churn out an enormous amount of power as soon as it receives a trickle of radio emission from outside itself. The next step, I suppose, is to speculate on how the feedback mechanism works, and why it works as it does. Anybody got any ideas?"

Alexandrov cleared his throat. Everybody waited to catch one of the Russian's rare remarks.

"Bastard in Cloud. Said so before."

There were wide grins and a giggle from Yvette Hedelfort. Kingsley, however, remarked quite seriously:

"I remember you did. Were you serious about it, Alexis?"

"Always serious, damn it," said the Russian.

"Without frills, what exactly do you mean, Chris?" someone asked.

"I mean that the Cloud contains an intelligence. Before anybody starts criticizing, let me say that I know it's a preposterous idea and I wouldn't suggest it for a moment if the alternative weren't even more outrageously preposterous. Doesn't it strike you how often we've been wrong about the behavior of the Cloud?"

Parkinson and Ann Halsey exchanged an amused glance.

"All our mistakes have a certain hallmark about them. They're just the sort of mistake that it'd be natural to make if instead of the Cloud being inanimate, it were alive."

CHAIN REACTION

BOYD ELLANBY
(Lyle and William C. Boyd)

As a husband and wife team, the Doctors Boyd collaborate equally well on writing—both scientific and science fiction works—and on scientific projects which have taken them all over the world, on such errands as blood-typing the 3,000-year-old tissues of mummies in Egypt and studying hereditary factors in various parts of Asia. The results have appeared not only in scientific journals but in such books as William Boyd's Genetics and the Races of Man, *probably the first and certainly the best-known popularly written book to point out that such visible features as skin color and hair are only a part of the story of "racial characteristics"—and that the relationships demonstrated by inheritance of blood-typing factors point to some strange and unexpected joinings at the roots of Man's family tree.*

As science fiction writers the Boyds employed the phonetic pseudonym of "Boyd Ellanby"; one of the best liked of their stories is this one, called Chain Reaction.

MacPherson shuffled the cards over and over again. His hands were almost steady.

"Want to place a limit on the bets?" he asked.

His two colleagues who had made the night drive with him from the University said nothing, but Rothman laughed.

"Today?" he said. "Today, the sky's the limit."

MacPherson rested the deck on the table and watched as Rothman stood up to look through the barred window at the glittering Arizona desert. Rothman had got thinner during his months of confinement; his shoulders were bony beneath the gray hospital robe and his balding head looked like a skull.

"Are you going to play?" asked MacPherson. "Or is poker too childish an amusement for a mathematician?"

Rothman turned his back to the window. "Oh, I'll play. When three old friends from the Project suddenly turn up for a visit, even a madman will string along."

Shuffling the cards again, MacPherson wished the other men would say something; it wasn't fair of them to make him carry the conversation. Professor Avery, who had cut his physics classes in order to join the morning's party, sat in glum silence. His plump face was pale, and behind thick-lensed spectacles which enlarged his eyes grotesquely, he blinked as he watched the flickering cards. Dr. Neill, from Physical Chemistry, was tapping his toe against the table leg, watching Rothman, who stood at the window, waiting.

"But we can't have much of a game with only four people," said Rothman. "We ought to have a fifth."

"Maybe we can find someone." MacPherson walked to the locked steel door and rattled the rectangular lattice set in at shoulder height, put his mouth to the metal bars and called out.

"Hey, Joe!"

An attendant in white uniform shuffled into the corridor of closed doors, carrying a tray with one hand and scratching his head with the other.

"How about joining us for a game of poker?"

Joe shook his head and grinned. "Not me, Professor! I start buddying around with the loonies, I lose my job."

"But we're not inmates!"

"Maybe not, but Dr. Rothman is."

"Doesn't prove I'm crazy, Joe," said Rothman. "Conversely, not being inmates doesn't prove these men are sane."

"It's a fact you don't look any crazier to me than a lot of professors," confessed Joe. "I don't know. All I know is, *I'm* not crazy enough to break the rules and lose my job. Besides, you longhairs wouldn't stand a chance at poker with me."

Still grinning, he shuffled out of sight down the hall.

MacPherson sighed and went back to the table. "Well, we'll have to get along with just the four of us."

"There's always the unseen guest," said Rothman, "but you won't need to deal him a hand. He already holds all the cards."

Neill looked up. "Stop hamming and sit down. Quit making like a maniac. It's not even a good act."

"Okay." Rothman drew up a chair. "Now what was said about limiting the bets?"

"Why bother setting a limit?" said Neill. "We're not likely to mistake each other for millionaires and we all got exactly the same pay when we were on the Project. Unless your sick pay has had two or three zeros tacked onto it, you're not going to be making any wild bets, and as for the rest of us—"

"University professors are still being paid less than night-club dancers," said Avery. "You're lucky to be out of the rat race, Rothman. While we worry about how to pay the grocery bill, you can relax, eating and sleeping at government expense. You never had it so good."

"Maybe you'd like to get yourselves committed and keep me company?"

MacPherson rapped the deck on the table. "Stop that kind of talk. We came here to play poker."

"Did you?" asked Rothman, grinning. "Then why don't you deal?"

"Cut, Neill?" said MacPherson. As he shot the slippery cards over the table top, each flick of his thumb watched by Rothman's intent eyes, he regretted this impulsive visit; it now seemed a gesture without meaning. He wondered whether the others were as nervous as he was.

On the drive over from Los Angeles during the night, Neill had seemed calm enough and even Avery, who had changed a lot during work on the Project, had chatted with them unconstrainedly. It was hard to be certain what other men were feeling, even when you had known them a long time, but it could not be pleasant for any of them to be visiting a former colleague who had been removed from the Project directly to a sanitarium.

"Tell me something," said Rothman as he picked up his cards. "Do you still think I'm crazy?"

"Don't be an idiot," MacPherson snapped. "Do you think we'd cut our classes and drive nearly five hundred miles just to play poker with a lunatic?"

"No," said Rothman. "That's how I know. But why aren't you frank about it? Why keep on pretending there wasn't a special reason for your visit?"

Neill was beating his foot against the table leg again and Avery's eyes were hard and staring as he examined his cards.

"Who'll open?" MacPherson asked. "I can't."

"I can," said Rothman. "I'm betting one blue chip. Listen, Avery, why won't you look at me? If you think I'm hamming, what do you call your own act? How long are we going to go on kidding each other? They've shut me up here, but that doesn't mean they've stopped me from logical thinking. My three old friends from the Project don't turn up in the middle of a Friday morning just to calm my fevered brain with a card game."

"What's wrong with poker?" demanded MacPherson.

"Poker? Nothing. I know—It must be the test. Total conversion of matter to energy. Not just a minute percentage any more—*total* conversion. They've finished the set, haven't they? They're ready to test. They're going to disintegrate Waaku, aren't they? It must be today. Then this is the day the world ends. Tell me, when is zero hour?"

Neill's cards had slipped from his fingers and he stooped to the floor, fumbling for them. Avery was bending one corner of a card, creasing it, smoothing it out, and creasing it again. Nobody was going to answer, MacPherson realized. They were leaving it up to him.

He spoke sharply. "You're getting onto forbidden ground, Rothman. You know we're not allowed to discuss the Project with you. We're allowed to visit you only under the strictest promise not to speak of it at all. You're certainly rational enough to understand what the therapists have told you, that you'd get well easily enough if you'd stop worrying. Forget about zero hour. Everything's going to be all right."

Rothman turned to look out the window. "Is it today?"

"How should we know? We're only innocent bystanders now, like you. Remember, we all left the Project over six months ago, except Avery, and last month they let him go."

Neill had rearranged his cards now and he looked at them instead of Rothman as he spoke. "There's nothing to worry about. Your calculations were wrong. The test is not going to get out of control—if and when they make it. But they don't tell us things any more."

"Since they fired you," said Rothman.

"That's right, since they fired us," Neill said. The creased corner of a card suddenly broke off in his fingers.

"If you didn't believe in my calculations, why did you back me up? I didn't ask you to. If you didn't believe in the danger, why didn't you stay out of the argument and keep your jobs? It wasn't your fight. You could have kept out of it—or attacked me, like Avery."

"All we did was insist that even if you had made a mistake in your calculations, that didn't necessarily prove you were crazy," said Neill. "We didn't know whether you were right or not. We couldn't argue about the math. Avery tore that to pieces and the boys at Columbia and Harvard backed him up. MacPherson and I aren't competent to check your math.

To us, you didn't seem any crazier than the people who sent you here. But after you'd scared them silly, they had to do something to stop your scaring other people."

He turned to pick up his cards again, but stopped at the sight of Avery. Avery was standing and crumpling a card spasmodically, his lips were moving without sound, and he was breathing rapidly.

"Look here," said MacPherson. "You'd better change the subject. If little Joe passes by the door and hears us talking about the Project, he'll have our visiting privileges revoked before you can say nuclear fission, and they'll stay revoked forever."

"How long is forever?" asked Rothman.

Avery threw down his cards and walked to the window. Through the bars, there was nothing to be seen but the expanse of sand, glinting in the morning sun, and a cactus plant casting a stubby shadow. He whirled to face the others.

"Look, MacPherson," he burst out. "I'm fed up with this game. Snookums Rothman mustn't think about the Project any more, so we mustn't say the naughty word. But we were all in it together at the beginning and there was a while when we were all every bit as scared as he was. Why not tell him we came this morning in case—just in case—he'd heard about the test and was worrying? What's the harm in telling him what the whole university knows? That zero hour is today, this morning, now!"

"Shut up, you fool!" said MacPherson.

But Rothman glanced at his cards again, then looked up. "When does it begin? What time is it now?"

"Don't answer!" shouted MacPherson. "Are you trying to knock him off balance again?"

"I will answer!" said Avery. "I'm going to tell him. He scared us silly with his calculations; now let us scare him with some cold facts. It'll do him good. Maybe when the test is over, if he finds—I mean *when* he finds—he was wrong, he'll be cured."

"Yes, and maybe he'll really be crazy."

Grabbing Avery fiercely by the arm, MacPherson tried to drag him to the door, but Avery broke away.

"Listen, Rothman!" Avery's breath was coming quick and shallow. "Today is the day! Zero hour is eleven o'clock this morning!"

MacPherson sagged. No one spoke or moved as they all watched Rothman.

At last Rothman sighed, once. "What time is it now?"

From the door came a scratching sound. MacPherson turned to see Joe, grinning at them through the steel lattice.

"How's things?" Joe wanted to know. "Thought I heard a commotion in here. Doc Rothman's not acting up, I hope?"

"Everything's under control, Joe," MacPherson assured him. "Just having a friendly game."

"Don't cheat while they're watching you," said Joe, and his face disappeared.

"Well, the murder's out," said MacPherson.

"No use kidding you any longer," Neill said, fanning his cards. "Eleven o'clock this morning. Six o'clock tomorrow morning, Waaku time. But it's just another test. Nothing's going to happen."

Avery took off his glasses and began to polish the lenses. "Any idea of a possible chain reaction is ridiculous. As a matter of fact, I recently spent a full week checking the math again myself, so I know. But we knew how you felt about it, Rothman, and we didn't want you to be worrying here all alone, in case you'd found out. That's why we came."

Rothman was looking out the window. He did not answer. Slowly MacPherson went back to his chair and picked up his cards. "And now how about playing some poker? Rothman, you opened for a blue. What about you, Neill?"

"I'm staying," said Neill, shoving in a chip. "Always was a gambler. I'm going to stay till the cows come home."

"What time is it?" Rothman asked. "I haven't got a wrist-watch. They think I might break the crystal and cut my throat."

MacPherson slammed down his cards and jerked his watch from his pocket. "What does it matter what time it is? Why couldn't they give you a watch with a plastic crystal? If you have to know, it's eleven-forty."

"And thirteen seconds," added Neill.

"Then it's already started," said Rothman.

He leaned his head against the back of his chair and closed his eyes. "It's on its way now. There's something more than a third of the Earth between us and Waaku—the place where Waaku was, I mean. The disintegration wave is moving slowly. The seismic wave of an earthquake would get here in about fifty minutes, more or less. But the shock wave from Waaku, traveling somewhere around five thousand miles an hour, will need about an hour and seventeen minutes, plus or minus a minute or so. That means it will reach us in about thirty-seven minutes from now, and the disintegration wave is following close behind. Well, nice to have known you, fellows. Anyone want to check my math?"

He waved toward the desk behind him, piled high with manuscript and a sprawling heap of books on which rested a slide-rule.

"Calm down," said MacPherson. "Nothing is going to happen. Damn you, Avery! Are you proud of what you accomplished?"

Avery glared. "It'll do him good! He's got to learn to face reality, like the rest of us. In a little more than half an hour, the test will be finished. The world will still be here. Rothman will have to admit his equations were wrong—and then he'll be cured."

Rothman leaned forward. "Or contrariwise, Rothman will *not* have to admit he was wrong and Rothman will *not* be cured! If I made a mistake in my math, why couldn't anybody put his finger on it? I'm not so crazy that I wouldn't be able to see an error in calculus when it was pointed out to me. If you're sure my calculations are wrong, why do you look so frightened?"

"Do we have to go over all that again?" said MacPherson. "The boys at Columbia told you where the mistake was. It's where you inverted that twelve-by-twelve matrix. Didn't you bother to check the inverted matrix?"

"The same old tale." Rothman picked up his cards. "No mathematician will ever admit that another mathematician could invent a method beyond his comprehension. Still harping on an error in my inverted matrix. What time is it now?"

"There's no doubt that your calculations are wrong," said Neill, "but I still don't see why we have to insist on proving it the hard way. With bombs, why do we need to fool around with the total disintegration of matter? Sure, I know the new model releases a googol times the energy you get out of uranium fission, but who cares? There's plenty of uranium for our needs."

"The trouble with uranium is that it doesn't make a big enough bang," said MacPherson. "People aren't impressed by it any more. The same goes for plutonium, even for lithium, at least for any size bomb we can make. The idea is to show the world something so convincing that they'll never even think of a war again. When they see every island in the Waaku chain wiped off the map, they'll get the point."

Avery creased another card and cleared his throat. "*Did* you check the inverted twelve-by-twelve, Rothman?"

"I suppose you think I forgot to. Have *you* checked it?"

"Yes, I have. I may not know much math, but I did check it."

"Even after the Columbia boys said it was nonsense? Well, does it come out right?"

"No, it doesn't! You multiply the inverted matrix by the original and you not only don't get zeros for all elements outside the diagonal, you get a haphazard assortment of ones and twos. Worse still, every element in the diagonal comes out equal to zero. The product of the two matrices is about as different from the identity matrix as anything could be. You're one of our most brilliant mathematicians—how could you manage to make so many mistakes in one set of calculations?"

"Did I tell you that was an inverted matrix? Maybe, for this problem, you need something a little more advanced than algebra. Anyhow, if my math is all wrong, why did your first report okay it?"

"What do you mean, my first report?"

"The one you sent to Prexy. The one you later called in and burned. Except Prexy showed it to me and I photostated it. Here." Rothman reached into the pile of papers on his desk and drew out a little envelope. It contained photographic prints. He held one before Avery's glasses. "Does that look familiar?"

Avery drew his hand across his forehead, but did not reply.

"Is that true, Avery?" asked MacPherson. "Did you make a report okaying Rothman's calculations and then withdraw it?"

"Well, what if I did? The report didn't seem to make me much more popular than Rothman was. What if some very influential people in Government explained to Prexy, and he explained to me, just how unpopular that first report might make me? Or suppose they didn't. Maybe I simply didn't find the mistakes in the math until later." Avery kept looking at his cards as he spoke.

"Oh, great," said MacPherson. "Rothman gets put away here, Neill and I lose our jobs, and there's hell to pay in Washington, all because Avery says Rothman's math is full of holes. Now it turns out he wasn't sure and maybe was pressured into it. Grand. Between a screwball and a skunk, I'll choose the screwball. Maybe if Avery had stuck to his guns, there wouldn't have been any test."

"It doesn't matter," said Rothman. "Avery was probably warned to mend his ways. I was. Or maybe he couldn't face the truth. I'm sure he's been much happier, the last few months, believing I'm crazy. Anyway, I don't blame him any more. Maybe my math will soon speak for itself. For your benefit—" he turned to Avery—"I may point out that the errors you said you found affect only the *velocity* of the wave of disintegration. So what if that isn't quite right? The proof that the reaction will be self-sustaining is independent of that."

Avery was white with rage. "The proof, as you called it, that the reaction will be self-sustaining and will consume the entire substance of the Earth doesn't make sense, either. You used D as an operator where it should have been a constant. That's what finally made them certain that you were insane."

There was a rap at the door and Joe poked his head in. "Lunch, Professors! Twelve o'clock, high noon, like they say. How about some turkey sandwiches?"

MacPherson began to sweat; the thought of food made him feel sick.

Was it possible, he wondered, that in spite of everything, he was not quite sure? He looked at Neill and Avery, but they had turned their heads away.

"We won't bother with lunch, Joe," said Rothman.

"Must be a pretty good game if you won't even knock off to eat," said Joe. "Well, will you at least mark your menu for tomorrow?"

"For tomorrow? Tomorrow isn't going to come, you know."

"Nuts," muttered Joe as he closed and locked the door. "Pure nuts."

Avery cleared his throat, and his voice was thin. "Look here, Rothman! If the Universe were composed of matter as unstable as you claim, it would have ceased to exist long ago. Somewhere, somehow, in the infinity of chance events since the creation of the Earth, something would have occurred to start the self-sustaining chain reaction, and all matter would have been annihilated."

"Are you trying to prove something to yourself?" asked Rothman. "Surely you don't equate infinity with a mere four billion years. That's a finite time—long enough for the more dangerous radioactives to disappear completely, of course, but not long enough for all possible chance events to have taken place. Anyway, I never have asserted that the reaction would reach from Earth to the other planets, or even to the Moon. The Universe, including the Solar System, will still go on. But our old Earth is going up like a pile of magnesium

powder mixed with potassium chlorate when you drop a
lighted match on it."

Avery wiped his forehead. "I don't know why I keep arguing with a lunatic. But you know yourself that the value
you give for the integration constant in those equations is a
pure guess, only you spend ten pages of doubletalk trying to
hide that fact. If the constant is the one you give, why, sure,
then you get a chain reaction. But you made it up! Who ever
heard of a constant of that magnitude in the solution of an
ordinary differential equation?"

"That's one criticism of my work the Harvard and Columbia boys never mentioned."

"Okay, then I mention it. You're crazy!"

"Are you sure?"

"Positive!"

"Then why can't you forget the approach of zero hour? I'll
tell you why and you aren't even making a good show of hid-
ing it. You know that, compared to mine, your knowledge of
mathematics is about on a level with that of a college sopho-
more. Deep down, you know that my calculations were correct. You are convinced—*convinced*—that the bombing of
Waaku has already started a chain reaction. And that about
seventeen minutes past twelve, around eight minutes from
now, the shock wave will reach us, and then the wave of disintegration. Look out of the window! See that cactus in the
sand, with its little yellow flower? It will be annihilated. All
that desert will go, too—every pebble, every grain of sand.
Everything you see, and you yourself, will be disintegrated,
transformed into energy!"

Suddenly he relaxed into a grin and softened his voice. "I
thought we were playing poker. We're waiting for you to bet.
Why don't you at least look at your cards?"

Avery opened his mouth, then closed it, and picked up his
hand, riffling the five cards.

"I'm staying," he said. "Here's your blue and I raise you a
blue."

Slowly the others picked up their hands and stared at the
cards. MacPherson scarcely looked at his as he spoke.

"I'm staying." He picked up the deck. "Cards, gentlemen?"

Rothman shook his head. "I'll play these."

Neill took two. "I like to hold a kicker," he explained.

Avery and MacPherson drew three.

"I opened," said Rothman, "and I'll bet five blue chips."

"See you and raise you a blue," Neill said.

"I'll string along," said Avery.

MacPherson threw his hand in. "I'll let you guys fight it out."

They all looked at Rothman, who was studying his cards.

"I'll see you," he began, and paused. Then he shoved all of his chips into the pot. "I'll see you and raise you a hundred blue chips."

"Damn it, Rothman!" MacPherson protested. "I know we agreed on no limit, but if you go on playing like this, you'll lose more than you can afford."

"I've already lost everything," said Rothman, "and so have you. Don't you know what time it is? In a few minutes, none of you will be around to try to collect. What time is it now?"

Avery reached for his watch, then stopped.

Rothman turned his head. "What's that?"

Nobody moved.

A noise like the roar of a swift freight train rushed into the room, rattling the windows. The walls shook, the floor trembled, the slide-rule slid off the pile of books and clattered to the floor.

They jumped to their feet and Avery ran to the window, clutching at the bars.

"Not yet," said Rothman calmly. "The cactus plant will still be there, casting its little shadow. You might as well sit down and finish the game. That was only the shock wave. Have you forgotten that it is transmitted through the Earth faster than the wave of disintegration? We still have a few minutes left. Isn't anybody going to see my bet?"

Avery lurched to the desk, grabbed a remnant of torn paper and scribbled on it.

"I'll see you," he yelled, "and raise you a hundred and twenty-five billion blues!"

MacPherson walked to the window. "Look at the sky. This is it."

They all jammed against his back, trying to see the horizon, waiting. Avery dropped the scrap of paper and covered his eyes.

"What is there to see?" Neill whispered.

"I thought—there was a flash . . ." MacPherson's voice trailed off, and he rubbed his eyes.

"But I didn't see anything," said Neill. "There's nothing to see."

A minute went by. The desert remained calm, the blue sky was unmarked by even a cloud, the air was still.

A second minute went by.

Neill drew out his watch, looked wonderingly at the steady

march of the second hand. Then he turned and stumbled into the lavatory. They could hear his dry heaves.

Rothman's eyes wavered from MacPherson to Avery, and back to MacPherson, and he sighed.

"Looks as if I was wrong, gentlemen," he said. "Maybe I am crazy, after all. I wonder if that integration constant could have been wrong." He reached down to the floor to pick up the fallen slide-rule, sat down and drew a pad of paper toward him.

MacPherson leaned against the window, too weak to move. He saw Avery take his hands away from his eyes. He could hear the chattering of Avery's teeth, could hear them click as he clamped them together, trying to control his lips. It seemed a long time before Avery managed to speak.

"*You!*" cried Avery. He lunged forward, grabbed Rothman by the shoulder and jerked him to his feet. "This—will teach you—not to make—mistakes—"

He smashed his fist into Rothman's face.

Still MacPherson could not move, could not even shout. He could only listen to Avery.

"And this will teach you—not to set up matrices—that don't multiply—that burn up—the world—"

Again Avery struck and knocked Rothman to the floor.

Breaking through his paralysis, MacPherson clutched Avery by the shoulder, but Avery kicked at the man on the floor, again and again.

"Avery!" shouted MacPherson. "Snap out of it, man! It's all over! The test is finished. We're still here. Rothman was wrong, just as we always knew he was!"

But Avery was on his knees, pounding Rothman with both fists, sobbing out meaningless words, oblivious to the shouts outside and to MacPherson's tugging.

The door burst open and Joe rushed in, followed by two other attendants.

"What goes on?" After a glance at Avery's contorted face, Joe grabbed for his legs. "Send for the doc, boys. We're going to need help."

One of the men ran down the corridor while Joe and the others succeeded in pulling Avery away from Rothman, who struggled to his feet. A doctor came in with a loaded hypodermic. He gave Avery an injection in the arm.

"Go easy there," said MacPherson. "He'll be all right in a few minutes. He's had a shock, that's all."

"Shock," Avery mumbled.

MacPherson gripped Avery's arm. "Try to relax, man. It's

finished. We never believed in it, of course. But I'll admit it's a relief, even to me, to be *sure* there was no danger of a chain reaction at all."

Suddenly he felt cold.

There was no understanding in Avery's eyes. He slumped to the floor.

"Do you think he'll be all right when he comes out from under the drug?" asked MacPherson.

"I can't say," said the doctor. "I only saw him a few minutes, when you came here this morning. I thought at the time he was pretty disturbed. Much more than Rothman here. Next week, I think, we're going to send Rothman home."

Rothman wiped the blood off his chin and grinned weakly. "You don't mean that, Doc. I used the wrong integration constant in a little calculation. I must be crazy."

THE MIRACLE
OF THE
BROOM CLOSET

W. NORBERT
(Norbert Wiener)

*"W. Norbert" is the Mr. Hyde of Dr. Norbert Wiener, it is
the personality he wears when he is neither the creator of cy-
bernetics as a new and separate discipline nor the celebrated
professor at the Massachusetts Institute of Technology. Norbert Wiener has had a remarkable career—as readers of his
autobiography (or for that matter, of the daily papers) know
—but it has dealt with facts; his alter ego lies under no such
restriction; "W. Norbert" can investigate such odd interactions
as those between Faith and the Electron—as he does in* The
Miracle of the Broom Closet.

Everybody has his own Mexico. For some it is seafishing in
Acapulco with the usual photograph of the fisherman and the
fish. I believe the fish take as much pride in the photographs
as the fishermen, only under the ocean things are turned upside down, and the pride of the fish is in the weight and size
of the American who appears beside him. Others sit on the
lawns at Cuernavaca and bask in the sunshine. I suppose that
on weekdays they are prominent leather manufacturers from
Mexico City or famous doctors; but I have merely seen them
in their basking costumes with their wives and children up
from the City in play suits of Jim Tillet's black patterns. I am
told that there are even a few people in Mexico who go up
Popo, and a slightly smaller number who come down again.
However, I do not wish to assert what I have not observed
with my own eyes.

For me Mexico means none of these. Instead, it means a
severely formal and efficient building, with plumbing painted
in three different colors, and the universal odor of the experimental laboratory. It means working with a friend of mine

who is a physiologist, and who will not be named in the sequel for reasons that will appear obvious. It means a highly energetic and competent group of young men of various nationalities, who are not averse to playing occasional tricks on one another, and who pursue their several careers as physiologists, chemists, and other varieties of scientists. There is also Sebastian.

Sebastian is the janitor. I do not mean to imply in the least that he is an ordinary janitor. In fact, he is the janitor to end all janitors. When I first met him, he was possessed of a flowery conversational style, and two equally flowery moustachios. The moustachios, alas, have passed into history, although I suspect them of having been stolen by one of the younger chemists. The style is still there.

When I first met him, Sebastian was only able to be flowery in one language. As a matter of fact, the general question asked in the laboratory when a new article is to be turned over to the press is, "Is this the way that Sebastian would have said it?" Since then, with the ebb and flow of foreign and largely North American scientists, English has become the second language of the laboratory, and Sebastian can manage to be quite as dignified in it as he can be in Spanish. He holds very high opinions as to the responsibility and the conduct of "international scientists" and speaks reverently of them.

Sebastian is thus an internationalist, but he is not himself an unnational being. He is most definitely a Mexican, and a very devout one at that. There is a Shrine in the broom closet, not unlike the portable affairs that Mexican chauffeurs carry around with them on the front window; and I need not tell you that the Saint to whom he prays is his namesake. I don't mean that there is not a portrait of the Virgin of Guadalupe somewhere in the Shrine—that would be too much to expect of a patriotic Mexican—but the main figure is that of a Roman soldier pierced through and through with arrows and looking very uncomfortable under the circumstances.

I must now report to you a sad event which happened some few years ago, and almost caused the disruption of our flourishing little institution. It all goes back to a visit the Boss paid to the National Pawn Shop. Why the Boss should visit the National Pawn Shop is more than I can understand, but I believe that it was under the pressure of some of his wife's American friends, who had heard there were to be found there rather remarkable opportunities for the purchase of Colonial jewelry. However, one of the lots to be auctioned off seemed to consist of a miscellaneous collection of hardware, and to be so little in demand that it was going to be knocked down at a ridiculously low price. There is always a need for odd bits of metal around a laboratory, for clamping the different parts of an apparatus together; and as about fifteen pieces of miscellaneous junk were to be knocked down for half a peso, the Boss couldn't resist the need of supporting the financial interests of his laboratory.

Most of the stuff was no use to anyone—it consisted of a few things that looked like picture frames, some miscellaneous brass work and a few bits of junk jewelry—but there were some iron rods which caught my friend's attention as just what he needed for the assembly of his new oscillograph. The oscillograph is located in the back of the room just opposite the broom closet I have mentioned, where the janitor keeps his washrags and brooms, and performs his private devotions.

It is the part of the ideal scientist to keep a magnificent impartiality in his decisions; but although this is so, in a long career extending over 40 years and three continents, I have never met the ideal scientist. The very least he wants is to get publishable results, and what he usually wants is to show that Professor So-and-So of the University of Patagonia has made a fool of himself in his last paper. Much as I admire my esteemed Mexican colleague, I cannot acquit him of a full measure of human frailty in such matters. He is quite as capable of chortling as the next man, and his long and successful scientific career has given him many occasions to chortle.

In the period in which this tale is laid, Professor Halbwitz, formerly of the University of Spiesburg, and now a refugee at the University of Patagonia, had presented a paper concerning nervous conduction which contained some features highly obnoxious to my friend. The dispute began with the fact that the Patagonian scientist used a certain German make of amplifier, while the Mexican scientist swore by an American amplifier which a friend of his had constructed. At any rate, there was a marked discrepancy between the results of the two men. For a while, my friend put it down not only to the other fellow's bad instrumentation, but in particular to the electrodes he was using. I may say bad electrodes or polarized electrodes are the continual excuse of the electrophysiologists.

Before long the whole laboratory knew that the combat between their director and Herr Professor Halbwitz was a grim battle to the death. The less respectful youngsters had heavy bets on the outcome, weighted decisively, I may say, by the fact that their boss had almost always come across in the pinches. On the other hand, as becomes a man of dignity and substance, the janitor, our Sebastian, was unable to relieve his emotions in such a trivial and undignified way. The Boss over whom he watched, the Boss who was a national asset of Mexico, the Boss to whose office he had often brought the bootblack and the barber—much, I may say, to the Boss's embarrassment—not only could not be wrong, but by some sort of contradiction, he needed the full support of Heaven in not being wrong. Far be it from me to expatiate on the fluency of the prayers which went up to Saint Sebastian. Neither the fluency of Sebastian's Spanish nor my own linguistic abilities permit me to do justice to the subject. At any rate, the first results of this devotion was most gratifying. The Mexican electrodes seemed to work perfectly, and the American amplifiers were all that a committee of Edisons could have wished. The paper proceeded flowingly; it seemed as if H. Halbwitz was doomed to be swallowed into the outer darkness in which he belonged.

Convincing as the results of our laboratory were, they appeared to have no effect whatever on the stream of publications arising in Patagonia. In one article after another, Herr Professor Halbwitz continued to maintain his indefensible thesis, and the controversy went on for a period of months. By this time somebody in the Morganbilt Institute in New York began to be intrigued by the blank opposition between the results of the two scientists. He was an old friend of the Boss, and we had full confidence that the results of our laboratory would be completely confirmed. We got a most apologetic letter from the Morganbilt Institute, in which our friend, Dr. Schlemihl, confessed himself unable to duplicate our results. He supposed that there had been some misunderstanding on his part about our setup, but as far as his work went, it seemed to be distinctly on Halbwitz's side. A long letter from our laboratory did not improve the situation. It appeared that Schlemihl's understanding of what we had done had been perfectly correct. It was really a nasty situation, because the controversy came to take on a rather personal tinge, and there wasn't anything we could do about it. An article appeared in an Argentine newspaper commenting on the corruption of Mexico by North American contacts, and declaring a national mission of Argentina to be at the lead in all branches of science and intellectual effort. This was followed by a rather chauvinistic article in the *Journal of the American Medical Association,* casting doubts on all Latin-American work.

We still kept getting the same results. The Boss began to look more and more strained. I don't know how we could have kept from an explosion if just about this time a totally new and unexpected piece of work of his in an entirely different field had not come off, and saved the reputation of the laboratory. Still it was a close thing; and to this day the name of Halbwitz is not to be mentioned in the laboratory without a certain feeling of humiliation.

It was only the other day that we got our first clue as to where the difficulty really lay. The Boss was looking a little more carefully over the collection of junk that he had bought before throwing it out as utterly useless. In the bottom of the box, between two flat pieces of metal, there had sifted down a little slip of parchment, indicating that the box had been the property of an old Mexican priest who had excavated some of the material in the neighborhood of one of the early churches. This church was devoted to Saint Sebastian, and the priest offered as a theory, perhaps not too well substantiated but perfectly probable, that the pieces of metal he had dug up were relics; in fact, probably some of the original arrows of Saint Sebastian.

I don't know just the process by which the engines of the death of Saint Sebastian acquired special miraculous powers, but we have the True Cross as a prototype, and relics are of the most diverse character. The miracle of Joshua, when he made the sun stand still, was a really good-sized one; but within the frame of science there are minor miracles as well. Now, to upset scientific experiment at all requires a very small miracle indeed, and with a devout and faithful servant praying to Saint Sebastian in the direct presence of his arrows, what can one expect? After all, as we understand it, the Saint was a Roman soldier, and the very special needs of the modern scientist must be well beyond him. The needs of an eloquent and faithful though simple soul are matters much more suited to his comprehension.

We have no complete evidence that this is what happened. However, since then I have noticed on the part of the Boss a distinct disinclination to use any material emanating from a quasi-clerical source. I don't think he is any more religious than he was before, but he is very much annoyed, and last year when there was a question of hiring a fellow by the name of Sebastian as laboratory boy, the youngster lost the job. And I am very sure I know why.

At any rate, the moral of this little tale, if there is any moral, is that saint and scientist should each stick to his own business. Meanwhile, the janitor Sebastian flourishes, and I believe that in his self-satisfaction he is beginning to grow his moustachios again.

HEAVYPLANET

LEE GREGOR
(Milton A. Rothman)

Like Chan Davis, Isaac Asimov, and one or two others in this collection, Milton Rothman was a science fiction fan long before he was a scientist: there are few scientists at the age of twelve, which is when Milt Rothman began his interest in the field. Your editor well remembers the Sunday afternoon in Philadelphia, a quarter of a century ago, when four or five fans from New York journeyed to meet four or five Philadelphia fans, thus conducting what was called "The First American Science Fiction Convention." I was one of the guests, and Milt Rothman one of the hosts.

Since then Rothman, torn between music and science scholarships, elected ultimately to take his doctorate in physics. His present work is with the Princeton University Plasma Physics Laboratory (once called Project Matterhorn), where his principal investigations have to do with the behavior of various types of wave motion in highly ionized gas.

Ennis was completing his patrol of Sector EM. Division 426 of the Eastern Ocean. The weather had been unusually fine, the liquid-thick air roaring along in a continuous blast that propelled his craft with a rush as if it were flying, and lifting short, choppy waves that rose and fell with a startling suddenness. A short savage squall whirled about, pounding down on the ocean like a million hammers, flinging the little boat ahead madly.

Ennis tore at the controls, granite-hard muscles standing out in bas-relief over his short, immensely thick body, skin gleaming scalelike in the slashing spray. The heat from the sun that hung like a huge red lantern on the horizon was a tangible intensity, making an inferno of the gale.

The little craft, that Ennis maneuvered by sheer brawn, took a leap into the air and seemed to float for many seconds before burying its keel again in the sea. It often floated for long distances, the air was so dense. The boundary between air and water was sometimes scarcely defined at all—one merged into the other imperceptibly. The pressure did strange things.

Like a dust mote sparkling in a beam, a tiny speck of light above caught Ennis' eye. A glider, he thought, but he was puzzled. Why so far out here on the ocean? They were nasty things to handle in the violent wind.

The dust mote caught the light again. It was lower, tumbling down with a precipitancy that meant trouble. An upward blast caught it, checked its fall. Then it floated down gently for a space until struck by another howling wind that seemed to distort its very outlines.

Ennis turned the prow of his boat to meet the path of the falling vessel. Curious, he thought; where were its wings? Were they retracted, or broken off? It ballooned closer, and it wasn't a glider. Far larger than any glider ever made, it was of a ridiculous shape that would not stand up for an instant. And with the sharp splash the body made as it struck the water—a splash that fell in almost the same instant it rose—a thought seemed to leap up in his mind. A thought that was more important than anything else on that planet; or was to him, at least. For if it was what he thought it was—and it had to be that—it was what Shadden had been desperately seeking for many years. What a stroke of inconceivable luck, falling from the sky before his very eyes.

The silvery shape rode the ragged waters lightly. Ennis' craft came up with a rush; he skillfully checked its speed and the two came together with a slight jar. The metal of the strange vessel dented as if it were made of rubber. Ennis stared. He put out an arm and felt the curved surface of the strange ship. His finger prodded right through the metal. What manner of people were they who made vessels of such weak materials?

He moored his little boat to the side of the larger one and climbed to an opening. The wall sagged under him. He knew he must be careful; it was frightfully weak. It would not hold together very long; he must work fast if it were to be saved. The atmospheric pressure would have flattened it out long ago, had it not been for the jagged rent above which had allowed the pressure to be equalized.

He reached the opening and lowered himself carefully into the interior of the vessel. The rent was too small; he enlarged it by taking the two edges in his hands and pulling them apart. As he went down he looked askance at the insignificant plates and beams that were like tissue paper on his world. Inside was wreckage. Nothing was left in its original shape. Crushed, mutilated machinery, shattered vacuum tubes, sagging members, all ruined by the gravity and the pressure.

There was a pulpy mess on the floor that he did not examine closely. It was like red jelly, thin and stalky, pulped under a gravity a hundred times stronger and an atmosphere ten thousand times heavier than that it had been made for.

He was in a room with many knobs and dials on the walls, apparently a control room. A table in the center with a chart on it, the chart of a solar system. It had nine planets; his had but five.

Then he knew he was right. If they came from another system, what he wanted must be there. It could be nothing else.

He found a staircase, descended. Large machinery bulked there. There was no light, but he did not notice that. He could see well enough by infrared, and the amount of energy necessary to sustain his compact gianthood kept him constantly radiating.

Then he went through a door that was of a comfortable massiveness, even for his planet—and there it was. He recognized it at once. It was big, squat, strong. The metal was soft, but it was thick enough even to stand solidly under the enormous pull of this world. He had never seen anything quite like it. It was full of coils, magnets, and devices of shapes unknown to him. But Shadden would know. Shadden, and who knows how many other scientists before him, had tried to make something which would do what this could do, but they had all failed. And without the things this machine could perform, the race of men on Heavyplanet was doomed to stay down on the surface of the planet, chained there immovably by the crushing gravity.

It was atomic energy. That he had known as soon as he knew that the body was not a glider. For nothing else but atomic energy and the fierce winds was capable of lifting a body from the surface of Heavyplanet. Chemicals were impotent. There is no such thing as an explosion where the atmosphere pressed inward with more force than an explosion could press outward. Only atomic, of all the theoretically possible sources of energy, could supply the work necessary to lift a vessel away from the planet. Every other source of energy was simply too weak.

Yes, Shadden, all the scientists must see this. And quickly, because the forces of sea and storm would quickly tear the ship to shreds, and, even more vital, because the scientists of Bantin and Marak might obtain the secret if there was delay. And that would mean ruin—the loss of its age-old supremacy —for his nation. Bantin and Marak were war nations; did they obtain the secret they would use it against all the other worlds that abounded in the Universe.

The Universe was big. That was why Ennis was so sure there was atomic energy on this ship. For, even though it might have originated on a planet that was so tiny that *chemical energy*—although that was hard to visualize—would be sufficient to lift it out of the pull of gravity, to travel the distance that stretched between the stars only one thing would suffice.

He went back through the ship, trying to see what had happened.

There were pulps lying behind long tubes that pointed out through clever ports in the outer wall. He recognized them as weapons, worth looking into.

There must have been a battle. He visualized the scene. The forces that came from atomic energy must have warped even space in the vicinity. The ship pierced, the occupants killed, the controls wrecked, the vessel darting off at titanic speed, blindly into nothing. Finally it had come near enough to Heavyplanet to be enmeshed in its huge web of gravity.

Weeaao-o-ow! It was the wailing roar of his alarm siren, which brought him spinning around and dashing for his boat. Beyond, among the waves that leaped and fell so suddenly, he saw a long, low craft making way toward the derelict spaceship. He glimpsed a flash of color on the rounded, gray superstructure, and knew it for a battleship of Marak. Luck was going strong both ways; first good, now bad. He could easily have eluded the battleship in his own small craft, but he couldn't leave the derelict. Once lost to the enemy he could never regain it, and it was too valuable to lose.

The wind howled and buffeted about his head, and he strained his muscles to keep from being blasted away as he crouched there, half on his own boat and half on the derelict. The sun had set and the evening winds were beginning to blow. The hulk scudded before them, its prow denting from the resistance of the water it pushed aside.

He thought furiously fast. With a quick motion he flipped the switch of the radiophone and called Shadden. He waited with fierce impatience until the voice of Shadden was in his ear. At last he heard it, then: "Shadden! This is Ennis. Get your glider, Shadden, fly to a45j on my route! Quickly! It's come, Shadden! But I have no time. Come!"

He flipped the switch off, and pounded the valve out of the bottom of his craft, clutching at the side of the derelict. With a rush the ocean came up and flooded his little boat and in an instant it was gone, on its way down to the bottom. That would save him from being detected for a short time.

Back into the darkness of the spaceship. He didn't think he had been noticed climbing through the opening. Where could he hide? Should he hide? He couldn't defeat the entire battleship singlehanded, without weapons. There were no weapons that could be carried anyway. A beam of concentrated actinic light that ate away the eyes and the nervous system had to be powered by the entire output of a battleship's generators. Weapons for striking and cutting had never been developed on a world where flesh was tougher than metal. Ennis was skilled in personal combat, but how could he overcome all that would enter the derelict?

Down again, into the dark chamber where the huge atomic generator towered over his head. This time he looked for something he had missed before. He crawled around it, peering into its recesses. And then, some feet above, he saw the opening, and pulled himself up to it, carefully, not to destroy the precious thing with his mass. The opening was shielded with a heavy, darkly transparent substance through which seeped a dim glow from within. He was satisfied then. Somehow, matter was still being disintegrated in there, and energy could be drawn off if he knew how.

There were leads—wires of all sizes, and busbars, and thick, heavy tubes that bent under their own weight. Some must lead in and some must lead out; it was not good to tamper with them. He chose another track. Upstairs again, and to the places where he had seen the weapons.

They were all mounted on heavy, rigid swivels. He carefully detached the tubes from the bases. The first time he tried it he was not quite careful enough, and part of the projector itself was ripped away, but next time he knew what he was doing and it came away nicely. It was a large thing, nearly as thick as his arm and twice as long. Heavy leads trailed from its lower end and a lever projected from behind. He hoped it was in working condition. He dared not try it; all he could do was to trace the leads back and make sure they were intact.

He ran out of time. There came a thud from the side, and then smaller thuds, as the boarding party incautiously leaped over. Once there was a heavy sound, as someone went all the way through the side of the ship.

"Idiots!" Ennis muttered, and moved forward with his weapon toward the stairway. Noises came from overhead, and then a loud crash buckled the plates of the ceiling. Ennis leaped out of the way, but the entire section came down, with two men on it. The floor sagged, but held for the moment. Ennis, caught between the downcoming mass, beat his way free. He came up with a girder in his hand, which he bent over the head of one of the Maraks. The man shook himself and struck out for Ennis, who took the blow rolling and countered with a buffet that left a black splotch on a skin that was like armor plate and sent the man through the opposite wall. The other was upon Ennis, who whirled with the quickness of one who maneuvers habitually under a pressure of ten thousand atmospheres, and shook the Marak from him, leaving him unconscious with a twist in a sensitive spot.

The first opponent returned, and the two grappled, searching for nerve centers to beat upon. Ennis twisted frantically, conscious of the real danger that the frail vessel might break to pieces beneath his feet. The railing of a staircase gave behind the two, and they hurtled down it, crashing through the steps to the floor below. Their weight and momentum carried them through. Ennis released his grip on the Marak, stopped his fall by grasping one of the girders that was part of the ship's framework. The other continued his devastating way down, demolishing the inner shell, and then the outer shell gave way with a grinding crash that ominously became a burbling rush of liquid.

Ennis looked down into the space where the Marak had fallen, hissed with a sudden intake of breath, then dove down himself. He met rising water, gushing in through a rent in the keel. He braced himself against a girder which sagged under his hand and moved onward against the rushing water. It geysered through the hole in a heavy stream that pushed him back and started to fill the bottom level of the ship. Against that terrific pressure he strained forward slowly, beating against the resisting waves, and then, with a mighty flounder, was at the opening. Its edges had been folded back upon themselves by the inrushing water, and they gaped inward like a jagged maw. He grasped them in a huge hand and exerted force. They strained for a moment and began to straighten. Irresistibly he pushed and stretched them into their former position, and then took the broken ends in his hands and *squeezed*. The metal grew soft under his grip and began to flow. The edges of the plate welded under that mighty pressure. He moved down the crack and soon it was watertight. He flexed his hands as he rose. They ached; even his strength was beginning to be taxed.

Noises from above; pounding feet. Men were coming down to investigate the commotion. He stood for a moment in thought, then turned to a blank wall, battered his way through it, and shoved the plates and girders back into position. Down to the other end of the craft, and up a staircase there. The corridor above was deserted, and he stole along it, hunting for the place he had left the weapon he had prepared. There was a commotion ahead as the Maraks found the unconscious man.

Two men came pounding up the passageway, giving him barely enough time to slip into a doorway to the side. The room he found himself in was a sleeping chamber. There were two red pulps there, and nothing that could help him, so he stayed in there only long enough to make sure that he would not be seen emerging into the hall. He crept down it again, with as little noise as possible. The racket ahead helped him: it sounded as though they were tearing the ship apart. Again he cursed their idiocy. Couldn't they see how valuable this was?

They were in the control room, ripping apart the machinery with the curiosity of children, wondering at the strange weakness of the paperlike metal, not realizing that, on the world where it was fabricated, it was sufficiently strong for any strain the builders could put upon it.

The strange weapon Ennis had prepared was on the floor of the passage, and just outside the control room. He looked anxiously at the trailing cables. Had they been stepped on and broken? Was the instrument in working condition? He had to get it and be away; no time to experiment to see if it would work.

A noise from behind, and Ennis again slunk into a doorway as a large Marak with a colored belt around his waist strode jarringly through the corridor into the control room. Sharp orders were barked, and the men ceased their havoc with the machinery of the room. All but a few left and scattered through the ship. Ennis' face twisted into a scowl. This made things more difficult. He couldn't overcome them all singlehanded, and he couldn't use the weapon inside the ship if it was what he thought it was from the size of the cables.

A Marak was standing immediately outside the room in

which Ennis lurked. No exit that way. He looked around the room; there were no other doors. A porthole in the outer wall was a tiny disk of transparency. He looked at it, felt it with his hands, and suddenly pushed his hands right through it. As quietly as he could, he worked at the edges of the circle until the hole was large enough for him to squeeze through. The jagged edges did not bother him. They felt soft, like a ragged pat of butter.

The Marak vessel was moored to the other side of the spaceship. On this side the wind howled blankly, and the sawtooth waves stretched on and on to a horizon that was many miles distant. He cautiously made his way around the glistening rotundity of the derelict, past the prow, straining silently against the vicious backward sweep of the water that tore at every inch of his body. The darker hump of the battleship loomed up as he rounded the curve, and he swam across the tiny space to grasp a row of projections that curved up over the surface of the craft. He climbed up them, muscles that were hard as carborundum straining to hold against all the forces of gravity and wind that fought him down. Near the top of the curve was a rounded, streamlined projection. He felt around its base and found a lever there, which he moved. The metal hump slid back, revealing a rugged swivel mounting with a stubby cylindrical projector atop it.

He swung the mounting around and let loose a short, sudden blast of white fire along the naked deck of the battleship. Deep voices yelled within and men sprang out, to fall back with abrupt screams clogged in their throats as Ennis caught them in the intolerable blast from the projector. Men, shielded from actinic light, used to receiving only red and infrared, were painfully vulnerable to this frightful concentration of ultraviolet.

Noise and shouts burst from the derelict spaceship alongside, sweeping away eerily in the thundering wind that seemed to pound down upon them with new vigor in that moment. Heads appeared from the openings in the craft.

Ennis suddenly stood up to his full height, bracing himself against the wind, so dense it made him buoyant. With a deep bellow he bridged the space to the derelict. Then, as a squad of Maraks made their difficult, slippery way across the flank of the battleship toward him, and as the band that had boarded the spaceship crowded out on its battered deck to see what the noise was about, he dropped down into a crouch behind his ultraviolet projector, and whirled it around, pulling the firing lever.

That was what he wanted. Make a lot of noise and disturbance, get them all on deck, and then blow them to pieces. The ravening blast spat from the nozzle of the weapon, and the men on the battleship dropped flat on the deck. He found he could not depress the projector enough to reach them. He spun it to point at the spaceship. The incandescence reached out, and then seemed to waver and die. The current was shut off at the switchboard.

Ennis rose from behind the projector, and then hurtled from the flank of the battleship as he was struck by two Maraks leaping on him from behind the hump of the vessel. The three struck the water and sank, Ennis struggling violently. He was on the last lap, and he gave all his strength to the spurt. The water swirled around them in little choppy waves that fell more quickly than the eye could follow. Heavier blows than those from an Earthly trip hammer were scoring Ennis' face and head. He was in a bad position to strike back, and suddenly he became limp and sank below the surface. The pressure of the water around him was enormous, and it increased very rapidly as he went lower and lower. He saw the shadowy bulk of the spaceship above him. His lungs were fighting for air, but he shook off his pretended stupor and swam doggedly through the water beneath the derelict. He went on and on. It seemed as though the distance were endless, following the metal curve. It was so big from beneath, and trying to swim the width without air made it bigger.

Clear, finally, his lungs drew in the saving breaths. No time to rest, though. He must make use of his advantage while it was his; it wouldn't last long. He swam along the side of the ship looking for an opening. There was none within reach from the water, so he made one, digging his stubby fingers into the metal, climbing up until it was safe to tear a rent in the thick outer and inner walls of the ship.

He found himself in one of the machine rooms of the second level. He went out into the corridor and up the stairway which was half-wrecked, and found himself in the main passage near the control room. He darted down it, into the room. There was nobody there, although the noises from above indicated that the Maraks were again descending. There was his weapon on the floor, where he had left it. He was glad that they had not gotten around to pulling that instrument apart. There would be one thing saved for intelligent examination.

The clatter from the descending crowd turned into a clamor of anger as they discovered him in the passageway.

They stopped there for a moment, puzzled. He had been in the ocean, and had somehow magically reappeared with the derelict. It gave him time to pick up the weapon.

Ennis debated rapidly and decided to risk the unknown. How powerful the weapon was he did not know, but with atomic energy it would be powerful. He disliked using it inside the spaceship; he wanted to have enough left to float on the water until Shadden arrived; but they were beginning to advance on him, and he had to start something.

He pulled a lever. The cylinder in his arms jerked back with great force; a bolt of fierce, blinding energy tore out of it and passed with the quickness of light down the length of the corridor.

When he could see again there was no corridor. Everything that had been in the way of the projector was gone, simply disappeared.

Unmindful of the heat from the object in his hands, he turned and directed it at the battleship that was plainly outlined through the space that had been once the walls of the derelict. Before the men on the deck could move, he pulled the lever again.

And the winds were silenced for a moment. The natural elements were still in fear at the incredible forces that came from the destruction of atoms. Then with an agonized scream the hurricane struck again, tore through the spot where there had been a battleship.

Far off in the sky Ennis detected motion. It was Shadden, speeding in a glider.

Now would come the work that was important. Shadden would take the big machine apart and see how it ran. That was what history would remember.

THE TEST STAND

LEE CORREY
(G. Harry Stine)

When Sputnik I roared into orbit, the heat and thrust its rockets generated were easily exceeded by the heat and thrust of thousands of American voices raised in protest and criticism. One voice critical of American rocket efforts belonged to a man who had more knowledge of what we had failed to do than most, a man who was actively at work on the missile development program at White Sands, who spoke up forthrightly with facts and figures—and found himself out of a job for his pains.

That man is G. Harry Stine, now working in space research on a private-enterprise basis, the same G. Harry Stine who, under his own name and the pseudonym "Lee Correy," has written a large number of first-rate science fiction stories . . . including the present The Test Stand.

With rockets making regular trips on schedule out to the space station now, I guess they've licked most of the old problems we had years ago. The rocket motors start smooth and burn smooth, and they don't have mixture-ratio troubles any more. And they've made terrific strides toward increasing combustion efficiency and specific impulse.

Sure, I talk the language. I was a rocket engineer—once. But I just plain didn't have the guts to stay with it, I guess.

We called it "the world's safest business"—until we started building them for men to ride in. The problems got tough then. With instrument and sounding rockets, you can afford a failure now and then. But put a man in the bird and you've got to have a rocket motor that's reliable. It's got to start, run, and stop with complete, one-hundred-per cent reliability. And it's got to do it over and over again.

Some of the techniques had been worked out with rocket planes like the *"Skyrocket"* and the X-1, but scale up from six thousand pounds thrust to something in the neighborhood of several hundred tons, and you'll get some idea of what we were up against.

It may be commonplace today, but we certainly had some rough times with it in the beginning.

I'll admit that it got too tough for me. I finally quit and went to selling refrigerators. But I made the mistake of keeping my drawing board and slide rule. Give those to an engineer—any engineer—and what do you get? Gadgets. That's why I'm building the air-refrigeration units that keep the spacemen cool when the ships come tearing back into the Earth's atmosphere.

I know it's difficult for an engineer to quit the rocket business after the bug has bitten him. It took a good, hard scare to make me quit. I got scared so badly that I couldn't listen to a motor running in a test stand without shaking in my boots.

Back at White Sands in '65, we finished Test Stand Number Seven. It was a concrete and steel monster perched up on the side of a cliff and tied right to the granite bedrock of the Organ Mountains. We built it specifically to test the rocket motors for Project *Nomad*, the first orbital man-carrying rocket.

We had trouble with that propulsion system for *Nomad*. Today they don't think anything of igniting a whole rack of motors at the same time, but in those days we didn't know much about it. We didn't have catalyst propellants, and we considered ourselves mighty lucky to get *one* chamber going. Getting a fire started in more than one was considered a miracle.

Those of us with the Rocket Division of the Karlter Ship & Drydock Corporation worked out the multiple start technique for our transoceanic rockets, but the motors would slobber around and waste a couple tons of propellants—liquid oxygen and liquid hydrogen—before the system built up enough thrust to get off the ground.

Then some bright design engineer back in the plant got the brilliant idea that those tons of fuel could be saved if the motors started at full thrust. We got a test directive telling me to work out the details.

Details, mind you. That meant figuring flow rates, mixture ratios, lag times, ignition delay, and valve timing. Oh, we had a lovely time! We had four blows with single chambers on Test Stand Three before we got an inkling of how to do it.

Those were the cut-and-try days; nobody knew very much about what went on inside a rocket motor.

Then Project *Nomad* went crash priority. They suddenly wanted that orbital rocket and wanted it *bad*.

My crew chief on Test Stand Seven didn't like it a bit. "Pete, they oughta give us some time to run cold-flow tests with water before we try to light-off all those chambers at once," he complained to me that day when I told him about it.

"They didn't give us *any* time, Dan," I had to explain. "Karlter and the boys on Staff want the reduced data by the end of the week. That means we get a starting test off today and a full run tomorrow."

"What do them guys want? Miracles?"

"That's our specialty."

Dan went out on the stand to get things ready while I pushed the morning paperwork over my desk in the field office. Just as I got around to tackling the silly problem of having to justify an air-conditioning system for our closed control room buried in the mountainside, Jerry Tedder, the controls technician, came in.

Jerry was a young squirt straight out of I. C. S. who'd been on the stand for about six months. You couldn't exactly call him a greenhorn at rocket motor testing because you're not a greenhorn when you've gained a deep respect for high-performance rocket engines. But Jerry was still inclined to get panicky at times, so I'd put him under McDougal's wing until he steadied down and got reliable. He was good; he knew *Nomad*'s electrical controls; but he was pretty young. He was also impulsive. In fact, he was definitely that way right then.

"Mr. Edwards, what's the story Dan's been giving me about haywiring the system for a full-thrust start?"

I pushed back my chair, lit up a cigarette, and asked him, "What's the matter, lad? You got troubles? What's wrong with our revised control wiring?"

"Mr. Edwards, it's going to blow all to hell!"

"Is it, now? What makes you think it's going to blow?" I said slowly. Jerry had the tendency to get scared blue when we ran a test that had the slightest amount of danger involved. Right then, it irked me more than usual because I'd spent most of the night before going over the calculations, diagrams, and details of the test. As far as I was concerned, figures based on engineering calculations made from valid data didn't lie.

"The whole system's too marginal right now! If we modify it, we can't expect it to be reliable," he told me, sitting down on the edge of the desk. "And those pressure-regulating valves have a tendency to hang-up on surges."

"Look, youngster," I replied quietly, looking him straight in the eye, "I know what this system will do and what it won't do. That's my job. Now get out there with Mac and rig the sequence controls the way I show in the wiring diagram. That's an order. Understand?"

"But we're liable to get into trouble—"

"Not if you do it right. Let me know when you're ready to run the functional checks." I turned back to my desk work, implying that he'd better hop-to if he wanted to remain on the crew. This wasn't the first time Jerry Tedder had shown he was afraid of that chained monster on the edge of the cliff. The unbridled fury of a rocket motor tied down to a mountainside and shaking the very granite itself is enough to make strong men tremble if they haven't seen it before. But, since Jerry had been with Project *Nomad* for six months, I was beginning to suspect that he just didn't have any guts.

The functional tests went fine. They checked out to the last wiggly ink line on the charts in the control room. Pressures, valve timing, everything was just as I had figured. I finally straightened up and told Dan, "I'll buy it. Start loading propellants."

Dan had to nudge Jerry, who was staring at the charts with a wooden expression. He was scared blue again. When he snapped back to life, he stepped up to the control console and picked up the public-address mike.

"Attention, all personnel! We are commencing to load propellants! No smoking in the stand area! All arc welders and torches out! Stand is in yellow condition!"

I pulled Dan over into a corner behind the instrument recorders. "Put Mac on the control board today," I instructed him. "Tedder's so shaky he might abort the run."

My crew chief shook his head. "Can't. Mac got an upset stomach and a headache, so I had to send him home."

"When did this happen?"

"Just before the functionals."

"Great! We'll have to leave Jerry where he is then—but you stand next to him and hold his hand, will you?"

"Sure thing," Dan replied with a grin, then added a reminder, "Say, don't forget to call your wife this time."

"Judas! I almost forgot!" I went over to the phone and called Doris.

Ever since Number Seven had been in operation, she'd wanted to bring Bobby down to see his daddy "make smoke." The little guy was pretty sharp for his four years. Whenever Number Seven would make a run, he'd hear the noise and tear out on the front porch of our house, see the big dust cloud, and jump up and down shouting, "That's my Daddy making smoke!"

Doris said she'd be down at the road-block in time, so I got back to the business at hand. Jerry was a bit steadier now as he operated the banks of switches studding the control console. Looking out through the heavy windows toward the test stand, I could see the frost collecting on the pipes as the tanking progressed. Liquid oxygen and liquid hydrogen were flowing down from the storage areas on the mountain behind and into their separate tanks mounted above the motors in the stand.

When I saw my old green Chevvy pull up at the road-block a half-mile away, I got on the field phone and had them put Doris on.

"Hi, baby! How's Bobby?"

"Excited," she told me.

"I'll bet. He's *really* going to see Daddy making smoke today!"

"You're sure we're not too close. If something happens—"

"Nothing can happen."

"Suppose it explodes?"

"My dear, sweet wife," I kidded her, "do you think I'd let you come this close if I thought it was going to blow up? Just stay where you are, and you'll see a real show. I'll be down after the run."

"Five minutes," Dan warned me.

I hung up and got on the job. The control room was quiet the way it always was before a test, a sort of strained silence with an air of tension all around. The instrument technicians were standing by their recorders, and Jerry was behind the firing console with Dan beside him. The youngster was visibly nervous; there was no color in his cheeks. I knew his symptoms pretty well, and I was glad old Dan was standing by to hold him in check.

Picking up my pear-shaped cut-off switch, I checked the connections. If something *did* go wrong, I'd have little time to push that switch and shut the motors off. Everybody else in the room had a switch in his hand, too, and I knew they were thinking the same thing.

Taking up my position in front of the heavy windows where I could see, I looked out on the test stand silhouetted

against the sky, a fantastic lacework of steel beams a yard
thick, pipes, tubing, walkways, and the rocket nozzles with
their big tanks above them, all rearing up as high as a ten-
story building.

"One minute," Dan announced.

"May we have it quiet, please?" I raised my voice over the
noise of the recording instruments. A dead hush fell over the
room, broken only by the low voices of the instrument men.

"Energize the cut-off circuit!"

"Cut-off hot!" Jerry sang out, his voice quavering a bit.
The little switch in my hand was armed now.

"Instruments zero?"

"Instruments zero!" came the reply from the instrument
engineer far back in the control room.

"Twenty-second warning!" I said quietly to Jerry.

Outside, an air horn blasted its voice across the hills and
desert.

My hands were sweaty. They always got that way just before a test. I guess it was tension which I never noticed. But
Jerry's hands, I could see they were trembling as he poised
them over the switches of the console.

"Flame quench on!" I snapped. A white fountain of water
sprang from a pipe and gushed down into the concrete flame
pit to protect it from the hell-fire of the rocket flame.

"Close vents and pressurize!"

From the back of the room amidst the banks of recording
instruments, someone read the tank pressures by percentage
as they came up: "Eighty—eight-five—ninety—ninety-five
—pressurized!"

This was it, the supreme moment of tension and suspense
in rocket-motor testing.

"Charts and cameras on! Fire on count-down!" I sang out.

The chart recorders started with a groan accompanied by
the *clack-clack-clack* of the timing relays.

"Three—two—one—FIRE!" Jerry leaned on the firing
button. He missed it the first time, but got it on the second
try.

I switched my eyes to the motors on the test stand.

Nothing happened.

Nothing. No glow of igniters. No cloud of liquid oxygen
or hydrogen. No sudden splash of flame laced with shock dia-
monds. Nothing.

"Misfire! Cut!" I yelled at the same time Jerry and Dan
did likewise. I bore down on the switch in my palm.

"No cut-off! No cut-off! It's still hot!" Jerry yelled back, panicky.

"Are the valves frozen?" I wanted to know.

"Valve seat temperatures O.K.!" an instrument man called out.

A plume of vapor suddenly spurted from one of the tanks. "Relief vents are working," Dan reported.

I discovered I was shaking, but managed to pull myself back under control out of sheer necessity. This was no time for me, the test engineer, to lose my head. But it was one of those times when a second stretches out as long as an hour. It seemed to take me forever to move; I was simply rooted to the spot.

Finally, I got out, "Everybody stay put! Emergency condition! Jerry, stay at the board and watch things!" I backed away from the window until I bumped into the control-sequence recorders. Then I got a look at the ink lines on the paper.

"Dan! Come here!" I called.

Stepping away from Jerry's side, my crew chief looked over my shoulder at the chart. "Something shorted," he observed. "Looks like the igniter relay stuck."

"There's more than that," I pointed out. "Instrumentation! What's the pressure upstream of the gas-generator valve?"

"No pressure yet," came the reply.

"Then the pressure regulator jammed," Dan concluded.

My mind ran over the schematic drawings of the electrical and pneumatic control systems of the unit. I came to two conclusions:

The unit would blow sky-high if (a) the sticking igniter relay decided to work, or (b) the jammed pressure regulating valve suddenly functioned. There wasn't a chance that they would decide to work at the same time, in which case the unit would run instead of blow.

I recalled Jerry had said something earlier about the reliability of the electrical controls and the regs having a tendency to jam on surges. Maybe I should have listened to him; maybe he had more savvy than I thought.

But why couldn't we shut down the unit right now? That didn't make sense to me until Jerry spoke up.

"Mr. Edwards, I think I know where our trouble is."

"Where?"

"Mac put in some jumper wires so we could make our functional checks. He was going to remove them before the test."

But Mac had gone home sick, and nobody had remembered the jumpers! If I hadn't had years of test experience behind me, I would have blown my top over this stupid oversight. But even the most experienced crews pull blunders on occasion; every man has his assigned job, and the tension prior to a run is usually so high that you think of nothing except your specified job as outlined in the "cook book," the operating procedure manual. You haven't got time to worry about everyone else's job.

Sometimes the blunders are funny—like forgetting to turn the recorders on or neglecting to load the film in the cameras. But it's not so funny when a man has to go outside to disarm a hot, misfired unit.

Jerry went on, "Dan, if you'll take the board here, I'll go and get us out of trouble."

If the misfire had been a shock, this statement from Jerry Tedder completely floored me. Hadn't he been scared blue a minute before? I was too upset right then to make much of it. Instead, I asked, "What do you think you can do?"

"I'll jumper a few things myself. I'll disarm the igniter relay and safety the system."

"That's half the job. Can you release the regulator?"

"I've never done it, but all you have to do is pound on it with a mallet after you've disconnected the line downstream."

"Yeah, but you've got to know *where* to pound," I reminded him. With three-thousand pounds-per-square-inch gas pressure on a regulator, you only have to hit it once in the wrong place to get killed very dead. High-pressure is like an explosive; it's perfectly safe if you know how to handle it, but it can kill you if the tubing bursts.

"I'll be careful," Jerry replied.

I knew he would, but I didn't trust him on pneumatic hardware yet. And he couldn't go out on that stand alone; you can't expect *that* much out of a man.

I don't know what it was. Perhaps it was the fact that I wanted to show Jerry that I wouldn't let him do anything his boss refused to do. I must have been crazy, but I said, "Grab your hard hat. You jumper that relay first, and I'll release the regulator. Take the board, Dan, and if anything happens, hit the water deluge quick!"

Jerry grabbed a few wires with clips on the ends, and I rummaged around in Dan's tool box until I found a box wrench, a crescent wrench, and a mallet. Thus armed, we walked down the long tunnel cut through the granite of the mountain toward the steel door sealing the far end.

Our steps echoed from the concrete walls, and we didn't say a word. I was sweating pretty badly; I could feel the sweat running down my sides under my shirt. And my stomach was tight. It was the old, familiar signal that comes when danger is around. I don't like it. I didn't like it then, but *somebody* had to go out on that test stand, somebody who knew what he was doing.

Thank God Dan hadn't volunteered to go! I might have taken him up on it!

Jerry pulled the door open with a clang and we stepped out into the afternoon sunlight.

As we approached the stand, I suddenly realized that I no longer had the protection of the control room around me. I was out in the open. If the unit fired now, we'd be shaken up pretty badly; but if it exploded, we were through.

Test stands had been beautiful things to me until that moment. All at once, that gray mass of steel and concrete was ugly. It had no grace in its lines; it was built to keep the tons of thrust from pushing the motors and tanks toward the sky. It was bulky, massive, solid, forbidding, and I hated it.

I got one look at the bottom of the mountain and saw my green Chevvy and a bunch of people standing around—waiting. Doris and Bobby were down there, and if we had an explosion, they were too close! Sure, I hadn't expected an explosion; if things had gone right, there wouldn't have been a chance. But as I thought of the tons of liquid oxygen and hydrogen in those tanks—equal to a dozen times the force of a like amount of TNT if they mixed and ignited—I wanted to yell to them to run. But I couldn't. I couldn't even walk. I just stood in my tracks.

Jerry went a few steps ahead of me, then turned to look back. "Come on, Pete," he urged.

I was on a crate of mental eggs as we got to the base of the stand and started up the ladder. I was shaking a little, but I rationalized that I was right in the middle of things now; I had to take whatever came.

We climbed up to the electrical control box, and Jerry plugged in his telephone headset. "O.K., Dan," he told the crew chief inside the control room, "I'm disarming the igniter circuit."

"Careful," I warned him unnecessarily. "Don't jar that box, or the relay is liable to function."

He nodded and gingerly started to remove the cover. If he had been shaking in the control room because of fear, it wasn't obvious now; his hands were steady and his movements careful as he lifted off the cover and set it on the steel grating of the walkway. Carefully, he took one of the clip wires from his pocket and connected one end.

There were lines in his face I had never seen before, and sweat was standing out on his forehead. I think I detected a split-second of hesitation before he connected the other end of the clip wire. But he looked carefully at the maze of wires and connections, then slowly reached in, the clip opened between two fingers.

He came out of there in a hurry, so fast that I thought something was wrong. I was all ready to hit the deck, useless as it might have been. "Got it!" he snapped. "Igniter disarmed! Hold everything for a minute!" Working rapidly now, he clipped on several more jumpers and removed some that were already there.

I felt partially relieved. Half the job was done. He stepped back and said to Dan on the phones, "O.K., the unit is electrically safe. No, no! Don't try the cut-off switch! That regulator's still hung-up!" Then he turned to me.

That was my cue. I walked out on the platform to the unit and started tracing pneumatic lines. The tense, vibrant hiss of compressed gas was all around. As I took out my box wrench to loosen the B-nut on the fitting, the tank relief valve let loose just over my head.

I dropped the wrench. It fell through the grating and bounced on the platform below. It slipped through the grating there and fell . . . and fell . . . and fell down into the flame pit. After seconds, it bounced off the bottom over a hundred feet down.

Without the correct wrench, I was forced to use the adjustable crescent wrench—the "knuckle-buster" so maligned by mechanics.

The fitting came loose without trouble, so I moved around to where I could get at the regulator. In order to reach it, I had to clamber off the platform onto the thrust mount and stand on a narrow beam. Since I had to swing the mallet, I was forced to hang on with only one hand. I didn't look down; it was a clear fall to the bottom of the pit.

I gave the regulator a careful visual check, but I didn't touch it. I had to free it first. Aiming closely, I swung the mallet back.

A ton-and-a-half of pressure on each square-inch of surface there! If I missed, too bad. Five hundred pounds of pressure had been known to tear a man in half.

What in blue blazes, I thought savagely, *made me come out here?* This was no place for a man with a wife and kid!

This was the sort of stuff a crazy guy with no responsibilities does!

Hit it, boy! But *don't* miss!

I got it squarely on the first swing. It released. The sharp, hissing roar of low-pressure gas coming out the end of the disconnected tube deafened me, but it was music to my ears right then.

We canceled the test that day and pumped the propellants back into their storage tanks where they were safe.

Crash program or not, we couldn't have made a run that day.

I guess I shook pretty badly for about fifteen minutes, although I hadn't been shaking when the boys tore me loose from where I had "frozen" on my lofty perch over the flame pit.

After three chain cigarettes and two cups of very black coffee, I went down to see Doris and Bobby.

They were disappointed, of course, but I didn't tell them what had gone on. No use worrying them about it. But Bobby was in tears.

"Daddy didn't make smoke. Daddy didn't make any smoke at all!"

I swung him up into my arms. "Sorry, Bozo. I know Daddy didn't make smoke."

I didn't add a fervent "Thank God!" The smoke might have been me.

It was never the same after that, not for an old codger like me. I stuck to my desk and turned the stand over to the younger boys. As far as I'm concerned, the test stands are strictly for the youngsters because they're something more than rocket-test stands. They test men, too.

AMATEUR IN CHANCERY

GEORGE O. SMITH

Twenty years ago the readers of Astounding Science Fiction *discovered a new series called "Venus Equilateral" by a previously unpublished author named George O. Smith. These were stories about interplanetary radio communication. They made an immediate hit; and what set them apart from similar, but lesser, yarns was that the author clearly knew what he was talking about. The technical jargon was accurate. The physical concepts were correct. The engineering data was taken from authoritative sources and slipsticked to the future extrapolations needed on the spot.*

And well these things should be true. For Smith was then, as he is now, a radio engineer with a fat file of patents in his name. He goes on doing electronics engineering research—presently as an information analyst working on communications problems—as he goes on writing science fiction stories that draw heavy fan mail from the readers, like Amateur in Chancery.

Paul Wallach came into my office. He looked distraught. By some trick of selection, Paul Wallach, the director of Project Tunnel, was one of the two men in the place who did not have a string of doctor's and scholar's degrees to tack behind their names. The other was I.

"Trouble, Paul?" I asked.

He nodded, saying, "The tunnel car is working."

"It should. It's been tested enough."

"Holly Carter drew the short straw."

"Er—" I started and then stopped short as the implication became clear. "She's—she's—not—?"

"Holly made it to Venus all right," he said. "Trouble is we can't get her back."

"Can't get her back?"

He nodded again. "You know, we've never really known very much about the atmosphere of Venus."

"Yes."

"Well, from what little came through just before Holly blacked out, it seems that there must be one of the cyanogens in the atmosphere in a concentration high enough to effect nervous paralysis."

"Meaning?"

"Meaning," said Paul Wallach in a flat tone, "that Holly Carter stopped breathing shortly after she cracked the airlock. And her heart stopped beating a minute or so later."

"Holly—dead?"

"Not yet, Tom," he said. "If we can get her back in the next fifteen or twenty minutes, modern medicine can bring her back."

"But there'll be brain damage!"

"Oh, there may be some temporary impairment. Nothing that retraining can't restore. The big problem is to bring her back."

"We should have built two tunnel cars."

"We should have done all sorts of things. But when the terminal rocket landed on Venus, everybody in the place was too anxious to try it out. Lord knows, I tried to proceed at a less headlong pace. But issuing orders to you people is a waste of time and paper."

I looked at him. "Doc," I asked, giving him the honorary title out of habit, "Venus is umpty-million miles from here. We haven't another tunnel car, and no rocket could make it in time to do any good. So how can we hope to rescue Holly?"

"That's the point," said Wallach. "Venus, it appears, is inhabited."

"Oh?"

"That's what got Holly caught in the first place. She landed, then saw this creature approaching. Believing that no life could exist in an atmosphere dangerous to life, she opened the airlock and discovered otherwise."

"So?"

"So now all we have to do is to devise some way of explaining to a Venusian the difference between left and right. I thought you might help."

"But I'm just a computer programmer."

"That's the point. We all figured that you have developed a

form of communication to that machine of yours. The rest of
the crew, as you know, have a bit of difficulty in communicating among themselves in their own jargon, let alone
getting through to normal civilians. When it comes to a
Venusian, they're licked."

I said, "I'll try."

Project Tunnel is the hardware phase of a program started
a number of years ago when somebody took a joke seriously.

In a discussion of how the tunnel diode works, one of the
scientists pointed out that if an electron could be brought to
absolute rest, its position according to Heisenberg Uncer-
tainty would be completely ambiguous. Hence it had as high
a possibility of being found on Venus as it had of being
found on Earth or anywhere else. Now, the tunnel diode
makes use of this effect by a voltage bias across the diode
junction. Between narrow limits, the voltage bias is correct to
upset the ambiguity of Mr. Heisenberg, making the electron
nominally found on one side of the junction more likely to be
found on the other.

Nobody could deny the operability of the tunnel diode.
Project Tunnel was a serious attempt to employ the tunnel
effect in gross matter.

The terminal rocket mentioned by Paul Wallach carried
the equipment needed to establish the voltage bias between
Venus and the Earth. Once established, Project Tunnel was in
a state that caused it to maroon the most wonderful girl in
the world.

Since the latter statment is my own personal opinion, my
pace from the office to the laboratory was almost a dead run.

The laboratory was a madhouse. People stood in little
knots, arguing. Those who weren't talking were shaking their
heads in violent negation.

The only one who appeared unupset was Teresa Dwight,
our psi-girl. And here I must confess an error. When I said
that Paul Wallach and I were the only ones without a string
of professorial degrees, I missed Teresa Dwight. I must be
forgiven. Teresa had a completely bland personality, zero
drive, and a completely unstartling appearance. Teresa was
only fourteen. But she'd discovered that her psi-power could
get her anything she really wanted. Being human, therefore,
she did not want much. So forgive me for passing her by.

But now I had to notice her. As I came in, she looked up
and said, "Harla wants to know why can't he just try."

Wallach went white. "Tell that Venusian thing 'NO!' as
loud as you can."

Teresa concentrated, then asked, "But why?"

"Does this Harla understand the Heisenberg Effect?"

She said after a moment, "Harla says he has heard of it as a theory. But he is not quite prepared to believe that it does indeed exist as anything but an abstract physical concept."

"Tell Harla that Doctor Carter's awkward position is a direct result of our ability to reduce the tunnel effect to operate on gross matter."

"He realizes that. But now he wants to know why you didn't fire one of the lower animals as a test."

"Tell him that using animals for laboratory experiments is only possible in a police state where the anti-vivisection league can be exiled to Siberia. Mink coats and all. And let his Venusian mind make what it can of that. Now, Teresa—"

"Yes?"

"Tell Harla, very carefully, that pressing the left-hand button will flash the tunnel car back here as soon as he closes the airlock. But tell him that pushing the right-hand button will create another bias voltage—whereupon another mass of matter will cross the junction. In effect, it will rip a hole out of this laboratory near the terminal, over there, and try to make it occupy the same space as the tunnel car on Venus. None of us can predict what might happen when two masses attempt to occupy the same space. But the chances are that some of the holocaust will backfire across the gap and be as violent at this end, too."

"Harla says that he will touch nothing until he has been assured that it is safe."

"Good. Now, Tom," he said, addressing me, "how can we tell right from left?"

"Didn't you label 'em?"

"They're colored red on the right and green on the left."

"Is Harla color-blind?"

"No, but from what I gather Harla sees with a different spectrum than we do. So far as he is concerned both buttons look alike."

"You could have engraved 'em 'COME' and 'GO.' "

Frank Crandall snorted. "Maybe you can deliver an 'English, Self-Taught' course through Teresa to the Venusian?"

I looked at Crandall. I didn't much care for him. It seemed that every time Holly Carter came down out of her fog of theoretical physics long enough to notice a simpleton who had to have a machine to perform routine calculations, we were joined by Frank Crandall who carted her off and away from me. If this be rank jealousy, make the most of it. I'm human.

"Crandall," I said, "even to a Hottentot I could point out that the engraved legend 'GO' contains two squiggly symbols, whereas the legend 'RETURN' contains 'many.' "

Wallach stepped into the tension by saying, "So we didn't anticipate alien life. But now we've got the problem of communicating with it."

Crandall didn't appear to notice my stiff reply. He said, "Confound it, what's missing?"

"What's missing," I told him, "is some common point of reference."

"Meaning?"

"Meaning that I could define left from right to any semi-intelligent human being who was aware of the environment in which we live."

"For example?"

I groped for an example and said, lamely, "Well, there's the weather rule, valid for the northern hemisphere. When the wind is blowing on your back, the left hand points to the low pressure center."

"Okay. But how about Venus? Astronomical information, I mean."

I shook my head.

"Why not?" he demanded. "If we face north, the sun rises on our right, doesn't it?"

"Yes. Even in the southern hemisphere."

"Well, then. So it doesn't make any difference which hemisphere they're in."

"You're correct. But you're also making the assumptions that Venus rotates on its axis, that the axis is aligned parallel to the Earth's and that the direction of rotation is the same."

"We know that Venus rotates!"

"We have every reason to believe so," I agreed. "But only because thermocouples measure a temperature on the darkside that is too high to support the theory that the diurnal period of Venus is equal to the year. I think the latest figures say something between a couple of weeks and a few months. Next, the axis needn't be parallel to anything. Shucks, Crandall, you know darned well that the solar system is a finely made clock with no two shafts aligned, and elliptical gears that change speed as they turn."

"Practically everything in the solar system rotates in the same direction."

I looked at him. "Would you like to take a chance that Venus agrees with that statement? You've got a fifty percent

chance that you'll be right. Guess wrong and we have a metric ton of hardware trying to occupy the same space as another metric ton of matter."

"But—"

"And furthermore," I went on, "we're just lucky that Po-
laris happens to be a pole star right now. The poles of Mars
point to nothing that bright. Even then, we can hardly expect
the Venusian to have divided the circumpolar sky into the
same zoo full of mythical animals as our forebears—and if
we use the commonplace expression, maybe the Venusian
never paused to take a long-handled dipper of water from a
well. Call them stewpots and the term is still insular. Sure,
there's lots of pointers, but they have to be identified. My
mother always insisted that the Pleiades were—er—was the
Little Dipper."

Teresa Dwight spoke up, possibly for the second or third
time in her life without being spoken to first. She said, "Harla
has been listening to you through me. Of astronomy he has
but a rudimentary idea. He is gratified to learn from you that
there is a 'sun' that provides the heat and light. This has been
a theory based upon common sense; *something* had to do it.
But the light comes and goes so slowly that it is difficult to
determine which direction the sun rises from. The existence
of other celestial bodies than Venus is also based on logic. If,
they claim, they exist, and their planet exists, then there
probably are other planets with people who cannot see them,
either."

"Quoth Pliny the Elder," mumbled Paul Wallach.

I looked at him.

"Pliny was lecturing about Pythagoras' theory that the
Earth is round. A heckler asked him why the people on the
other side didn't fall off. Pliny replied that on the other side
there were undoubtedly fools who were asking their wise men
why we didn't fall off."

"It's hardly germane," I said.

"I'm sorry. Yes. And time is running out."

The laboratory door opened to admit a newcomer, Lou
Graham, head of the electronics crew.

He said, "I've got it!"

The chattering noise level died out about three decibels at
a time. Lou said, "When a steel magnet is etched in acid, the
north pole shows selective etching!"

I shook my head. "Lou," I said, "we don't know whether
Venus has a magnetic field, whether it is aligned to agree

with the Earth's—nor even whether the Venusians have discovered the magnetic compass."

"Oh, that isn't the reference point," said Lou Graham. "I'm quite aware of the ambiguity. The magnetic field does have a vector, but the arrow that goes on the end is strictly from human agreement."

"So how do you tell which is the north pole?"

"By making an electromagnet! Then using Ampere's Right Hand Rule. You grasp the electromagnet in the right hand so that the fingers point along the winding in the direction of the current flow. The thumb then points to the north pole."

"Oh, fine! Isn't that just the same confounded problem? Now we've got to find out whether Harla is equipped with a right hand complete with fingers and thumbs—so that we can tell him which his right hand is!"

"No, no," he said. "You don't understand, Tom. We don't need the right hand. Let's wind our electromagnet like this: We place the steel bar horizontally in front of us. The wire from 'Start' leaves us, passes over the top of the bar, drops below the bar on the far side, comes toward us on the under side, rises above the bar on the side toward us, and so on around and around until we've got our electromagnet wound. Now if the 'start' is positive and the 'end' is negative, the north pole will be at the left. It will show the selective etching in acid."

I looked at him. "Lou," I said slowly, "if you can define positive and negative in un-ambiguous terms as well as you wound that electromagnet, we can get Holly home. Can you?"

Lou turned to Teresa Dwight. "Has this Harla fellow followed me so far?"

She nodded.

"Can you speak for him?"

"You talk, I hear, he reads me. I read him and I can speak."

"Okay, then," said Lou Graham. "Now we build a Le Clanche cell. Ask Harla does he recognize carbon. A black or light-absorbing element. Carbon is extremely common, it is the basis of life chemistry. It is element number six in the periodic chart. Does Harla know carbon?"

"Harla knows carbon."

"Now we add zinc. Zinc is a light metal easily extracted from the ore. It is fairly abundant, and it is used by early civilizations for making brass or bronze long before the culture has advanced enough to recognize zinc as an element. Does Harla know zinc?"

"He may," said Teresa very haltingly. "What happens if Harla gets the wrong metal?"

"Not very much," said Lou. "Any of the light, fairly plentiful metals that are easily extracted from the ore will suffice. Say tin, magnesium, sodium, cadmium, so on."

"Harla says go on."

"Now we make an electrolyte. Preferably an alkaline salt."

"Be careful," I said. "Or you'll be asking Harla to identify stuff from a litmus paper."

"No," said Lou. He faced Teresa and said, "An alkaline substance burns the flesh badly."

"So do acids," I objected.

"Alkaline substances are found in nature," he reminded me. "Acids aren't often natural. The point is that an acid will work. Even salt water will work. But an alkaline salt works better. At any rate, tell Harla that the stuff, like zinc, was known to civilized peoples many centuries before chemistry became a science. Acids, on the other hand, are fairly recent."

"Harla understands."

"Now," said Lou Graham triumphantly, "we make our battery by immersing the carbon and the zinc in the electrolyte. The carbon is the positive electrode and should be connected to the start of our electromagnet, whereas the end of the winding must go to the zinc. This will place the north pole to the left hand."

"Harla understands," said Teresa. "So far, Harla can perform this experiment in his mind. But now we must identify which end of the steel bar is north-pole magnetic."

"If we make the bar magnetic and then immerse it in acid, the north magnetic pole will be selectively etched."

"Harla says that this he does not know about. He has never heard of it, although he is quite familiar with electromagnets, batteries, and the like."

I looked at Lou Graham. "Did you cook this out of your head, or did you use a handbook?"

He looked downcast. "I did use a handbook," he admitted. "But—"

"Lou," I said unhappily, "I've never said that we couldn't establish a common frame of reference. What we lack is one that can be established in minutes. Something physical—" I stopped short as a shadowy thought began to form.

Paul Wallach looked at me as though he'd like to speak

but didn't want to interrupt my train of thoughts. When he could contain himself no longer, he said, "Out with it, Tom."

"Maybe," I muttered. "Surely there must be something physical."

"How so?"

"Tue tunnel car must be full of it," I said. "Screws?"

I turned to Saul Graben. Saul is our mechanical genius; give him a sketch made on used Kleenex with a blunt lipstick and he will bring you back a gleaming mechanism that runs like a hundred-dollar wrist watch.

But not this time. Saul shook his head.

"What's permanent is welded and what's temporary is snapped in with plug buttons," he said.

"Good Lord," I said. "There simply *must* be something!"

"There probably is," said Saul. "But this Harla chap would have to use an acetylene torch to get at it."

I turned to Teresa. "Can this psi-man Harla penetrate metal?"

"Can anyone?" she replied quietly.

Wallach touched my arm. "You're making the standard, erroneous assumption that a sense of perception will give its owner a blueprint-clear grasp of the mechanical details of some machinery. It doesn't. Perception, as I understand it, is not even similar to eyesight."

"But—" I fumbled on—"surely there must be some common reference there, even granting that perception isn't eyesight. So how does perception work?"

"Tom, if you were blind from birth, I could tell you that I have eyesight that permits me to see the details of things that you can determine only by feeling them. This you might understand basically. But you could never be made to understand the true definition of the word 'picture' nor grasp the mental impression that is generated by eyesight."

"Well," I persisted, "can he penetrate flesh?"

"Flesh?"

"Holly's heart has stopped," I said. "But it hasn't been removed. If Harla can perceive through human flesh, he might be able to perceive the large, single organ in the chest cavity near the spine."

Teresa said, "Harla's perception gives him a blurry, incomplete impression." She looked at me. "It is something like a badly out-of-focus, grossly under-exposed X-ray solid."

"X-ray solid?" I asked.

"It's the closest thing that you might be able to understand," she said lamely.

I dropped it right there. Teresa had probably been groping

in the dark for some simile that would convey the nearest
possible impression. I felt that this was going to be the nearest that I would ever get to understanding the sense of perception.

"Can't he get a clear view?"

"He has not the right."

"Right!" I exploded. "Why—"

Wallach held up his hand to stop me. "Don't make Teresa
fumble for words, Tom. Harla has not the right to invade the
person of Holly Carter. Therefore he can not get a clearer
perception of her insides."

"Hell!" I roared. "Give Harla the right."

"No one has authority."

"Authority be damned!" I bellowed angrily. "That girl's
life is at stake!"

Wallach nodded unhappily. "Were this a medical emergency, a surgeon might close his eyes to the laws that require
authorization to operate. But even if he saved the patient's
life, he is laying himself open to a lawsuit. But this is different, Tom. As you may know, the ability of any psi-person
is measured by their welcome to the information. Thus
Teresa and Harla, both willing to communicate, are able."

"But can't Harla understand that the entire bunch of us are
willing that he should take a peek?"

"Confound it, Tom, it isn't a matter of our permission! It's
a matter of fact. It would ease things if Holly were married
to one of us, but even so it wouldn't be entirely clear. It has
to do with the invasion of privacy."

"Privacy? In this case the very idea is ridiculous."

"Maybe so," said Paul Wallach. "But I don't make the
rules. They're *natural* laws. As immutable as the laws of
gravity or the refraction of light. And Tom, even if I were
making the laws I might not change things. Not even to save
Holly Carter's life. Because, Tom, if telepathy and perception
were as free and unbounded as some of their early propo-
nents claimed, life would be a sheer, naked hell on earth."

"But what has privacy to do with it? This Harla isn't at all
humanoid. A cat can look at a king—"

"Sure, Tom. But how long would the cat be permitted to
read the king's mind?"

I grunted. "Has this Harla any mental block about examining the outside?"

He looked at me thoughtfully. "You're thinking about a
scar or some sort of blemish?"

"Yes. Birthmark, maybe. No one is perfect."

"You know of any?"

I thought.

It was not hard for me to conjure up a picture of Holly Carter. Unfortunately, I looked at Holly Carter through the eyes of love, which rendered her perfect. If she had bridge-work, I hadn't found it out. Her features were regular and her hair fell loose without a part. Her complexion was flaw-less . . . at least the complexion that could be examined whilst Holly sunned herself on a deck chair beside the swim-ming pool.

I shook my head. Then I faced an unhappy fact. It hurt, because I wanted my goddess to be perfect, and if she were made of weak, mortal flesh, I did not want to find it out by asking the man who knew her better than I did.

Still, I wanted her alive. So I turned to Frank Crandall.

"Do you?" I asked.

"Do I what?"

"Know of any scars or birthmarks?"

"Such as?"

"Oh, hell," I snapped. "Such as an appendix scar that might be used to tell left from right."

"Look, Tom, I'm not her physician, you know. I can only give you the old answer: 'Not until they wear briefer swim suits.' "

My heart bounced lightly. That Holly was still in mortal danger was not enough to stop my elation at hearing Frank Crandall admit that he was not Holly's lover, nor even on much better terms than I. It might have been better to face the knowledge that Holly was all woman and all human even though the information had to come from someone who knew her well enough to get her home.

Then I came back to earth. I had my perfect goddess—in deadly peril—instead of a human woman who really did not belong to any man.

I hadn't seen Saul Graben leave, but he must have been gone because now he opened the door and came back. He was carrying a heavy rim gyroscope that was spinning in a set of frictionless gymbals. He looked most confused.

He said, "I've spent what seems like an hour. You can't tell me that this gizmo is inseparable from the selfish, insular intellect of terrestrial so-called homo sapiens."

He turned the base and we all watched the gymbal rings rotate to keep the gyro wheel in the same plane. "It should be cosmic," he said. "But every time I start, I find myself bit-ing myself on the back of the neck. Look. If you make the axle horizontal in front of you and rotate the gyro with the top edge going away from you, you can define a common reference. But motion beyond that cannot be explained. If the axle is depressed on the right side, the gyro will turn so the far edge looks to the right. But that's defining A in terms of A. So I'm licked."

Frank Crandall shook his head. "There's probably an absolute to that thing somewhere, but I'm sure none of us know it. We haven't time to find it. In fact, I think the cause is lost. Maybe we'd better spend our time figuring out a plausible explanation."

"Explanation?" blurted Wallach.

"Let's face it," said Crandall. "Holly Carter's life is slipping away. No one has yet come close to finding a common reference to describe right from left to this Harla creature."

"So what's your point?"

"Death is for the dying," Crandall said in a monotone. "Let them have their hour in peace and dignity. Life is for the living, and for the living there is no peace. We who remain must make the best of it. So now in about five minutes Holly will be at peace. The rest of us have got to answer for her."

"How do you mean?"

"How do you propose to explain this unfortunate incident?" asked Crandall. "Someone will want to know what happened to the remains of Holly Carter. I can see hell breaking loose. And I can see the whole lot of us getting laughed right off the Earth because we couldn't tell right from left. And I can see us all clobbered for letting the affair take place."

"You seem to be more worried about your professional reputation than about Holly Carter's life!"

"I have a future," he said. "Holly doesn't seem to. Hell," he groaned, "we can't even gamble on it."

"Gamble?"

"How successful do you think you'd be in getting this Venusian to risk his life by closing his eyes and making a fifty-fifty stab in the dark at one of those buttons?"

"Well—" started Wallach—"we'd be gambling too, you know. But—"

"Wait a moment," I said. "I've got a sort of half-cracked theory. May I try?"

"Of course."

"Not 'of course.' I'll have to have quiet, with just Teresa to communicate through."

"If you have any ideas, try them," said Wallach.

"Do you really know what you're doing?" demanded Frank Crandall.

"I think so," I replied. "If it works, it'll be because I happen to feel close to Holly."

"Could be," he said with a shrug. I almost flipped. Duels have been fought over less. But instead of taking offense, Crandall topped it off by adding, "You could have been a lot closer if you'd tried. You always said you had the alert, pixie-type mind that was pure relaxation instead of a dead letdown after a period of deep concentration. But you were always scuttling off somewhere. Well, go ahead and try, Tom. And good luck!"

I took a deep breath.

"Teresa?" I asked.

"Yes, Mr. Lincoln?"

"Tell Harla to concentrate on the buttons."

"He is."

"There is a subtle difference between them."

"This he knows, but he does not know what it is."

"There is a delicate difference in warmth. One button will be faintly warmer than the other."

"Harla has felt them."

I dropped the third-person address and spoke to Teresa as if she were but one end of a telephone line. "Harla," I said, "only part of the difference lies in the warmth to physical touch. There should be another kind of warmth. Are you not affected by a *feeling* that one is better than the other?"

Harla's reply came direct through Teresa: "Why yes, I am indeed drawn to the warmer of the two. Were this a game I would wager on it. But that is emotion and hardly suitable as a guide."

"Ah, but it is!" I replied quickly. "This is our frame of reference. Press the warmer of the but—"

I was violently interrupted. Wallach shook me violently and hurled me away from Teresa. Frank Crandall was facing the girl, shouting, "No! No! The warm one will be the red one! You must press the green—"

And then he, too, was interrupted.

Displaced air made a near-explosive *whoosh!* and the tunnel car was there on its pad. In it was a nightmare horror holding a limp Holly Carter across its snakelike tentacles. A free tentacle opened the door.

"Take her while I hold my breath," said Harla, still talking through Teresa. "I'll return the tunnel car empty. I can, now that I know that warmth is where the hearth is."

Harla dropped the unconscious girl in my arms and snapped back into the car. It disappeared, then returned empty just as the doctor was bending over Holly.

So now I have my Holly, but every now and then I lie awake beside her in a cold sweat. Harla could have guessed wrong. Just as Wallach and Crandall had been wrong in assuming the red button would be warmer than the green. Their reaction was as emotional as Harla's.

I hope Harla either forgives me or never finds out that I had to sound sure of myself, and that I had to play on his emotions simply to get him to take the fifty-fifty chance on his—hers—*our* lives.

And I get to sleep only after I've convinced myself that it was more than chance . . . that somehow our feelings and emotions guided Harla where logic and definition fail.

For right and left do not exist until terrestrial man defines them.

THE
MARK GABLE
FOUNDATION

LEO SZILARD

Leo Szilard's credentials as a scientist are of the highest order, his work as a pioneer in nuclear studies having contributed very greatly to the present state of advancement of the field. To this towering reputation he has recently added two new ones. The first is as a "television personality"—particularly in the assorted panel shows dealing with nuclear testing and atomic warfare, where his polemical remarks add the weight of authority and the reason of a keen mind to the debate. The second is as a sort of belle-lettrist of science—and science fiction—with the publication of his book of short stories, The Voice of the Dolphin.

Pointed and revealing, Szilard's comments on world affairs are even better expressed through science fiction stories than over the television air, as attested by the present story, The Mark Gable Foundation.

As soon as I saw the temperature of the rabbit come back to normal, I knew that we had licked the problem. It took twenty-four hours to bring his temperature down to one degree centigrade, injecting three grains of dorminol every ten minutes during that period. Sleep set in between the third and fourth hours, when the body temperature fell below twenty-six centigrade; and after twenty-four hours, at one centigrade, there was no longer any appreciable metabolic activity. We kept him at that low temperature for one day, after which time, having completed our measurements, we injected metaboline and allowed the temperature to rise to normal within one hour.

There was never any doubt in my mind that once we got this far, and got the temperature down to one centigrade, we could keep the rabbit "asleep" for a week, a year or a hundred years just as well as for a day. Nor had I much doubt that if this worked for the rabbit it would work for the dog; and that if it worked for the dog, it would work for man.

I always wanted to see what kind of place the world will be three hundred years hence. I intended to "withdraw from life" (as we proposed to call the process) as soon as we had perfected the method, and to arrange for being returned to life in 2260. I thought my views and sentiments were sufficiently advanced, and that I had no reason to fear I should be too much behind the times in a world that had advanced a few hundred years beyond the present. I would not have dared, though, to go much beyond three hundred years.

I thought at first that one year should be plenty for perfecting the process as well as for completing the arrangements; and that I should be *in statu dormiendi* before the year was over. As a matter of fact, it took only six months to get ready; but difficulties of an unforeseen kind arose.

A section of public opinion was strongly opposed to "withdrawal from life," and for a time it looked as though the Eighty-sixth Congress would pass a law against it. This, fortunately, did not come to pass. The A.M.A., however, succeeded in obtaining a court injunction against my "withdrawal" on the basis that it was "suicide," and suicide was unlawful. Since a man *in statu dormiendi* cannot of his own volition return to life—so the brief argued—from the legal point of view he is not living while in that state.

The ensuing legal battle lasted for five years. Finally Adams, Lynch and Davenport, who handled my case, succeeded in getting the Supreme Court to accept jurisdiction. The Supreme Court upheld the injunction, with three justices dissenting. Mr. Davenport explained to me that the ruling of the Supreme Court, though on the face of it unfavorable, was in reality a very fortunate thing for me because it removed all obstacles that might have stood in the way of my plans. The ruling of the Supreme Court, Mr. Davenport explained, established once and for all that a man is not legally living while *in statu dormiendi*. Therefore, he said, if I should now decide to act against the advice of his firm, disregard the court injunction and proceed to withdraw from life, no legal action could be taken against me under any statute until I was returned to life three hundred years hence, at which time my offense would come under the statue of limitations.

All arrangements having been completed in secrecy, and

having named Adams, Lynch and Davenport as executors of
my estate, I spent my last evening in the twentieth century at
a small farewell party given to me by friends. There were
about six of us, all old friends, but somehow we did not understand each other very well on this occasion. Most of them
seemed to have the feeling that they were sort of attending
my funeral, since they would not see me again alive; whereas
to me it seemed that it was I who was attending their funeral,
since none of them would be alive when I woke up.

According to the records, it took about two hours until
sleep set in, but I do not remember anything that was said
after the first hour.

The next thing I remember was the prick of a needle, and
when I opened my eyes I saw a nurse with a hypodermic sy-
ringe in one hand and a microphone in the other.

"Would you mind speaking into the microphone, please?"
she said, holding it at a comfortable distance from my face.

"We owe you an apology, as well as an explanation," said
a well-dressed young man standing near my bed and holding
a microphone in his hand. "I am Mr. Rosenblatt from
Adams, Lynch, Davenport, Rosenblatt and Giannini. For reasons of a legal nature we deemed it advisable to return you to
life, but if you wish to complete the three hundred years,
which appears to be your goal, we hope we shall be able to
make the necessary arrangements within one month. At least
we shall try our best to do so.

"Now, before you say anything, let me explain to you that
the gentleman sitting next to me is Mr. McClintock, the may-
or of the city—a Democrat, of course. Subject to your ap-
proval, we have agreed that he may give you an interview
which will be televised. The proceeds will go to the Senile
Degeneration Research Fund. The broadcasting companies understand, of course, that it's up to you to agree to this arrangement, and they have an alternate program ready which
can be substituted if you should object. If you agree, however, we shall go on the air in one minute. Naturally, the
broadcasting companies are anxious to catch your first re-
sponses rather than have something rehearsed put on the air.
I'm certain you'll appreciate their point of view."

"Before I answer this," I said, "would you mind telling me
how long I've been asleep?"

"I should have told you this before," he said. "You were
out ninety years."

"Then," I said after a moment's reflection, "I have no
friends left from whom to keep any secrets. I have no objection to the broadcast."

As soon as the announcer finished with his somewhat lengthy introduction, the mayor came in. "As chairman of the Senile Degeneration Research Fund, I wish to express my thanks to you for having graciously consented to this interview. Senile degeneration is one of our most important diseases. One in eight die of senile degeneration, and more than half of those who reach the age of a hundred and five. Given ample funds for research, we cannot fail to discover the causes of this disease, and once the cause of the disease is known it will be possible to find a cure. But I know that I should not monopolize the air; there must be many things that you would want to know about our society. Please feel free to ask anything you like."

"Why was I returned to life?" I asked.

"I'm certain," the mayor said, "that Messrs. Adams, Lynch, Davenport, Rosenblatt and Giannini will want to give you a detailed explanation of that. It was their decision, and I have no doubt that it was a wise one in the circumstances. I'm not a lawyer, but I can tell you something about the political background of their decision. Politics—that's my field.

"I wonder whether you realize how much trouble your process of 'withdrawal from life' has caused the government. For a few years only a few persons followed your example, mostly political scientists and anthropologists. But then, all of a sudden, it became quite a fad. People withdrew just to spite their wives and husbands. And I regret to say that many Catholics who could not obtain a divorce chose this method of surviving their husbands or wives, to become widowed and to remarry, until this practice was finally stopped in 2001 by the papal bull 'Somnus Naturae Repugnans.'

"The Church did not interfere, of course, with the legitimate uses of the process. Throughout the latter part of the century doctors encouraged patients who suffered from cancer and certain other incurable diseases to withdraw from life, in the hope that a cure would be found in the years to come and that they could then be returned to life and cured. There were legal complications, of course, particularly in the case of wealthy patients. Often their heirs raised objections on the ground that withdrawal from life was not yet an entirely safe process; and equally often the heirs demanded that they too should be permitted to withdraw from life for an equal period of time, so that the natural sequence of the generations would be left undisturbed. There are about one million cancer patients at present *in statu dormiendi,* and half a million of their heirs."

"Then cancer is still not a curable disease?" I asked.

"No," the mayor said, "but with all the funds which are now available it can take at the most a few years until that problem is solved. The most important, even though a somewhat controversial, application of your process," he continued, "came about twenty-five years ago. That was when the present great depression started. It came as a result of seventy-five years of Republican mismanagement. Today we have a Democratic President and a Democratic Congress; but this is the first Democratic President since Donovan, and the first Democratic Congress since the Hundred and Fifth. As more and more of the Southern states began to vote Republican, our party was hopelessly outvoted, until gradually its voting strength began to rise again; and today, with a Democratic majority solidly established, we have nothing to fear from coming elections."

"So finally there's a truly progressive party in the United States?" I asked.

"Yes," the mayor said, "we regard ourselves as progressives. We have the support of the Catholic Church, and eighty per cent of the voters are Catholics."

"What brought about such mass conversions?" I asked.

"There were no mass conversions," the mayor said, "and we wouldn't want any. Families of Polish, Irish and Italian stock, having a stronger belief in the American way of life than some of the older immigrant stocks, have always given birth to more children; and so today we have a solid Catholic majority.

"Now that the Democratic Party is established in office, we're going to fight the depression by the proper economic methods. As I said before, there was a Republican Administration in office when the depression hit us twenty-five years ago. In the first year of that depression unemployment rose to ten million. Things looked pretty bad. There was no public-works program or unemployment relief, but Congress passed a law, the Withdrawal Act of 2025, authorizing the use of Federal funds to enable any unemployed who so desired to withdraw from life for the duration of the depression. Those unemployed who availed themselves of this offer had to authorize the government to return them to life when the government deemed that the labor market required such a measure.

"Seven out of ten million unemployed availed themselves of this offer by the end of the first year, in spite of the opposition of the Church. The next year unemployment was up another seven million, out of which five million were withdrawn from life. This went on and on, and by the time our party got into office, two years ago, there were twenty-five million withdrawn from life, with Federal support.

"Our first act in office was to make withdrawals from life unlawful; and the second was to institute a public-works program."

"What does your public-works program consist of?" I asked.

"Housing," the mayor said.

"Is there a housing shortage?" I asked. "No," the mayor said. "With twenty-five million unemployed *in statu dormiendi* there is, of course, no housing shortage."

"And will you now return these twenty-five million unemployed to life?" I asked.

"Only very gradually," the mayor replied. "The majority of the sleepers are non-Catholics and it would upset the political balance if they were returned to life all at once. Besides, operating the refrigerator plants of the public dormitories for twenty-five million sleepers is part of our public-works program.

"Incidentally," he added, "whether you yourself come under the Antiwithdrawal Act of 2048 is a controversial question. Your lawyers felt that you would not want to violate the law of the land, and they tried to get a court ruling in order to clear you; but the court refused to take the case, because you weren't legally alive; finally your lawyers decided to return you to life so that you may ask the court for a declaratory judgment. Even though there is little doubt that the court will rule in your favor, I personally hope that you'll find our society so pleasant, and so much more advanced than you would have expected, that you'll decide to stay with us in the twenty-first century."

"Thank you very much, Mr. Mayor," the announcer said. "This was beautiful timing. We're off the air," he said to me, thinking I needed more explanation.

The mayor turned to me. "If you feel well enough, I would like to take you home for dinner. It's a small party, four or five guests, my wife and my daughter Betty. The poor girl is brokenhearted. She has just called off her engagement, and I'm doing what I can to cheer her up. She's very much in love with the fellow."

"If she loves him so much, why did she break with him?" I asked.

"All her friends teased her about him because he wears teeth," the mayor said. "Of course, there's no law against it, it's just not done, that's all."

Something began to dawn upon me at this moment. The

nurse, a pretty young girl, had no teeth, Mr. Rosenblatt had no teeth, and the mayor had no teeth. Teeth seemed to be out of fashion.

"I have teeth," I said.

"Yes, of course," the mayor replied, "and you wear them with dignity. But if you should decide to stay with us you'll want to get rid of them. They're not hygienic."

"But how would I chew my food, how do *you* chew your food?" I asked.

"Well," the mayor said, "we don't eat with our hands. We eat from plates—chewing plates. They plug into sockets in the table and chew your food for you. We eat with spoons."

"Steaks, too?" I asked.

"Yes, everything," the mayor said. "But have no fear, we shall have knife and fork for you tonight, and flat plates such as you are accustomed to. My daughter kept them for her fiancé."

"I'm sorry that my second daughter will not be with us tonight," the mayor said as he was starting his car. "She's in the hospital. In college she's taking mathematics and chemistry. She could have talked to you in your own language."

"Nothing seriously wrong, I hope," I said.

"Oh, no!" the mayor said. "Just plastic surgery. She'll be out in a day or two."

"With a new nose?" I asked.

"Nothing wrong with her nose," the mayor said. "As a matter of fact, she has Mark Gable's nose. No, it's one of these newfangled operations. My wife and I don't approve of it, but this girl, she runs with the smart set. 'Esophagus bypass,' they call it. No longer necessary to watch your diet, you know. Eat as much as you please and switch it to the bypass—goes into a rubber container, of course. I tried to talk her out of it, but that girl has an answer for everything. 'Father,' she said, 'isn't there a food surplus in the world? If everybody ate twice as much, would that not solve the problem'?"

"Maybe she's right," I said, remembering with an effort that I always used to side with youth.

When we sat down at table I looked forward to the steak; I was pretty hungry by that time. But when it was served, after a few fruitless attempts with knife and fork I had to ask for a chewing plate.

"The choice cuts are always especially tough," my hostess explained.

"Tell me," I said, "when did people begin to discard their teeth, and why?"

"Well," the mayor said, "it started thirty years ago. Ford's chewing plates have been advertised over television for at least thirty-five years. Once people have chewing plates, what use do they have for teeth? If you think of all the time people used to spend at the dentist's, and for no good purpose, at that, you'll have to admit we have made progress."

"What became of all the dentists?" I asked.

"Many of them have been absorbed by the chewing-plate industry," the mayor explained, "Henry Ford VI gave them preference over all categories of skilled workers. Others turned to other occupations. Take Mr. Mark Gable, for instance," the mayor said, pointing to a man sitting at my right, a man about fifty, and of great personal charm. "He had studied dentistry; today he is one of the most popular donors, and the richest man in the United States."

"Oh," I said. "What is his business?"

"Over one million boys and girls," the mayor said, "are his offspring in the United States, and the demand is still increasing."

"That must keep you pretty busy, Mr. Gable," I said, unable to think of anything else to say.

Apparently I had put my foot in it. Mrs. Gable blushed, and the mayor laughed.

"Mr. Gable is happily married," the mayor said. "He donated the seed when he was twenty-four years old. The stock should last indefinitely, although the demand may not. The Surgeon General has ruled that no seed donated by anyone about twenty-five may be marketed in the United States."

"Has there been legislation about this, giving the Surgeon General such authority?" I asked.

"No," the mayor said. "Legislation was blocked by filibuster in the Senate. But the Surgeon General takes action under the Pure Food and Drug Act."

"How can he do that?" I asked.

"There was a decision by the Supreme Court thirty years ago," the mayor said, "that all ponderable substance which is destined to enter through any orifice of the human body comes properly under that act. There was no legislation in this whole field whatsoever. Any woman who wishes to bear a child of her own husband is perfectly free to do so. Over fifteen per cent of the children are born in this manner; but most wives prefer to select a donor."

"How do they make a choice?" I asked.

"Oh," the mayor said, "the magazines are full of their pictures. You can see them on the screen at home and in the movies. There are fashions, of course. Today over seventy per cent of the 'donated' children are the offspring of the thirty-five most popular donors. Naturally, they're expensive. Today a seed of Mr. Gable's will bring a thousand dollars; but you can get seed from very good stock for a hundred. Fashions are bound to change, but long after Mr. Gable passes away his estate will still go on selling his seed to connoisseurs. It's estimated that for several decades his estate will still take in more than thirty million dollars a year."

"I have earned a very large sum of money," said Mr. Gable, turning to me, "with very little work. And now I'm thinking of setting up a trust fund. I want to do something that will really contribute to the happiness of mankind; but it's very difficult to know what to do with money. When Mr. Rosenblatt told me that you'd be here tonight I asked the mayor to invite me. I certainly would value your advice."

"Would you intend to do anything for the advancement of science?" I asked.

"No," Mark Gable said. "I believe scientific progress is too fast as it is."

"I share your feeling about this point," I said with the fervor of conviction, "but then why not do something about the retardation of scientific progress?"

"That I would very much like to do," Mark Gable said, "but how do I go about it?"

"Well," I said, "I think that shouldn't be very difficult. As a matter of fact, I think it would be quite easy. You could set up a foundation, with an annual endowment of thirty million dollars. Research workers in need of funds could apply for grants, if they could make out a convincing case. Have ten committees, each composed of twelve scientists, appointed to pass on these applications. Take the most active scientists out of the laboratory and make them members of these committees. And the very best men in the field should be appointed as chairmen at salaries of fifty thousand dollars each. Also have about twenty prizes of one hundred thousand dollars each for the best scientific papers of the year. This is just about all you would have to do. Your lawyers could easily prepare a charter for the foundation. As a matter of fact, any of the National Science Foundation bills which were introduced in the Seventy-ninth and Eightieth Congresses could perfectly well serve as a model."

"I think you had better explain to Mr. Gable why this foundation would in fact retard the progress of science," said a bespectacled young man sitting at the far end of the table, whose name I didn't get at the time of introduction.

"It should be obvious," I said. "First of all, the best scientists would be removed from their laboratories and kept busy on committees passing on applications for funds. Secondly, the scientific workers in need of funds would concentrate on problems which were considered promising and were pretty certain to lead to publishable results. For a few years there might be a great increase in scientific output; but by going after the obvious, pretty soon science would dry out. Science would become something like a parlor game. Some things would be considered interesting, others not. There would be fashions. Those who followed the fashion would get grants. Those who wouldn't would not, and pretty soon they would learn to follow the fashion, too."

"Will you stay here with us?" Mark Gable said, turning to me, "and help me to set up such a foundation?"

"That I will gladly do, Mr. Gable," I said. "We should be able to see within a few years whether the scheme works, and I'm certain that it will work. For a few years I could afford to stay here, and I could then still complete the three hundred years which were my original goal."

"So you would want to go through with your plan rather than live out your life with us?" asked the mayor.

"Frankly, Mr. Mayor," I said, "before Mr. Gable brought up the plan of the foundation, with science progressing at this rapid rate I was a little scared of being faced with further scientific progress two hundred years hence. But if Mr. Gable succeeds in stopping the progress of science and gives the art of living a chance to catch up, two hundred years hence the world should be a livable place. If Mr. Gable should not go through with his project, however, I would probably prefer to live out my life with you in the twenty-first century. How about it, Mr. Mayor?" I said. "Will you give me a job if I decide to stay?" "You don't need a job," the mayor said. "You don't seem to realize that you're a very famous man."

"How does being famous provide me with a livelihood?" I asked.

"In more ways than one," the mayor said. "You could become a donor, for instance. Now that over half of our professional men are medical doctors, more and more wives want children with some measure of scientific ability."

"But, Mr. Mayor," I said, "I'm above twenty-five."

"Of course," the mayor said, "the seed would have to be marketed abroad. The rate of exchange is none too favorable," he continued, "but even so you should be able to earn a comfortable living if you decided to stay."

"I don't know, Mr. Mayor," I said. "The idea is a little novel for me; but I suppose I could get accustomed to it."

"I'm sure you could," said the mayor. "And incidentally, whenever you decide to get rid of that junk in your mouth, I shall be glad to get an appointment for you with Elihu Smith, the dental extractor. He took care of all our children."

"I appreciate your kindness very much, Mr. Mayor," I said, smiling politely and trying to hide a suddenly rising feeling of despair. All my life I have been scared of dentists and dental extractors, and somehow I suddenly became aware of the painful fact that it was not within the power of science to return me to the twentieth century.